SOME SORT OF *Love*

Special Edition

Melanie Harlow

USA TODAY BESTSELLING AUTHOR

Copyright © 2022 by Melanie Harlow

All rights reserved.

No part of this book may be reproduced in any form or by any electronic or mechanical means, including information storage and retrieval systems, without written permission from the author, except for the use of brief quotations in a book review.

This book is dedicated with gratitude and respect to the mothers who shared stories about their beautiful children with me during research for this book. Thank you for your candor, your generosity, your wisdom, and your time. Your love and devotion inspired me.

Laura Barnes
Jennifer Eastwood
Sarah Ferguson
Ella James
Kelley Jefferson
Melissa Quintanilla
Rachel Todd

From the complications of loving you
I think there is no end or return.
No answer, no coming out of it.

Which is the only way to love, isn't it?

MARY OLIVER

CHAPTER 1
Jillian

YOU KNOW that stomach ache you get when you have to go to a family function, and everyone's in a couple but you, and they all pretend they don't think it's a big deal that you're thirty and single and don't have a date for your sister's wedding tomorrow, but really they're all wondering what's wrong with you and they're too polite to ask?

That's the stomach ache I had as I drove to Skylar and Sebastian's rehearsal dinner.

And the closer I got to Abelard Vineyards, the winery where Skylar worked and where the wedding would take place, the worse it got.

Because maybe they wouldn't be polite.

No date tonight? Must be hard to find a man once you're past a certain age.

So why aren't you married yet, Jillian? That clock is ticking!

You're not one of those lesbians, are you?

One of these days I was just going to go with that one. It was *so* much more interesting than the truth—I just hadn't found the right guy yet and didn't have a clue where to look. In fact, was it too late to get a hot lesbian date for tomorrow night? That would shut them up.

Stop it. Just stop it.

I took a few deep breaths and tried to focus on what mattered. *You're being ridiculous. This is not about you. This is about Skylar. She's your sister, and you love her, and you're thrilled for her. She deserves to be happy. Just because she met the love of her life first doesn't mean it's never going to happen for you. Now get over yourself.*

The knot in my gut loosened a little. I *was* being ridiculous, wasn't I? Maybe tonight wouldn't be so bad. I had nothing to be ashamed of. In fact, I had a lot to be proud of—M.D. after my name, a job I loved at a thriving pediatric practice, a great relationship with my parents and sisters, a beautiful condo with a riverfront view, a healthy body with the Nixon metabolism but *not* the Nixon ears, and a salary that allowed me to occasionally indulge my expensive taste in shoes and wine.

At the end of the day, I was right where I wanted to be.

It's just…I was lonely. And worried I'd waited too long to make a relationship a priority. And scared that I'd never meet someone who'd make me fall head over heels like both my sisters had.

No. Don't start. You don't have to let anyone see that. You just have to stand tall and smile, hopefully with a big-ass glass of wine in your hand.

Ah, wine. Wine was my friend. Wine understood me. Wine knew that it was entirely possible to be one hundred percent happy for your sisters and also ten percent jealous, because Wine does not care about mathematics. And Wine would never ask why I didn't have a man by age thirty. Wine and I had spent enough alone time together that Wine knew it wasn't that I didn't *want* to find love—of course I did.

But it was fucking hard!

It's not like they were handing out soul mates at the deli counter. *I'll take one tall, dark, and handsome with a steady job and a good sense of humor—oh, not the six-inch, the footlong. Thanks.*

Sighing, I pulled up at the winery and parked in the side lot next to Miles's Jeep. Around the back of the sprawling French Provençal style main building, a huge white tent for the reception had already been constructed. The rehearsal was supposed to start at six, and it was a few minutes after, but I took a minute to refresh my lipstick and fuss with my hair. If I had to walk in late and alone, I could at least do it looking better than I felt.

After a final once-over in the small rectangular mirror on the visor, I took one more deep breath and told myself, *There is nothing wrong with you.*

Then I whispered it. "There is nothing wrong with you."

Then I said it louder. "There is nothing wrong with you. Other than the fact that you're talking to yourself in the car."

A knock on the driver's side window made me jump—it was Natalie.

I opened the door and got out, my heart still pounding. "Jesus, Nat. You scared the shit out of me."

"Sorry. I came out to get my sweater because the A/C is on in there, and I was chilly." She held up a navy blue cardigan and gave me a quizzical look. "What were you doing in there?"

I locked my car, and we began walking across the gravel lot toward the main entrance. "I was...practicing my speech for the toast tomorrow. Are you sure I should be the one to give it? I feel like you'd be better at it."

"Tough. You're the maid of honor."

"More like the old maid of honor."

She laughed as she elbowed me. "Oh, stop. You are not an old maid."

"*Someone* will make that joke tonight—I guarantee it."

"That's ludicrous! You're young and beautiful!"

"I'm not young; I'm thirty. That's like ninety in judgey years."

"Oh Jesus." She shook her head as we climbed the stone

steps leading to the massive double doors. "You're gorgeous and smart and fun. You don't need to settle for anything less than perfect, and perfect can take a while to find, especially with your schedule."

I groaned. "Tell me about it. I don't even know where to look anymore."

"No more bites from that online thing?"

I shook my head. "I got off that after the convicted felon contacted me."

"Oh. Well, what about that surgeon you met for drinks last week?"

"Turns out he exaggerated the state of his divorce. As in, his wife didn't know about it yet."

"Jeez, what is *wrong* with people?"

"I don't know." I exhaled as we got to the top. "Sorry I'm being so negative, but with your engagement and pregnancy, and Skylar's wedding, I've just been feeling sorry for myself lately. It's stupid."

She paused with one hand on the door. "It's not stupid, Jilly." Her voice had softened. "I was jealous of Skylar too, before Miles came along."

"Really?" That surprised me, since Natalie wasn't the jealous type. "You never said anything."

She took her hand off the door. "I know, but I was. Things with Dan were so shitty, and I'd look at Sky and Sebastian and think, *that's* how you're supposed to feel. *That's* what being in love looks like. I didn't have that, and I wanted it."

"But then you found it."

"I did, but that doesn't mean you won't. Love isn't a finite thing in the universe. It's not like it gets used up by people who got there first."

I sighed. "I know. You're right. I need to stop comparing myself and just be patient. I fucking hate how whiny I sound. This is not me at *all*."

"I don't think you're whining. I think you're frustrated,

and I get it. But hang in there." She grinned. "And keep kissing those frogs. One of them is bound to be a prince, right?"

I had to chuckle at her hopeful smile, which sparkled like the diamond on her finger. Natalie had always been able to find the bright side in any situation, and I loved that about her. I pulled open the door. "Come on, crazy. Let's go in. Thanks for the pep talk—I needed it."

"Thanks for coming, everyone." Skylar stood at the front of the winery's tasting room, which had been transformed into a dining room for fifty tonight. The crowd hushed, and I marveled at the way she was able to command everyone's attention so completely. Maybe it was her theater training and experience onstage, maybe it was just her uncommon beauty, but she held everyone rapt, as usual. "We're so happy to see you here tonight."

As she began talking about what it meant to them to see so many loved ones gathered in one place, I admired her style, which was so different than mine. Skylar looked good in everything, but tonight she wore a simple black sleeveless crop top and a pale peach tulle skirt that billowed to her knees. Around her neck was a chunky gold necklace, and her long blonde hair spilled over both shoulders. She'd borrowed a fabulous pair of black Jimmy Choo heels from me—shoes were the one obsession we shared—but I could *never* have pulled off that outfit. With my height, the crop top would have looked like an accident, and that skirt would have made me look like an overgrown ballerina. I stuck to classics like pencil skirts, blouses, and trousers, but Skylar could pull off any trend she liked.

Next to her, Sebastian looked gorgeous in his dark blue suit, albeit a bit uncomfortable to be the center of attention. I noticed that Skylar held his hand as she talked, and a lump formed in my throat. I tried to dissolve it with the last sip of wine left in my glass, but it remained.

"I want to thank my soon-to-be father-in-law, Denny Pryce, for hosting this dinner tonight." She blew him a kiss, and the handsome older man smiled back at her, clearly smitten with his new daughter-in-law.

"We'd also like to recognize the best man and groomsmen, Sebastian's brothers Malcolm and David; their wives Kelly and Jen; our flower girls, Emily and Hannah Pryce; and our ring bearer, Caleb Pryce."

The young girls blushed and four-year-old Caleb took a bow as the room applauded, their parents beaming with pride. *How incredible to gain so much at once, not only a husband but a built-in family with brothers and sisters-in-law, nieces and nephews, and a bonus dad. She's so lucky.*

"I want to thank Mia and Lucas Fournier for allowing us to hold the wedding and all related events here," Skylar went on. "This is a dream setting, and I'm so grateful for everything they've done to make my vision come to life." She put her hand over her heart and made eye contact with the beautiful couple who owned the winery, and were standing at the back of the room. Mia blew her a kiss, and Lucas smiled and nodded, his arm around his wife.

"We also want to thank everyone who came in from out of town to share this weekend with us. We know you're all busy, and we truly appreciate the effort you made to be here. We love you." Skylar's eyes swept over the crowd again, but I noticed that Sebastian was focused solely on her. The love and admiration in his gaze made my throat get tight. Skylar was so *lucky*.

I bit my lip as she turned to our family table, her blue eyes shining. "Finally, we want to say thank you to my parents,

Bill and Grace Nixon, for hosting the wedding and for giving us an example of what true, committed love and marriage are. We know it's not easy, but you make it look that way. Congratulations on thirty-five years together."

As everyone applauded, my dad kissed my mom on the cheek, and the lump in my throat thickened.

"To my baby sister and bridesmaid Natalie, I want to say I love you and I couldn't be happier for you and Miles, who's been my brother all along." Taking a breath, she turned to me. "To my big sister and maid of honor Jillian, you're the smartest, kindest, strongest person I know. Thanks for always being there for me. I love you."

"Love you too," I whispered, my throat too tight to speak. Skylar wasn't the only one who was lucky. We all were.

I vowed right then to stop comparing myself to my sisters or anyone else. *Listen to what Skylar is saying. Happiness is about family and friends and being grateful for what you have, which is a hell of a lot.*

"We raise our glasses to all of you for being here tonight, and to love for bringing us together. Cheers!" she cried happily.

Suddenly I remembered my glass was empty, and my shoulders slumped in disappointment. Then I figured I'd raise it anyway, and to my surprise, when I went to grab it, I discovered someone had filled it when I wasn't looking.

That seemed like a good sign.

I actually smiled as I lifted it up. "To love!"

Maybe there was hope for me after all.

CHAPTER 2
Jillian

BY NINE THE FOLLOWING NIGHT, my positive attitude was somewhat diminished. All the rude questions and comments I hadn't heard at the rehearsal dinner had clearly been saved up for the main event.

No boyfriend yet? Maybe you're being too picky.

Last Nixon sister standing, huh?

Hard to believe you're still single, Jillian. You're so pretty! (Then they'd study me carefully, like they were trying to figure out what the problem was, since it couldn't be my face. If I were a car, they'd have asked me to pop the hood so they could take a look.)

One well-meaning great-aunt even dragged me over to meet someone who was seated at a nearby table. The fact that he was gay and even had a male date seemed lost on her, and she kept insisting we dance. The poor guy took me out on the floor just to shut her up, and we swayed awkwardly to "Ain't That a Kick in the Head" while my sisters howled with laughter at the head table.

After that, I decided to hide out near the bar and get tipsy.

I was creeping behind a row of topiary trees with my third —or maybe my fifth—glass of champagne when my mother's oldest friend, Irene Mahoney, spotted me. Irene meant well, but she was the kind of woman who always managed to compliment and insult me in one breath.

"Jillian! Are you hiding?" She stuck her hands on her ample hips.

"No, Aunt Irene. Just taking a break." Lifting my glass, I downed the rest of my champagne and immediately wanted more. Why were champagne flutes so small? Would it be wrong to ask for a bigger glass? Or maybe the whole bottle?

"Well, you should be dancing! You look so pretty in that dress, and you're never going to meet anyone if you don't put yourself out there. You know what they say, always a bridesmaid…" Her voice trailed off as she pointed one pudgy finger at me.

I squeezed the stem of my glass so hard I thought it might snap, but I managed a smile. "I'm not much of a dancer."

"How's the new job going? Your mother said you're loving it."

I nodded enthusiastically. "I am."

"Are the hours any less grueling? Do you have any time to yourself?"

"They're a little better, not much. But I love getting to know the families. Last week I—"

"What about your own family? Don't you want one?"

I bristled. "Sure. Eventually."

"Well, you're never going to meet anyone hiding over here with that frown on your face, silly girl."

Actually, I wasn't frowning until you came over here.

"You need to stand where you can be seen. Smile. Look more approachable," she admonished, patting my arm. "Let me find you a partner."

"No, really. I don't want to dance right now."

"Well, you're much too lovely to be standing over here so single—I mean, so alone. You're at that age where you have to be proactive about these things, Jillian. You have to let men see what a prize you are or risk being sad and lonely forever." She grabbed my arm and began to drag me toward the tent.

"Please. I'm not a prize, Aunt Irene. And I'm not sad, either."

"Of course you are! Every woman wants a man in her life."

Digging my heels in, I wrenched my arm away. "Actually, what *this* woman wants is another drink. Excuse me." I spun away from her and slammed immediately into a big, solid wall. Wait, no—it wasn't a wall. Walls don't have strong hands that reach out to steady you, huge dark eyes full of concern, and a thick, brown beard you're pretty sure would feel like velvet against your cheek. And your thighs.

They don't know your name, either.

"Jillian?"

For a second, I couldn't place him. Then my jaw dropped. *Oh my God.* "Levi?"

"You two know each other?" Irene, still right behind me, sounded pleased.

"Uh…yeah." Levi and I looked at each other, half stunned, half embarrassed. He took his hands from my upper arms, and I immediately felt unbalanced.

"We've, um…" Our eyes locked, exchanging a silent word. *Fucked.*

"Met." Levi finished my sentence, his lips tipping up.

I smiled too. What we'd done was have fumbling, frantic sex in a dorm utility closet the way only two desperately hormonal (and drunk) college students can do. To this day, every time I think about that encounter, I go a little weak in the knees.

Was it horrible that I didn't know his last name?

"Isn't this wonderful?" Irene looked back and forth between Levi and me, smiling approvingly. "And just look how nice and tall he is, Jillian. My word, he must be over six feet. You should ask her to dance," she ordered him.

Levi's eyes widened in alarm, and I smiled at him reassuringly. "Don't worry about it. I'm not much of a dancer." But Irene was right about one thing—he was nice and tall. He had a few solid inches on me, and at five foot eight plus my four-inch heels, that was pretty impressive. He wore a black suit with a white dress shirt, and the knot in his tie was loose and a little haphazard, as if he'd been in a rush to get dressed. His dark hair was parted on the side, longer on top and neatly combed back. Something stirred inside me—something I hadn't felt in a long time.

At least not without charging up Magik Mike first. And Mike had three speeds, seven functions, and rotating ball bearings, so this was pretty impressive.

"How about a drink instead?" I asked.

He smiled, looking relieved. "I'd like that."

"Perfect." Taking his elbow, I steered him toward the patio bar, tossing a placating smile at Irene over my shoulder. "Nice chatting with you, Aunt Irene. Enjoy the music."

When we were a safe distance away from her, I let go of Levi's arm, although I really wished I had a reason to keep holding on to it. What was he *doing* here? "Sorry about crashing into you like that. I'm a little clumsy. Plus..." I held up my empty champagne glass. "This doesn't help."

He laughed a little. "I didn't mind."

"So." I tried to think of where to begin, since *hey, remember that time we banged in a closet?* seemed a little too off-color for this occasion. "It's been a while. I almost didn't recognize you."

Grinning, he ran a hand over his chin. "Didn't have the beard back in college."

"I like it." I liked it a lot, actually. He'd been tall, skinny and cute at twenty-one, all arms and legs, floppy hair and cocky smile, but he was tall, broad, and gorgeous at thirty-two. I glanced at the darkening sky. *Please, God—please let him be single.*

"Thanks. My son likes it too."

I gave God the stinkeye. "Wow. You have a son?"

"Yes." We reached the bar and stood in the short line. "Scotty."

"How old is he?"

"He's eight."

"Got a picture?"

He pulled out his phone and scrolled through a couple photos before handing it to me. On the screen was an adorable young boy sitting on a swing. He had messy dark hair, his father's huge brown eyes and long limbs, a smattering of freckles across his nose, and ears that stuck out a little. His expression was thoughtful and serious, and he wore a shirt with a drawing of a T. Rex on it that said Scottasaurus.

"He's beautiful," I said, handing the phone back.

"Thank you."

Some quick math told me he must have gotten married fairly soon after college. I'd met him my sophomore year at U of M, but he'd only been visiting friends there. I hadn't even planned to go out that night—I'd had on a Harry Potter t-shirt, for heaven's sake, and I think it had a hole in it—but my friends had dragged me to the bar, insisting I needed a study break. I'd noticed Levi right away, and we'd eyed each other across the room for a good portion of the night before he finally came over to me and said, "Harry Potter fan, huh? So what are the chances I can Slytherin to your chamber of secrets tonight?"

Two drinks later, we were kissing, and two after that, we were racing hand in hand to my dorm, where he'd yanked me into the hallway broom closet after we'd discovered my roommate was already asleep in my room.

For a moment, I was distracted by the memory of giggling breathlessly as I listened to him tear open the condom wrapper and put it on, the sight of him lost to me in the dark. I remembered the way my heart pounded as I slid my underwear down my legs, terrified we'd rouse my RA, whose room was right next door. I remembered the scent of bleach and Pine Sol, his lips on mine, his hands on my shoulders as he turned my body toward the wall and lifted my jean skirt. Most of all, I remembered the way he whispered as he thrust up inside me again and again and again, so deep and hard it teetered on the edge between pleasure and pain, one hand over my mouth to stifle my cries. *You're so fucking hot, I wanna fuck you so hard, oh fuck I'm gonna come.*

OK, maybe not terribly poetic or imaginative, but hey, he was young.

And for me, a bookworm whose Saturday nights were usually spent reading bio-chem textbooks or romance novels, broom closet sex with a hot guy was a pretty erotic experience. Until that point I'd only had missionary sex in dorm room beds with two other guys, neither of whom had said anything except "uuuuuuuhhhhhhhhh" the entire time. And by "the entire time," I mean all five minutes.

But with Levi, it was different. Not that it was much slower—in fact, it may have been faster—but it was more illicit. More unexpected.

Dirtier.

Rougher.

And I'd liked it—it had shocked me how much I liked it. In fact, it was still one of my go-to fantasies when I was alone with Magik Mike.

Too bad he was married.

I cleared my throat in an effort to clear my head. "Is your wife here?"

"We aren't together anymore." He didn't look or sound particularly sad about it.

"Oh." My pulse picked up, and I sent God a silent apology for the stinkeye. "So tell me how you know Sebastian. Skylar is my sister."

He cocked his head. "Is she? Sorry, I probably would

know that if I hadn't been so late that I missed the ceremony. I never saw a program or anything."

"That's OK, most people wouldn't guess it. We don't look much alike." Skylar and Natalie had our mother's blonde hair and petite, curvy body. I had our dad's tall, thin frame and dark hair, although we all had the same blue eyes. "And we, um, might not have exchanged last names that night."

Levi laughed, a deep throaty sound that heated up my insides. "Maybe not."

"Jillian Nixon." I held out my hand.

He took it. "Levi Brooks."

I have a bit of a hand fetish and couldn't resist glancing down at his. It was solid and strong, with long fingers, nails neatly trimmed. A thick black watch peeked out from the crisp white cuff of his dress shirt, which made my heart skip a few beats. I *love* a nice wristwatch on a man. There's something so classic and masculine about it.

His grip was firm, and he gave my hand an affectionate little squeeze before letting go. "I met Sebastian at the gym a couple years ago, but I'm also his architect."

"You're an architect? Did you design his cabin?" I asked, impressed. "It's beautiful!"

"Thanks." He shrugged, sticking his hands in his pockets. "That was a pretty simple project, really. And Sebastian had a lot of input. He just needed someone to draw up the plans and supervise the construction."

"I hear they're adding on, though, right? I knew my sister wouldn't be able to live with so little closet space."

Levi chuckled, and I raised my eyebrows. "Sorry," he said. "It's just…" He glanced sideways at me, a boyish grin on his face. "Closet space."

My face warmed, and I couldn't help smiling either. "Ah. Yes. Closet space."

The group in front of us moved away from the bar, and Levi put a hand lightly at the small of my back as we stepped forward. It wasn't overtly suggestive, but it sent a flutter through my belly all the same.

In fact, every part of my body felt fluttery—my heart, my hands, my knees. Even my head, which can usually find something wrong with a guy in under five minutes, wasn't telling me no. So he had a son, so what? He was handsome and smart and funny, and I hadn't been this attracted to someone in a long time.

So I was glad when he left his hand on my back while we ordered drinks, his thumb rubbing softly at the base of my spine.

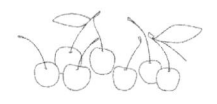

We took our drinks to an unoccupied table in one shadowy corner of the winery's stone terrace, where the ceremony had taken place hours before. Since then, the rows of chairs had been replaced by cocktail tables fashioned with giant oak barrels and round glass table tops covered with ivory linen. Party lights were strung in the trees above, and the table held small votive candles, which flickered in the falling dark.

"Hard to believe we've never run into each other before," I said, setting my glass on the table. "Have you lived in this area long?"

"About three years. Before that I was in Charlevoix. That's where my family is."

Impulsively, I reached over and fixed his tie, pulling the knot tighter and straightening it out. "Sorry. Couldn't resist."

"Was it crooked?" Grimacing a little, he took over the task, and a tingle swept up my arms when his fingers closed over mine. "I was so rushed tonight. My sister was late, and then I had trouble getting out of the house. Did I even remember to put pants on?"

I laughed. "Yes, you did." *Although I wouldn't mind if you took them off.*

"Oh, good." He picked up his drink and took a sip. "So tell me about you. I know your last name now, I know you used to like Harry Potter, and I know you're a little clumsy when you drink champagne, but other than that, I got nothing."

Heat rushed my face, and I giggled. "I am a little clumsy, and not just when I drink champagne. But in addition to that, I still like Harry Potter, and I'm a pediatrician."

He cocked his head. "Are you? I always wondered if you went to med school. Back then you were planning on it."

I smiled, pleased that he'd remembered something about me. And had he said *always wondered*? "Yes. I finished up my undergrad at Michigan and then went to medical school at Wayne State. I completed my residency up here and took a job in private practice about six months ago."

"In this area?"

I nodded. "Yes. In Traverse City. I'm really close to my family, so I was happy about that. Now catch me up more with *you*," I said, tucking my hair behind my ear. "If memory serves, you were at State—but there's a good chance it does not, since I believe there *may* have been some liquor consumed the night we, um…*met*—"

"Uh, yeah. A lot of liquor, as I recall." Levi laughed. "Sometimes I'm amazed my liver survived undergrad. OK, let's see. I think I met you my senior year, when I was at State, and then I ended up in Boston for grad school. Scotty was born during my final year there."

I blinked. "Wow. That must have been tough, trying to finish school and care for a wife and baby."

He hesitated. "Actually, Scotty's mom and I were never married."

"You weren't?"

He shook his head. "No. I offered to marry her when we

found out she was pregnant, but she didn't want that. She said she couldn't handle grad school and marriage and pregnancy all at once. Sometimes I wonder if she knew then she was leaving."

"She *left*?"

He nodded, lifting his drink again. "Shortly after Scotty was born. Said she wasn't cut out to be a mother and she'd made the wrong choice."

"My God." I tried to imagine what that must have been like for Levi, suddenly on his own with a newborn baby. "So you're raising him alone?"

"He's my son. For me, there was no choice." He rotated his glass slowly on the table, staring into it. "She wanted a career in finance, so she went to New York, and I moved back to Charlevoix so my family could help out. My uncle had an architectural firm and offered me a job."

"Do you ever see her or hear from her?" I hoped he didn't think I was being too nosy, but I was so curious about him.

"No, and that's how I wanted it. That's how we both wanted it." He met my eyes and lifted his broad shoulders. "The relationship wasn't good to begin with. I definitely got the best part of it—in fact, as far as I'm concerned, I got everything. She walked away with nothing."

My heart thumped hard. "I bet you're an amazing father."

He smiled, but he shook his head. "Actually, most of the time, I have no idea what I'm doing and I'm just trying to get through the fucking day." After another big swallow of whiskey, he squared his shoulders and set his glass down hard. "But you know what? I rarely get out on Saturday nights—in fact, I can't even remember the last time—so let's talk about something more fun." His dark eyes glittered. "Like broom closets."

I laughed, shaking my head. "That *was* fun. I still can't believe I did that."

"Are you saying you didn't make a habit of luring innocent college boys into your lair with your blue eyes and long legs and sexy Harry Potter t-shirt?"

"Ha! No, I certainly did not. And you were not that innocent." I tossed back the last of my champagne, the bubbles tickling my tongue.

"I wasn't?"

"No. You knew exactly what you were doing, and you did it very well."

"Thank you." He looked pleased with himself.

"And very fast."

His face fell as he groaned. "God, don't tell me. All I remember thinking is, 'oh fuck don't come oh fuck don't come oh fuck I came.'"

I couldn't resist. "That's pretty much what you said, too."

"Is it?" He groaned even louder and slammed the rest of his drink. "I need more whiskey. Want something?"

I bit my lip and looked at my empty glass. What number was that? I felt light-headed, but I didn't know if it was the champagne or the flirting. I felt light-hearted too. "I shouldn't."

"Why? Are you driving?"

"No."

"Are you married?"

"No."

"Are you worried I'm going to get you drunk and drag you into a closet for round two?"

I smiled coyly. "Maybe."

He leaned in closer, so close I felt his breath on my lips. "Good."

CHAPTER 3
Jillian

BEFORE LEVI CAME BACK with our next round, Skylar and Sebastian appeared on the patio. Noticing I was by myself, Skylar tugged on her new husband's hand, whispered in his ear, and left his side to join me at the table.

"Hey, you." She fanned her face, which was dewy and flushed, but other than the fact that her lipstick had faded, she looked just as radiant and flawless as she had at three o'clock this afternoon. "What are you doing hiding out all alone over here?"

"I'm not hiding, and actually, I'm not alone." I gave her a cryptic little smile, and her eyes widened.

"What's that mean?"

Over her shoulder, I saw Sebastian and Levi greet each other with a handshake and a back-thumping man-hug. I knew I'd only have a minute before they came over here, so I spoke fast. "OK, remember the guy I told you about, the one in the dorm closet?"

"Pine Sol?"

"Yeah. He's here."

"Pine Sol is *here*?" Her jaw dropped, and she craned her neck to look over her shoulder as I shushed her.

"Yes. He's talking to Sebastian right now."

She faced me again, her eyes huge and sparkling. "Pine Sol is *Levi Brooks*? The architect? I don't believe it!"

"Shhhhhhh!" I flapped my hands between us to get her to quiet down. "Will you hush, please? I don't want him to know I told you about the closet."

"I'm sorry, I can't help it. Oh my God, this is amazing. I can't wait to tell Natalie." She shook her head and moved around the table to make room for the guys, who were headed our way with drinks. "Wait, isn't he married? He's got a kid, I think."

I shook my head. "Nope. Not married. But yes, one son." There was no time to get into everything he had told me. "Do you know anything else about him?"

"Not really," she said, frowning. "Sebastian never gossips about anyone, it's so annoying."

"OK, quiet now. Here they come." Meeting Levi's eyes as he approached, I smiled, my heart tripping faster.

He set my champagne and his Old Fashioned down and came around the table to kiss my sister on the cheek. "Congratulations, Skylar. You look beautiful."

She flashed him her ten thousand watt smile. "Thank you. I'm so glad you're here. You've met my big sister, Jillian, I see."

He came back to his place beside me, standing a little closer this time, his body angled toward mine. "Yes. Actually, we met years ago."

"So I hear." Skylar gave him a smile that said I Totally Know What You Did, and I elbowed her. Did she have to be so obvious?

Natalie and Miles strolled up. "What's going on?" Natalie asked, eyeballing me and Levi and then me again.

Skylar scooted over to make room for them between her and Sebastian. "Levi, this is the youngest Nixon sister, Natalie, and her fiancé, Miles Haas."

While Miles and Natalie shook hands with Levi and Sebastian explained the connection, Skylar and I had a silent conversation with our facial expressions and eyebrows, the way only two sisters can. It went something like this:

Knock it off!

What? I'm not doing anything.

Yes you are, and you know it.

Relax, I'm only having a little fun. He doesn't know you told me.

He's standing right there! You're making it obvious! Now stop.

But the glint in her eye made me nervous.

"So Jillian, Sebastian was just saying you and Levi met at U of M?" Natalie sounded curious.

"We were *just* talking about your time at Michigan, weren't we?" Skylar turned to Natalie. "Remember, Nat? She was telling us about how clean the dorms were? How she loved the way they smelled like *Pine Sol*?"

If it hadn't been her wedding day, I might have strangled her. I couldn't even make eye contact with Levi, I was so mortified, but I thought I heard him chuckle.

"Pine Sol? Wasn't that the hot guy from college, the one she—wait a minute." Natalie's face screwed up in confusion until she noticed the way that Skylar was tilting her head toward Levi. "Ohhhhh."

"Is anyone else totally fucking confused?" Miles asked, looking around the table.

"Yes," Sebastian said.

I cleared my throat. "So Nat, how are you feeling tonight? That baby kicking yet?" I knew it was way too early in her pregnancy for that, but I was desperate to change the subject.

She beamed. "Not yet."

"Congratulations," said Levi. "Do you know what you're having?"

"Girl," said Skylar with confidence.

"I think boy," said Natalie.

"We'll know next month." Miles moved behind her and wrapped his arms around her waist, which had just started to disappear within the last few weeks. He kissed her shoulder. "I can't wait."

"Levi has a son." I smiled up at him over one shoulder. "Any advice for the parents-to-be?"

"Sleep. Now. As much as you can." He shook his head and grinned wryly. "Once that baby comes, sleep will be a distant memory. Other than that..." He shrugged, and his smile softened. "Just remember you're human. You're going to have days where you're like, 'This is awesome, my baby is a genius and I'm the most amazing parent on the planet' and days where you'll go, 'Fuck that, my baby is an asshole and needs to go the fuck to sleep.'"

Natalie laughed. "How old is your son?"

"Eight. But depending on the mood he's in, he can act like he's two or like he's eighty." He tipped back the rest of his cocktail and set down the glass. "Speaking of my little man, I should probably call home. Will you excuse me for a minute?"

"Of course."

"Thanks. Be right back." He placed a hand on my back before heading through the glass double doors into the winery's tasting room.

As soon as the door shut behind him, Skylar whacked me on the shoulder. "I still can't believe that's Pine Sol!"

"OK, what happened with you two?" Miles pushed his glasses farther up on his nose. "I feel like there's a story there."

"There is, and you'll like it," said Natalie. "They banged in a broom closet."

"Which smelled like Pine Sol," Skylar added.

"My God, is nothing sacred?" I threw a hand in the air. "I'm never telling you two big mouths anything ever again."

"What? We're all family here." Skylar gave me her innocent face. "And that was like ten years ago."

"Eleven."

"Whatever. Let's talk about him *now*. He's so hot! And so bearded! Plus he's, like, mature and responsible. And single. And perfect for you." Skylar ticked off his attributes on her fingers. "So you should marry him and have his hot bearded babies immediately."

"Slow down, Aunt Irene," I said, laughing. "I just learned this guy's last name like half an hour ago, and I'm not having *anyone's* bearded babies." *But I won't complain if he wants to go through the motions later tonight.*

"You're no fun." She stuck her tongue out at me and turned to Sebastian. "What do we know about this guy? Is he good enough for my big sister?"

Sebastian smiled. "He's a great guy. Really devoted to his son. Smart. Talented."

"Does it bother you?" Skylar asked. "That he has a son? Because it seems like he's into you."

"I don't know. I mean, I've never dated anyone with kids before, but…" I bit my lip. "You really think he's into me?"

"He'd be a fucking fool if he wasn't," Miles said.

Flashing him a grateful smile, I set down my glass half-full. "Thanks. You know what, I think I'll go in too. I need to use the bathroom." Maybe Levi and I could sneak out a different door when he was done with his call. Not that I didn't adore my family, but I was dying to be alone with Levi again.

That fluttery feeling was like a drug.

I thought I heard his voice in the darkened tasting room, but I went straight up the stairs to the winery's bridal suite where my sisters and I had dressed. After using the bathroom, I touched up my hair and makeup a little, frowning at the tiny lines around my eyes that had recently appeared. Leaning closer to the mirror, I scrutinized my face. I wasn't nineteen anymore, or even twenty-five. Did it matter? What did he see when he looked at me?

Straightening up, I ran my hands over my breasts and hips, shivering a little at the thought of *his* hands on me. At the thought of his body beneath that black suit. At the thought of his body beneath *me*—and above me and next to me and inside me.

You're so fucking hot, I wanna fuck you so hard, oh fuck I'm gonna come.

My mouth fell open, and I closed my eyes as a rush of arousal swept through me. God, I hadn't had sex in so long, it would probably be *me* who went off like a cannon in less than three minutes tonight.

If there was a tonight—I was getting a little ahead of myself.

(In my defense, we're talking a year-long dry spell and a hot bearded man here. I think I can be forgiven.)

As I came down the steps, I saw Levi standing off to my right, and the phone was still to his ear. He faced the tasting room bar, his back to me, and I wasn't sure if I should wait for him or go back out to the patio to give him some privacy.

When my heels clicked on the stone floor, he turned and held up one finger, like he wanted me to stay there while he finished his call. I took a seat on one of the couches clustered near the fireplace, and he came closer to me. The minute I heard him speak, I could tell he was agitated.

"I know he does. But I—"

Whoever he was talking to cut him off, and he exhaled loudly.

"But it's not behavioral. I've explained this. It's—"

Interrupted again, he closed his eyes, took a deep breath, and pinched the bridge of his nose.

"Listen to me." Dropping his hand, he turned toward the window so I only saw his profile and spoke quietly but firmly. "I don't care what your friend the doctor says. He's not Scotty's doctor, and he doesn't know the first fucking thing about him."

Uh oh. It sounded like maybe an argument—with his sister?—and I wasn't sure he wanted me to hear it. I kept my eyes on him, waiting for a signal, but he kept staring out the large windows, left hand at his side, fist clenching and unclenching. It probably shouldn't have turned me on, but that hand looked so solid and strong. I bet if he did throw a punch, the other guy would go down hard and fast. But something about him made me think he knew how to be gentle too. Maybe it was the way his eyes lit up when he talked about his son. Maybe it was the way he called Scotty his little man. Maybe it was the way he'd leaned in to me, his lips barely brushing mine…

"Look, we'll talk about this another time." Levi faced me again, and I jumped up as if I'd been caught staring at his crotch, not his hand.

"I have to go, Monica. I'll be home soon." Holding the phone slightly away from his ear, he grimaced, then spoke again. "Fine. Thank you." He ended the call and slipped his phone in his pocket as he came toward me, tension creasing his forehead. "I'm sorry about that."

"That's OK."

"My sister, Monica. I love her, but she has all sorts of opinions about how I should be raising my son and she likes to lecture me about it. Drives me fucking nuts."

"Sisters do that sometimes." I gave him a sympathetic smile. "Everything OK at home?"

He exhaled, and some of the worry lines on his face disappeared. "Yes. Scotty's finally asleep. For now."

"He doesn't sleep well?"

"Not really."

"Have you tried melatonin?"

"Yes. With mixed results." He hesitated before going on. "Scotty has autism, and routine is really important to him. He can be difficult at bedtime if the littlest thing is different."

As a doctor, I could've asked a bunch of questions and offered some more advice, but based on the conversation I'd just overheard, he wasn't looking for that. And I didn't want to be Dr. Nixon tonight. I just wanted to be Jillian.

And Jillian found it hotter than fuck that he was raising a child with autism on his own and was so devoted to him.

"So," he said, coming so near to me that the toes of his shoes met mine.

"So."

He glanced out the windows to the patio. "You want to go back out there?"

"Not really," I said, my pulse quickening.

A hint of a smile appeared as he met my eyes again. "You want to get out of here?"

My toes tingled. "Yeah. I do."

CHAPTER 4
Levi

I WATCHED her rush up the stairs to get her things, and as soon as she was out of sight, I adjusted myself in my pants. My dick had jumped to life the second she said *yeah, I do*, as if the question had been *you want to get naked and fuck?* rather than something much less suggestive. Not that I didn't want to get naked and fuck—hopefully I'd last a little longer than I had in the broom closet eleven years ago—but I didn't want to make her feel like that's what I expected. She wasn't a horny nineteen-year-old college student anymore; she was a doctor, for fuck's sake. She was beautiful and smart and mature and sophisticated, and a woman like her did not want some Neanderthal who probably needed a haircut and a new pair of shoes to throw her up against a wall for a five-minute fuck.

A woman like that deserved attention all night long. She deserved someone who would undress her slowly and delight in each new inch of her skin as it was revealed. Someone who would run his hands all over her body and find out where she liked to be touched, how she liked to be touched, what she wanted to hear whispered to her in the dark. Someone who would wrap those gloriously long legs around his neck and use his tongue until she begged for his cock, then use his cock until she begged for mercy.

Fuck. I could be that guy.

Except I couldn't be. Not tonight. Because I wasn't a horny college student anymore either—I was just a horny single dad who didn't have the luxury of taking a woman home and lavishing all my time and attention on her the way I wanted to.

As soon as I had the thought, I felt guilty. Scotty was the love of my life and always would be, and whenever I felt the slightest bit resentful about something I couldn't do because of him, that resentment was immediately crushed by shame. He didn't ask to be born wired differently, into a terrible relationship, to a mother who would decide she couldn't handle being a parent, to a father who wasn't prepared for any of it. He was completely innocent, and he needed me to be a better man.

You're spoiling him, Monica had scolded me tonight, as usual. She'd tried to make him wash and comb his hair before bed, which had resulted in a meltdown. Granted, the kid's hair was dirty and disheveled, but washing it was such a battle I permitted him to wash it only once a week, on Sunday nights. She'd also wanted him to change his pajama top, since he'd gotten chocolate milk on the front of the one he was wearing. But in Scotty's world, there is no pairing the dinosaur pajama bottoms with a plaid pajama top. There is also no changing into the plaid pajama bottoms, because he'd already planned on wearing the dinosaurs. Plaid was for school nights.

You let him run the house. He's the child; you're the adult. He's manipulating you.

I'd heard it from everyone in my family, which was a huge part of the reason Scotty and I had moved away. They meant well, but they didn't understand that Scotty's inflexibility wasn't just him being a brat—he experienced physical pain when something felt "wrong" for him. I wasn't letting him get away with things; I was making compromises the way all parents do, trying to find the right balance between being strict and being compassionate. Why couldn't they understand that?

Running a hand through my hair, I exhaled and wondered if I should ask Jillian for a rain check on a night when Scotty's usual sitter could be there. If he woke up again and I wasn't home yet, he might never get back to sleep. We'd be up all night, tomorrow would be miserable, and the whole start to the week would be off.

But she was so *beautiful*. And I hadn't been this attracted to someone in *so long*.

"Fuck," I muttered, checking my watch. What was the right thing to do? If she were a different sort of woman, if her brother-in-law weren't my friend and client, if we lived three states apart...if any number of circumstances were changed, I'd grab her hand, drag her out to my car, and spend the next thirty minutes fucking her brains out in the back seat. It would feel so good to take control that way, to *lose* control that way, to release some of this fucking tension. But was that fair to her?

My phone buzzed in my pocket.

"Hello?"

"He's up again." Monica's voice was strained, and in the background I heard the familiar keening of a nighttime meltdown. My chest hurt, the way it always did when Scotty was upset.

"Shit. OK, I'm on my way. Twenty minutes, OK? Thirty at the most."

"OK."

"Tell him he can play on his iPad."

"That'll just rile him up more. He's tired. He needs to go back to sleep."

I clenched my fist. "Just do it, OK? It will help calm him until I get there."

As I ended the call, I heard footsteps above, and then Jillian appeared at the top of the stairs carrying a small suitcase. I watched her descend, the tightness in my chest growing. Also the tightness in my pants. "Hey."

"Hey," she said, her face concerned as she reached the ground and saw my expression. She set down the suitcase. "What's up?"

Sighing, I put my phone back in my pocket. "I have to get home. Scotty woke up and he's upset."

"Oh." She tried to hide it, but I saw the disappointment in her eyes.

"I'm really sorry. I'll make it up to you, I promise."

"That's OK. I understand."

"Can I call you?"

"Of course." She smiled, and her lips looked so soft and inviting, I took a step closer.

If you kiss her, it will be that much harder to leave.

I knew it was the truth, but I couldn't help myself. *One kiss. Just one. And then I'll go.* I moved even closer and took her head in my hands.

The curve of her smile deepened. "What are you doing?"

"I'm thinking about kissing you."

"Stop thinking."

I lowered my lips to hers and let them rest there, fully intending the kiss to be short and sweet, just a goodnight.

But I couldn't break it off. I wanted more—I wanted to taste her. Slanting my head, I changed the angle of the kiss, teasing her mouth open with mine, slipping my tongue between her lips. A little sigh escaped her, and my dick jumped to life again.

You have to go, you have to go, you have to go.

But her hands were moving up my chest and my fingers were sliding into her soft brown hair and I could smell something sweet and citrusy on her skin and it mingled with the taste of whiskey on my tongue and oh God, I wanted my tongue everywhere on her body. I wanted to make her come with it just so I could hear that little sigh again and again and again. And I wanted to feel my hands in her hair just like this while she got on her knees and took my cock between her lips, looking up at me with those big blue eyes…

Groaning, I forced myself to take my lips off her before I completely lost my senses. "God, I wish I could stay," I said, resting my forehead against hers. "I wish a lot of things."

"I know." She played with my tie again. "I wish I was taking this tie off you, not straightening it."

"What a coincidence, that's one of my wishes too."

She laughed and kissed me quickly. "Another time, maybe. You better go."

I sighed and wrapped my arms around her, pulling her close. Her hair smelled good, too. I inhaled, trapping the scent of her in my lungs, memorizing the feel of her in my arms, so that later when the house was dark and quiet and I was alone in bed with my dick in my hand, I could imagine she was with me.

If I could get the house dark and quiet, of course. Sometimes I couldn't.

And before the cycle of resentment, guilt, and shame could set in, I dropped a kiss on her head and let go of her. Pulling my phone from my pocket, I unlocked the screen and handed it to her. "Will you put your number in here so I can call you?"

"Sure." She tapped her number onto the keypad and saved the contact info before handing it back to me. "There you go."

"Thanks. I'm so glad I came tonight. I almost didn't."

"I'm glad too. It was really good seeing you."

"You too. I haven't had the chance to tell you this yet, but you're even more beautiful now than you were then."

She smiled and shook her head, but I could tell she was flattered. "Stop."

"Truth. I swear." I kissed her cheek. "Night, Jillian."

"Night."

When I pulled into my garage twenty minutes later, I couldn't resist sending her a quick text, even though I'd talked to my sister on the way home and knew she still couldn't get Scotty back to sleep. It would be probably be a long night, but I was feeling oddly optimistic right now.

Hey. Pine Sol here.

Just wanted to tell you again how glad I am your clumsy ass ran into me tonight.

Can't stop thinking about you.

CHAPTER 5
Jillian

I MISSED him after he left. How crazy was that? We'd only spent a couple of hours together, but once I was alone again, I kept thinking about him and wishing he was there. I sat and watched people dance for a while, but in my head all I did was replay my time with him, from the accidental body check to the goodnight kiss, over and over again. Every time I thought about his lips on mine, his hands in my hair, his body pressing closer, I shivered.

When would I see him again?

When I was ready to leave, Skylar said to just have the limo driver take me home and come back for them, since she wasn't quite ready to call it a night. I said goodnight and went upstairs to get my stuff from the suite. As soon as I pulled my phone from my purse, I saw the text from Levi and gasped—first with embarrassment that he'd figured out the Pine Sol nickname, and second with pleasure...he couldn't stop thinking about me?

In the limo, I read the words over and over and over again, my insides dancing, until I could close my eyes and see them glowing on the back of my eyelids.

Can't stop thinking about you.

Can't stop thinking about you.
Can't stop thinking about you.

An hour later, when my dress was hanging in my closet and my face was scrubbed clean, I popped two Advil, pulled a soft cotton t-shirt over my head and stretched out between cool sheets with my phone in my hand. It was late, nearly one in the morning, but I texted him back.

Can't stop thinking about you either.
P.S. Totally embarrassed about the nickname. Sisters!

I set the phone on my nightstand and turned off the lamp. But I couldn't sleep. My body was tired but restless, with too much sexual energy trapped inside it, and all I could think about was Levi's kiss. And his voice in my ear. And his hands on me.

Sweet Jesus, those hands.

I sat up and reached into the nightstand drawer for Magik Mike.

But I hadn't charged him.

"Fuck!" I threw him back into the drawer and slammed it shut. Now what?

I was considering left-handing it when my cell phone buzzed.

Still awake?

Smiling, I picked it up again. **Yes.**

Cleaning the bathrooms with Pine Sol?

Hahaha no. You're up late. How is your son?

• • •

He's OK. He fell asleep in my bed, but I just put him in his, and he stayed asleep. Miracle.

Glad to hear it. Is your sister still there?

No, she went home. Did you have fun tonight?

Yes.

Did you have to dance?

NO, thank god. Aunt Irene let me be. She means well, but she drives me crazy.

Why?

Always bothering me about why I'm not married, don't I want a family, I work too much, the clock is ticking, etc.

Do you work too much?

I sighed and answered honestly. **Yes. But I love what I do, and I worked my ass off to get where I am.**

Do you want to get married and have kids?

. . .

I knew what he meant, but I had to tease him. **It's a little soon for that, isn't it?**

Ha. I guess I did just accidentally propose, didn't I? Oops.

Don't worry. I won't hold you to it. I do want it eventually. I just don't like the way people bug me about it. Like I have an expiration date or something.

My family bugs me too. They try to tell me how to live my life, raise my son, point out everything I'm doing wrong. Then they guilt me for not coming around enough.

Yes! God, why can't people leave well enough alone? Tonight I was told I'm not getting any younger, I'm too picky, and I'm unapproachable.

I approached you once.

With your smooth Harry Potter pickup line.

That was so ridiculous.

Hey, it worked.

. . .

It did. So clearly you are not that picky.

That made me smile. **You didn't even need a line tonight. I ran right into you.**

You did. I quite enjoyed it.

There was a long pause, during which I chewed my lip and considered the interesting places this little conversation could go. Maybe we hadn't gotten a second round in the closet, but that didn't mean we couldn't still have some fun tonight. **So. What are you up to now?**

Just lying here.

Me too.

Are you in bed?

Yes. I took a breath and wiggled my toes, which I do automatically when I'm excited about something. **Are you?**

Yes.

I grinned. **I feel like I should ask you what you're wearing. Is that pervy?**

. . .

Ha. No. Especially since I am not wearing anything too exciting. I never changed.

Still in your suit? Damn, that was exciting enough for me. I love a man in a suit and tie. Add a wristwatch, and my panties melt. I lay back on the pillows, getting more comfortable.

I took off the shoes and coat.

Tie?

Still wearing it.

My fingers trembled a little, but I typed the words I was thinking. **Take it off.**

He didn't answer right away, and I wondered if I'd gone too far, or if he was really doing it. This was the problem when you couldn't see someone's face. I chose to imagine he was taking it off, and pictured his hands loosening the knot and sliding it free from around his neck.

My phone buzzed.

Done. Your turn.

I'm not wearing a tie.

. . .

What are you wearing, smartass?

A t-shirt. Underwear. And I'm sorry to say they are not sexy at all.

Take your shirt off.

My heartbeat pattered faster as I set the phone aside, pulled my shirt over my head and lay back again. **Done. Unbutton yours.**

Done.

I hesitated, breathing hard and wondering what to do next. Was this really happening? **Undo your belt.**

Hey it's my turn.

I'm only wearing one more thing!

OK fine. But you're bossy.

I grinned and imagined those hands on his belt buckle, my stomach flipping. **Unzip your pants while you're at it.**

. . .

OK Bossypants. Done. Now take off your underwear.

I pushed them down my legs and kicked them off, leaving them under the covers at my feet. **Done.**

So you're naked?

Yes.

Fuck.

Are you hard?

Are you kidding?

No.

Fuck yes I am. I wish I was there.

I bent my knees and flattened my hand on my stomach. **What would you do to me?**

I'll tell you. But first tell me. Are you wet?

. . .

I slid my left hand between my legs, widening my knees a little, dipping a fingertip inside. **Yes.**

His next few messages came one by one, in no particular hurry.

I'd want to taste you first.

I'd bury my head in your thighs and lick you up down and sideways.

I'd do it softly just to make you beg for more.

I'd do it hard until your legs shook.

I'd fuck you with my tongue.

As he talked, I touched myself in just the ways he described, first with light, gentle strokes, soft little circles over my clit that made it ache and hum, feather-light brushes over tingling nerves. Then harder, pressing more firmly, dipping one finger inside myself, all the while imagining the feel of his beard against my skin, the sight of his dark hair between my thighs.

Yes yes yes was all I managed to type. The hum was building into a buzz, spreading throughout my whole body and I encouraged it, opening my legs wider, moving my fingers faster, dropping the phone on the bed and taking one hard nipple between my fingers. I glanced at the screen one last time.

I'd use my fingers inside you and my mouth on your pussy until you came so hard you couldn't breathe. I'd feel it happen on my tongue and fingers, hear you scream my name, watch your back arch off the bed.

. . .

At this point I stopped reading because my eyes were closing and my body was tight with tension, bursting with the need to come. His words and the thought of him doing what he described pushed me over the edge and I sighed his name as the orgasm crashed through me in blissful, rolling waves.

Then I lay there for a moment, panting and sweaty, until I recovered enough to pick up the phone.

Oh my god
Oh my god
I can't
Type

Are you breathing?

Heavily

Did you come?

Hard

Did you like it?

YES. My turn.

I rolled onto my stomach, smiling mischievously. **If you were here, I'd be begging you to fuck me right now.**

Would you?

. . .

Yes. You've got me hot and wet and wanting you.

What do you want?

First I want my hands on your cock.
    I want to feel how big and hard it is.
    I want to wrap my fingers around it and wonder how I'm going to take it all inside me. I'm remembering how hard you fucked me years ago, so deep it hurt.
    But I liked it.
    I think about it all the time.
    I make myself come when I fantasize about it. He wasn't typing back. I hoped his fingers were busy. **Can you feel my hands on you?**

Yes

Good. Now I want to straddle you and rub the tip of your cock against my pussy, so you can feel how wet I am.

oh fuck

I take my time, slide down onto you, inch by inch.
    I take you all the way in, so deep I can barely breathe.
    I move my hips over yours, slowly at first.
    I lean over you, kiss you, taste myself on your lips.
    You put your hands on my ass, force me to move faster, ride you harder.

            . . .

jesus fuck

I smiled even wider. This was like directing my own porn movie. I only wished I could see him, his white shirt and black pants undone, his hand on his dick, his eyes dark with lust. *God, I could come again just thinking about that.*

But I was on a mission.

Now for the big finish.

I can feel you getting even harder and bigger, you're hitting that perfect spot inside me, the one that makes my entire body clench up, my heart pound. I'm screaming your name as I come on your cock, and I bounce up and down even faster and harder, and it's so tight and wet and hot and you dig your fingers into my ass and tell me you're going to come. And then I feel you do it deep inside me and I don't stop moving until I've taken every last drop and feel your body go still.

OK, that had to do it, right?

I waited for him to text me back. It took a minute, and then the messages came in slowly.

Um
   Fuck
   That was
   So hot

I laughed softly. **It was.**

Be right back

     . . .

OK

I assumed he went to clean up a little, and I was thirsty, so I pulled on my t-shirt and took a minute to wash my hands and grab a water from the fridge. A few seconds after I got back into bed, he messaged me.

Hey.

Hey.

That was amazing.

Agreed.

I'm surprised I didn't wake up my kid.

I giggled. **Were you that loud?**

I don't know. Maybe. You were very vivid in your description.

It was very vivid in my head. I confess... I may have thought about it before.

You mentioned that.

. . .

It's the truth. I hesitated. **Did you ever think about me?**

You know I did.

I don't. Tell me.

I thought about fucking you. A lot.

Where?

Um, wherever I happened to be jerking off.

Hahaha that's not what I meant. I meant when you pictured it, where were we?

I have no idea. I don't think I pictured anything but bodies.

I sighed. **You're such a guy. But I'll take it. I like that you thought about fucking me.**

But now I want the real thing. Not in a closet. Not on the phone.

My breath caught. **Me too.**

. . .

Maybe we should go on a date first.

Haha maybe. Although we have already banged in a closet and sexted. The jig is up.

Right. But I would still like to take you out.

My whole body tingled, and I wiggled my toes. **OK.**

I'll call you this week.

Sounds good. Night.

Night.

I set the phone on the nightstand and pulled the covers up to my chin, unable to keep the smile off my face. All the worry in my head, and all the tension in my body, had been replaced by something else.

Exhilaration. Anticipation. Hope.
This felt like the beginning of something.

CHAPTER 6
Levi

SETTING MY PHONE ASIDE, I lay back on my bed and put my hands behind my head, my legs crossed at the ankles. Probably I should take off my pants and hang them up, put my shirt in the laundry basket, check on Scotty…but for a moment, I just wanted to lie there and think about her. Not about today's minor meltdowns over the yellow spoon or the seam in his socks, or the major ones about the hair-washing and stained pajamas. Not about the conversation with my mother in which she told me I wasn't severe enough in disciplining my son when he acted out. Not about the arguments with my sister in which she told me I can't keep letting Scotty make the rules. Not about the email I got yesterday from the school saying they still don't have his new IEP ready despite the testing results being sent to them weeks ago.

For a moment, I blocked all that out. I wasn't anyone's son or brother or father or advocate. I was just a man thinking about a woman.

But just for a moment.

A noise woke me, and I sat up quickly. Waited in the silent dark. Had I actually heard something? Or was the dull thud part of a dream? My mind was cloudy and my head hurt a little, probably from such an abrupt waking. I waited, scratching my beard and stifling a yawn. Then I heard it again. It was coming from downstairs, most likely Scotty trying to get a snack in the kitchen. He did that sometimes in the middle of the night. I picked up my phone to check the time—just after four. *I bet Jillian is sound asleep.* For a moment, I pictured her in bed, her skin warm and soft under the blankets, and imagined what it would be like to roll over at four in the morning and throw an arm around her slim waist. Pull her closer. Breathe in the scent of her hair.

Get hard against her ass.

Thump.

Sighing, I stood up and headed down the hall, where a nightlight kept the stairs well lit. They creaked as I went down, and the house felt a little chilly, the wood floors cool under my bare feet. We'd had a warm September, but soon I'd have to turn the heat on at night.

I went to the kitchen, where all the lights were on and Scotty was opening and closing cupboards. I figured he was looking for his cereal bowl, since the box of Fruity Pebbles was already out on the counter.

"Hey, buddy," I said.

"Do you want some cereal?" He meant that *he* wanted cereal. Pronouns still gave him trouble, and although his language and communication skills had improved a ton with therapy, he often repeated questions he'd heard asked before. Almost like he had scripts he recalled in certain situations when he couldn't find the right words to ask the question or make the statement he wanted.

"It's not time yet."

He ignored me and went on looking for his bowl, the dinosaur one he likes to use at breakfast. It was probably in the dishwasher, but I didn't want to tell him that. When he'd finished looking in all the cupboards he could reach, he stood still and fidgeted, facing away from me. "Let's have breakfast right now."

"Hey." I went over and hugged him from behind, hoping to head off his frustration. "It's only four in the morning, so we're not having breakfast yet, OK? We'll find the bowl at breakfast time. Come back upstairs with me."

"But I woke up, and after I have breakfast and get dressed, I can play on the iPad before church." He pointed at the fridge.

I laughed a little. Pinned to the fridge with a Detroit Tigers magnet was the Sunday chart with a symbol for each thing Scotty would do today. Once each thing was done, he'd move the little symbol, which was Velcro-ed to the chart, over to the column that said Done. If he got through three things on the chart without hassle, he got fifteen minutes of free iPad time. "That is the order of things, you're right. But look at the time. That order needs to start around seven in order for Dad to be sane. Let's go back upstairs now."

He let me lead him up the stairs, and I could almost taste the victory of a couple more hours of sleep, but he fussed when I tried to go back into his room, glancing down the hall like he might try to make a run for it.

"It's not time to wake up yet, Scotty," I said firmly.

"But you're dressed." He pointed to my clothes—the wrinkled, unbuttoned white shirt and rumpled black pants I'd fallen asleep in.

"Not really, bud. This is what I wore to the wedding last night."

"You slept in your clothes?" A hint of a smile.

"I guess I did."

"I want my iPad."

I sighed, exhaustion weighing down my bones. "How about if I lie down with you in your bed?" In my head I could hear my mother telling me this sent a confusing message. *Either you want him to follow the rules on his own or you don't.* She was probably right, but sometimes I just needed to buy myself a little more rest. Scotty loves to be close to me, and usually fell asleep right away if I lay next to him.

He considered it while he fidgeted. "OK. Yes."

We both climbed into his double bed, me on my right side and Scotty on his left. Immediately he reached over and started to play with my earlobe, almost like it was a security blanket. He's done it ever since he was a baby, and his therapist says it probably calms him, quiets his mind so he can relax. But sometimes he even does it during the day while he's playing—he'll just run over to me while I'm working at the table or folding laundry or cooking dinner and rub it for a few seconds, and then take off again. Those times make me laugh, which he loves, so maybe he's doing it for me as much as for himself. But in my heart I think it's his way of telling me he loves me and feels safe and happy. Those moments are gold to me.

Within minutes, he was asleep, his little palm resting on my cheek.

I watched him for a moment, listening to him breathe, adoring his peaceful expression. He was such a loving, sensitive soul. I wanted to shelter him forever, and yet I wanted others to know and experience his sweetness too. But it took time and patience—who would give it to him? Who would look past the quirks and grow to love the person beneath? I knew I couldn't follow him around for the next ten years, forcing kids to be more understanding and grown-ups to be less ignorant, teachers to be more tolerant and doctors to be less dismissive. Eventually I'd have to let go a little. Eventually.

I took his hand from my face, kissed it and held it between us, closing my eyes.

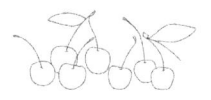

Scotty woke up for good about two hours later, and I left him in his bedroom playing with his dinosaurs while I went to shower. I hadn't gotten nearly enough sleep to feel rested, but I was in a good mood, partly because of the sweet quiet time I'd had with him this morning, and partly because of the memories of Jillian from the night before.

Stepping beneath the spray, I couldn't help smiling as I washed my hair and soaped up. First chance I got, I was going to read through our texts again. Just thinking about them made my cock start to swell. Groaning, I looked at the open bathroom door, wishing I had five minutes to lock it and jerk off before getting dressed. It would feel so good. But it never failed—every time I attempted that while Scotty was awake, he would come knocking. His timing was uncanny.

Gritting my teeth, I concentrated on other things—today's schedule, a client meeting I had tomorrow, the loads of laundry I had to get done, the dry cleaning that needed to be taken in. At this point, I was an expert in reclaiming control of my body like that. And sometime today I was going to look at the schedule for the coming week and weekend. I'd promised Jillian a date, but I needed to make sure I could get Sarah, the usual sitter, to watch Scotty. My sister was good in a pinch and only lived forty minutes away, and I *did* want my son to be close to my family—it was the only one he had—but I also wanted to keep my sanity. Scotty was dealing with enough frustration at school; placing additional stress on him at home wouldn't be good for him, and Monica stressed him out.

Hell, Monica stressed *me* out.

After drying off, I dressed in dark jeans and a clean white t-shirt, then went to get Scotty, so I could get him cleaned up before we went down for breakfast.

"Come on, bud. Shower time."

"I'm still playing."

"You want that iPad time, you better come with me now."

He thought about it for a moment and decided to come, taking my hand as we went down the hall to the bathroom we shared, the only one on the second floor.

The funny thing is, he never wants to get in the shower because he hates the feeling of soaping up, but once I get him in, he loves the water. He just doesn't want to do the things he's supposed to do—if I didn't stay in the bathroom and force him to use soap, he'd just play around, using his hands as characters, reciting lines from movies or TV shows or commercials or even just scripts he makes up based on whatever he's thinking about. Sometimes he sang them. Sometimes all I heard were sound effects.

After five minutes of growling and crashing noises I assumed were dinosaurs fighting, I opened the curtain a little. "Did you soap yet?"

"No."

"Scotty, come on. You've had five minutes already. Do it now."

He said nothing, just continued with the sound effects, his hands moving in front of his face. I sighed, reached in, and handed him the soap. "Do it. Now."

It would get done faster and better if I did it myself, but I told myself not to. Part of me wondered if eight years from now I'd be checking up on my sixteen-year-old, making sure he used soap in the shower.

"Done," he said a minute later.

"Good. Let's get that hair washed." I opened the curtain.

"Noooo," he whimpered, pleading with me with those big eyes.

"Yes. It's Sunday, you know the rule. And we've got to do it now if you want iPad time before church. Look at my hair, it's all wet too, see?" I tipped my head toward him. "I washed it already. We can brush our hair together. And you can brush my beard too."

He protested a little bit more but eventually gave in and let me wash it. (He counts while I do it, and I've mastered completing the chore in twenty seconds.) When he was clean and rinsed, he got out and dried off, then we went down to his room, where he got dressed on his own with only a couple prompts from me.

"Good job." I raised my hand and he gave me a high five.

We went back to the bathroom and stood in front of the mirror together combing our hair. I had to re-wet mine, which had dried flopping down onto my forehead. Scotty watched me, mimicking each step—put a little pomade in my hands, rub it through, comb it back. He got a big kick out of brushing my beard and using the dropper to put a few drops of beard oil into my palm and watching me work it in. I'd give him a drop or two as well, and he'd rub it into his chin and cheeks, a huge grin on his face. For his birthday last summer, I'd gotten him his own little bottle of Corktown oil from the Detroit Grooming Co. just like mine, and he treasured it.

When we were done, I leaned down as if to inspect his beard, and he threw his arms around my neck. Grinning, I wrapped my arms around his back and lifted him right off his feet. I never questioned these unexpected displays of affection —I just held his skinny little body close to mine, silently apologizing for everything I was doing wrong, everything I wanted him to have and couldn't give him.

"Great job this morning," I told him as we drove the short distance to St. Mary's. "If everything goes well at church today, we'll go to the park, OK?"

He looked happy about that, although I knew if we got to the park and it was crowded, he'd hang back a little, nervous about approaching groups of kids. His anxiety about crowds was a big reason we went to church. I wasn't very religious, and I had a lot of issues with the Catholic Church, but Sundays were an opportunity for Scotty to be among people in a controlled environment, one that wasn't likely to get too loud or chaotic or overwhelming for him. The church I chose had a program called the Buddy Ministry for special needs kids, which paired them with a trained teenager or college student who helped them participate in group activities related to the lesson for the day.

At the door, Scotty's usual Buddy was there to greet us, a local high school senior named Elliot who was fantastic with him. "Hey. How's it going, Scotty?"

"Hi, Elliot," I said, saying his name on purpose so that Scotty could hear it and maybe use it in saying hello. Despite his insane memory for facts, he wasn't good with names, even though he'd known Elliot for months. I also held out my hand for Elliot to shake so that Scotty would see how I greeted someone, but he didn't imitate me today.

"Do you want to play Climb the Ladder?" Scotty said instead of hello. Most likely it was a question Elliot had posed to him last Sunday.

"Sure, we can play that game today. Ready to go in?"

Scotty nodded, and I knelt down in the effort to make eye contact, which he wasn't always comfortable with, even with me. He once told me it was like a light that's too bright for him when he looks directly at someone's eyes. It just "feels wrong." I never push it, and sometimes he will do it on his own, but every now and then I initiate it to see if he'll respond. Today he met my eyes for a moment before looking off to the side.

"I'll see you after Mass, OK?" I rubbed his earlobe, and he smiled.

"OK."

Taking him by the arm, Elliot nodded at me and led Scotty down the hall toward the classrooms.

I headed into the sanctuary and chose a pew near the back that wasn't too crowded. Pulling my phone from my jacket pocket, I made sure the sound was off, and couldn't resist glancing at Jillian's thread from last night. I looked over both shoulders before tapping her name, feeling heat in my face. Scrolling through it, I felt the heat in other places, and the crotch of my pants grew tight.

Jesus, put the phone away before a bolt of lightning strikes you. You're probably going to hell as it is.

As the first notes of the opening hymn rang out, I dropped the phone back into my pocket and stood, trying to adjust my pants as stealthily as possible. But it was no use. I spent the entire service thinking about fucking Jillian Nixon in every possible position (and some impossible ones), and the only thing I prayed for was that no one would notice the massive erection I had.

Oh yeah. I was going to hell for sure.

But it might be worth it.

CHAPTER 7
Jillian

ON SUNDAY, I slept until nine—a huge luxury for me—and went over to Natalie and Miles's house for brunch. After that, I drove Skylar and Sebastian to the airport, where they'd catch a quick flight to Detroit, and then another to Cancun for a week. I admit, I felt a pang of envy seeing them off, but who wouldn't? I blamed that on the fact that I hadn't taken a vacation in forever, and I promised myself I'd take a trip somewhere in the next year, even if it was just a spa weekend with my sisters.

When I got home, I did some laundry, caught up on some paperwork, did some studying for the activities and tests I'd need to take to keep my board certifications, and took a power walk through the neighborhood.

Number of times I thought about Levi Brooks throughout the day: approximately one billion.

Number of times I read through our sext thread: at least one hundred.

Number of times I got myself off in my post-walk shower thinking about him: just one.

But it was a good one—I was glad the bathroom window was closed.

Afterward, I was putting my pajamas on when I heard my phone buzz on the nightstand. I glanced at it—Levi Brooks calling.

I tugged my shirt over my head and accepted the call. "Hello?"

"Hi."

"Hi. How are you?"

"Good. You?"

"Good. I just got out of the shower." *Thanks for the orgasm.* I jumped on the bed and criss-crossed my legs, which were clad in blue and pink plaid flannel pants. "I was a little sweaty after a walk."

"Do you have a dog?"

"No, it's just me here. What about you? Dog? Cat? Potbellied pig?"

"Nope. Just an eight-year-old boy and a thirty-two-year-old man here. That's enough animal for one house."

I laughed. "Maybe you're right."

"How was your day?"

"Good. I had brunch with my family at Natalie's this morning. Took Skylar and Sebastian to the airport. Did some work this afternoon. How was yours?"

"Really good, actually. Church and then the park, where there was only one minor meltdown over an ambulance siren and he actually played on the swings with a few kids. Then a few errands. I *am* a little tired today, though. I went to bed kinda late last night."

I smiled. "I'd say I was sorry, but…"

"Don't you dare. So what are your plans for this week?"

"The usual. Work."

"Are you busy on Friday evening?"

My heart thumped a few hard beats. "I don't think so."

"Can I take you out for a drink?"

"I'd like that."

"Is six at Low Bar OK? I wish I had time for dinner too, but I like to be around here at bedtime."

"I understand."

"Should I pick you up?"

"Actually, I'll probably have to meet you. I don't get out of the office much before that time. Unless you'd be able to do Saturday night instead?"

He paused. "Probably not. Scotty and I have movie nights at home on Saturdays, and I missed it last night because of the wedding. I'm sorry."

"That's OK. Friday will work fine, really."

"OK. Thanks." A little silence. "I thought about you a lot today."

I fell onto my back and smiled at the ceiling. "You did?"

"Yeah. I reread our texts from last night in church."

I burst out laughing. "I'm surprised you didn't burst into flames."

"Me too. Every time I heard the word God, I imagined you screaming it."

Gasping, I put a hand to my stomach, which felt like I was cartwheeling downhill. "You are so bad."

"I know. Because then I thought about all the things I could do to *make* you scream it."

It was a moment before I could speak again. "You did?"

"Yeah. Mass was over way too soon today."

I exhaled slowly, my eyes sliding over to my nightstand drawer. I needed to recharge Magik Mike right the fuck now. God, I *loved* the way he talked. If only I could record it!

"Silence. Have I shocked you? Told you I was an animal."

I laughed gently. "Um, no. I was just thinking that I wish I could somehow record this conversation, so I could hear you talk to me like that later on when it's just me and Magik Mike."

"Who the hell is Magik Mike?"

My face burned. Had I actually just admitted I had a

vibrator? There was feeling at ease with someone and then there was TMI. What if this turned him off? "It's, ah…a toy."

"A toy?"

"Yes." I sighed. *You might as well own it now, Nixon.* "For grown-ups."

He laughed, that deep throaty sound that melted my insides. And my panties. "I wish I could come play with you."

"Well, then I wouldn't need the toy, silly."

"Oh no, I'd put that toy to good use on you."

My jaw dropped. *Sweet Jesus.* "You would?"

"Definitely. And there wouldn't be a thing you could do about it."

"Why not?"

"Because I'd tie you to the bed first."

"Oh, God." I fanned myself as heat rose in my body, prickling on the surface of my skin.

"See? It works. Only I imagined it louder."

"It would be. Trust me."

He exhaled. "I don't want to, but I better go. Scotty's iPad break is about up, and it's time to get back to math."

"Ah, math homework. Can't say I miss it. How's it going?"

"It's OK. He's actually pretty good at math, he just struggles with directions. If a problem has more than one step, it's tough. He also hates any kind of writing because he doesn't have good fine motor skills. He gets frustrated and feels bad about it."

My heart ached a little. "You must be so patient."

"I try. Sometimes I need these breaks just as much as he does."

"I'll bet. Does he like school?"

"He did last year. He had a very understanding teacher who made him feel safe and capable. This year has had a rough start."

"What about friends at school?"

He sighed again. "Not many. Scotty struggles to relate to other kids his age. He wants to, but several things make it tough. He doesn't understand personal space, doesn't understand slang and sarcasm, doesn't like when kids deviate from the specific games he wants to play, or break the rules. He does better with younger kids, but I worry that he's going to be picked on for that as he gets older."

"Poor thing."

"And he worries constantly about things other kids don't understand."

I rolled onto my side and propped my head on my hand. "What does he worry about?"

"God, some days the list is endless. The weather, the schedule, his schoolwork. Crowds. Storms. The dark. Loud noises. Washing and brushing his hair. Hot food."

"Wow." I wanted to ask if Scotty had been diagnosed with an anxiety disorder or even OCD, but I also wanted to preserve the casual, friendly feel of our conversation. I was curious about his son, and my natural instincts were to help, but I wasn't his doctor and didn't want to act like it. Mostly I was just listening for *Levi,* to give him an ear without weighing in.

"And then there are his obsessive interests."

"Which are what?"

"Baseball stats, for one."

"Well, that's pretty typical for his age, right?"

"No. When the average second grader wants to talk about baseball, he wants to recap the awesome win from the night before or maybe say who their favorite players are. Scotty wants to recite the list of top MLB career batting averages, like fifty of them, complete with years played, games played, at bats, hits, runs, and RBI's."

"Whoa. He has all that memorized?"

"Completely. And hardcore eight-year-old fans might

know names like Ty Cobb or Joe Jackson, but even they don't really care about what happened in baseball in 1915. In St. Louis. On a Tuesday."

I laughed. "What else is he interested in?"

"Dinosaurs and Franz Liszt."

I laughed again. I couldn't help it. "Baseball and dinosaurs, I understand. But Franz Liszt? The composer?"

Levi chuckled too. "Yes. He loves classical music. He went through a Mozart phase, then a Bach, then a Vivaldi. Now it's Liszt."

"Have you taken him to the symphony?"

"Not yet. I want to, but I'm worried—one, about the volume level, and two, about the crowd. Same with a Tiger game."

"Well, he sounds like a very smart, interesting, well-rounded kid."

"He is. I wish more people knew him like I did. I worry that will never happen."

Something squeezed my heart. "Sounds like *you* have a lot of worries too."

"I guess so, but what parent doesn't? And maybe I'm making it sound worse than it is. We have plenty of good days too, including today. Anyway, I better get him refocused on math again."

"Of course. Sorry to keep you with all my questions."

"No, I'm glad you did. Thanks for asking. And for listening."

"Any time. I'm looking forward to Friday."

"Me too. And Jillian..." He sighed. "I'm sorry if I got a little overexcited about sex. I probably shouldn't say all that to you."

"Why not?"

"I don't know. It's been so long since I've talked to a woman this way, I don't even remember what I'm doing. I'm like a fucking teenage boy. You're going to think I'm no different than the asshole who couldn't last five minutes in the closet."

I laughed. "Hardly. I don't think that at all. I think you're like me. Really focused on one part of your life, so focused that the other parts feel like muscles we haven't used in a while."

"Exactly. But I promise I've learned a few things since the closet."

"Guess what?" I whispered. "I have too."

He groaned. "OK, I'm really going now. Or I never will."

"Night, Levi."

"Night."

I ended the call and dropped the phone next to me. A date. *A date!* One that I was actually excited about—when was the last time that had happened?

I frowned, thinking about the last few dates I'd been on. I hadn't even shaved my legs for those, but for Levi…

Scooping up my phone again, I made a note to call the salon on Tuesday and schedule a bikini wax. A full Brazilian.

I didn't do anything halfway.

CHAPTER 8

Levi

OF COURSE, I was fucking late. I'd been looking forward to seeing her all week long, we hardly had enough time to begin with, and I was fucking late.

But a client meeting had run long, which meant I was late getting to the bus stop to meet Scotty, which made him late for swim therapy and threw his whole sense of equilibrium off for the day, and even Sarah had a hard time getting him settled. He clung to my waist as I left, and I felt like the biggest asshole on the planet for thinking, *Let go, champ, Daddy wants to go get laid.*

Not that I was positive I'd get laid. In fact, as I sped toward Low Bar, my dick perking up at the mere thought of getting inside her, I told myself to calm the fuck down. *Maybe she wants to get to know each other a little better before getting naked, which is perfectly normal, and probably a good idea, so don't go charging at her like a bull at a red cape. Be a goddamn gentleman. Can you do that?*

I could do that. I could be a gentleman. A gentleman with a raging hard-on, but a gentleman.

I parked on a side street and grabbed my jacket from the passenger seat, adjusting myself in my jeans before shutting the door and locking the car. Shrugging into my jacket as I hurried down the block, I hoped she hadn't been sitting there for too long, although she seemed like the kind of person who liked to be punctual.

In front of the door, I was tempted to stop, take a breath, run a hand through my hair, fix my cuffs, and stroll in all cool and casual, like a badass.

But that just wasn't me.

I threw open the door and rushed down into the dark, intimate bar, stopping for just a moment to give my eyes time to adjust to the candlelight. As soon as I saw her, standing behind a stool at the bar, hanging a jacket over the back, I strode toward her.

"Jillian."

She looked up and smiled. God, she was so fucking pretty. Was she really here waiting for *me*? "Hey you."

"Hey. I'm so sorry I'm late. An afternoon meeting ran long, which threw off the entire rest of the day for Scotty, and..." I shook my head. "Anyway, I'm sorry."

"Stop apologizing. You're here. I just got here too."

I slipped a hand around her waist and pulled her close, pressing my lips to her cheek. "I'm here. And you're beautiful."

"Thank you." She slid onto her chair, and I eyed her legs as she crossed them. She had on a tight gray dress with short sleeves and a knee-length hem, black heels, and pearls at her throat. Jillian's curves were subtle, but the dress hugged every last one of them, and those legs were begging to be slung over my shoulders.

Easy there, caveman. Sit down. Order a drink. Say words. Make nice.

I took the seat next to her, and she slid the cocktail menu toward me. "I haven't ordered yet, but I've looked at this already."

"You're much nicer than I am," I said, dropping my keys

and phone into my pocket. "I probably would've slammed two drinks by now and bitched to the bartender about how inconsiderate people can be."

She laughed. "Really. No big deal."

I called the bartender over and gestured for Jillian to go first.

"I'd like Blue Coat gin, please. Up with a twist, and I like it extra dry. In and out with the vermouth."

I ordered a Sazerac and turned to face her. "I've never heard a woman so particular about her martini."

She shrugged guilelessly. "I know what I want."

"I like that about you. You're discerning."

"Some might even call it picky."

I grinned. "Then I'll take it as a compliment you're even here. Tell me about your week."

She sat up taller, clasping her hands around her knee. "It was good. I'd have liked to get a little more exercise, but it's hard to make myself get up at five and go to the gym, and by the time I leave work around seven or eight, I'm usually too tired. And already craving a glass of wine." She wrinkled her nose. "I'm not very disciplined."

"You're a doctor working long hours. I'd say that takes discipline."

"Thanks. How was *your* week?"

"Pretty good. Busy. I'm working on a vacation house in Harbor Springs, so I had to make a trip up there and back in one day, which was a little hectic."

"I love that area. We used to ski there all the time when I was younger."

I nodded. "We did too. Every year I say I'm going to go again, and I never do."

She put her hand on my arm. "I do the exact same."

"Oh yeah? We should promise each other we'll go together. And hold the other accountable."

"Deal." She held out her pinkie, and I stared at it. "Come on, give me your pinkie."

Laughing, I hooked mine through hers. "What's this, a pinkie swear?"

"Yes," she said, her face grave. "It's how the Nixon sisters seal deals, and we take it very, very seriously."

"You have my word. We will go skiing." I squeezed her tiny finger with mine—not too hard, since I probably could have snapped the delicate bones—and allowed myself the brief fantasy of making out with her in an outdoor hot tub while it snowed.

Then I had to adjust my pants again.

She took a small sip of her martini. "How was Scotty's week? Get that math homework done?"

I groaned. "Barely. Homework is always a struggle. But he had a good week too, I think. There was one episode at school where he got frustrated and threw his pencil, but nothing major."

"Good."

"The thing is, he notices the difference between himself and the other kids now, academically. He compares himself and sees that he struggles to do basic things they breeze through."

"Poor thing. Any word on the IEP?"

I clenched my jaw. "No. And I've called every day for two weeks. I'm beginning to think I need to just go in there and be an asshole until I get an answer on what's taking so long."

She sipped her drink again. "Have they told you what the holdup is?"

"I've been told it's 'administrative,' which I think is code for bullshit. And I hate to be a jerk about it, but..." I shrugged. "I have to. I'm the only soldier he's got. He won't fight for himself. He just gives up."

She set down her glass and patted my shoulder. "You're doing the right thing. At least, I think you are."

"Thanks. OK, enough about that. Tell me something fun you did this week."

She tilted her head to one side and chewed her bottom lip as she thought. "Oh! I attended a sign language workshop. We have a few patients and parents at the office who use it, so I decided to learn some basics."

"Oh yeah? I know a little sign language. It was part of Scotty's speech therapy when he was younger." I set my drink down and signed a few words at her, the only ones I could remember, which were basic things like *please, more, play, toy, Dad*. "Know what I'm saying?"

She looked adorably baffled. "Nope," she confessed, laughing a little. "I have no idea."

"Good, because it's *so dirty*."

Squealing, she grabbed my hands and pushed them down between us. "Hush, then. What if someone in here speaks sign language?"

"Then they'd know what I want to do to you right now."

Her jaw dropped. Our eyes stayed locked. "Like what?" she whispered.

"You sure you want to hear it out loud?"

She took a breath. "Maybe you could whisper it to me."

I leaned toward her and put my lips to her ear. "I want to set you up on this bar, throw your legs over my shoulders, and bury my tongue in your pussy."

She gasped and brought a hand to her stomach.

So much for the gentleman.

"Then I want to pull you onto my lap and watch you slide down onto my cock."

She made a small noise just then, something between a sigh and a squeak.

"I'd like to make you come so hard you forget to breathe. Would you like that?" I brushed my lips against her throat, just beneath her ear.

"Yes," she whispered.

"Fuck, you smell good," I said, inhaling the sweet scent of her hair and neck. Glancing down, I saw her chest rising and falling fast, her breasts straining against the material of her dress. I saw her hands flexing on her lap. And I saw those pearls at her throat, pictured her wearing them—and only them—while I slid into her.

Oh fuck. My cock is so hard right now.

I sat up straight and looked at her. "I'm just going to be honest, Jillian. I wish I had all night with you, but I don't. I only have another hour, maybe. I'd be happy to spend it right here talking to you, if that's what you want, but—"

"I want you." She leaned over and whispered in my ear. "I want you *right now*."

By the time she got to *now*, I was pulling out my wallet and tossing bills on the bar.

She stood up and threw her jacket over her arm, and I grabbed her hand as we raced through the bar, out the door, and up onto the sidewalk. "I'm parked over there," she said breathlessly.

"I'm the other way."

She gave me her address, and I took her head in both hands, kissing her hard before turning around to run down the street. No joke, I *ran*.

It was possibly the most uncool thing I have ever done in my life, but fuck it, I wanted to do things right this go around and that took time. I had maybe an hour, and I wasn't about to waste a precious minute of it walking to my car.

That was one more minute I could have making her scream, and I intended to use it.

CHAPTER 9
Jillian

THE WAY LEVI raced down the street reminded me of the way my sisters and I used to tear down the stairs on Christmas morning to see if Santa had come. I couldn't help giggling as I hurried to my car as quickly as I could without tripping on the sidewalk in my heels. I was just as anxious as he was, but skinned knees were not sexy.

As fast as I flew home, Levi must have driven even faster, because a black Audi SUV was already parked in front of my building when I pulled up, and he jumped out of it a second later. Deciding not to bother with the garage, I parked next to it, and Levi came around to open my car door. As soon as I stood up, he grabbed me, crushing his lips to mine, his hands threading through my hair. Pushing me back against my car, he pressed his lower body into me, and I felt the bulge in his pants through my dress as his tongue stroked inside my mouth, and it made me want to wrap my legs around him.

"Inside," I whispered. "Or we're going to give my neighbors a show they weren't expecting and don't deserve."

At the front door, he stood behind me while I fumbled with the lock, kissing the back of my neck and unzipping my dress while my shaky hands tried desperately to get the key in. The moment it turned and the door opened, I moved inside the dark hallway and turned around, dropping everything I held and throwing my arms around his neck.

Our mouths came together, hot and impatient, our tongues meeting between open lips. He pushed the door shut behind him and kept moving forward. "Where," he growled.

"This way." Without breaking the kiss, I walked backward down the hall and into my first-floor bedroom. Along the way, Levi shed his dark brown jacket and shoes, and I kicked off my heels. Inside my room, where the shades were pulled and a bedside lamp glowed softly, he lifted my dress over my head and tossed it onto my dresser.

His eyes, black as night and ravenous enough to make me shiver, roved over my entire body. My wardrobe might be conservative, but I had a small collection of exquisite, provocative French lingerie—one of my favorite little secrets—and beneath my dress I'd worn a beautiful black lace bra and panty set.

"Jesus, you wore that to work?"

I smiled. "Yes, but I kept my dress on there."

He ran his hands down the sides of my arms, making my whole body shiver. "Cold?"

"No. Just anxious." I slid my hands up the front of his shirt and started on the buttons.

"Jillian, wait." He grabbed my hands, pinning them to his chest. "I want this so badly, but I don't want to—" He broke off, his face uncertain. "I feel like I'm always rushing you. I told myself not to act like a fucking caveman tonight, and just take you out for a nice drink, and here I am in your bedroom tearing your clothes off."

"You're not rushing me." Rising up on tiptoe, I kissed him softly, my body aching for his touch. "I want this just as badly as you do, Levi. Maybe more."

"Impossible." Letting my hands go, Levi pushed one bra strap aside and kissed my bare shoulder, the other hand running down my side, over my hip, then up my inner thigh. "I could hardly concentrate at work. If you see a vacation house shaped like an erection in Petoskey, you'll know that was the one I worked on this week."

Laughing gently, I slipped one hand around his lower back and let the other slide down the front of his jeans and over the tight, hard bulge threatening to bust the seam. "Funny, I was thinking about an erection all week too. Bet it was the same one."

He groaned as he edged his fingers beneath the lace of my panties and felt how wet I was.

"I fucking love the lace," he whispered. "I almost want to leave it on."

"So leave it on."

"Next time." He bent down to drag my panties down my legs. "I want to see you this time. Twice now, you've made me come without even seeing your naked body...and those are just the times you know about. But the pearls..." He straightened and touched the necklace I wore. "The pearls can stay."

I stepped out of my panties as he reached behind me, unhooking my bra with one hand. I let it fall as his hand slid between my legs again. *His hands, his hands*...I couldn't stop thinking about them.

But it wasn't only his hands I wanted. I had to get him undressed—how the hell did he keep distracting me?

I went to work on his shirt buttons again as his mouth slanted over mine, his fingers stroking my clit. But seconds later my hands went still as he penetrated me with one fingertip. I moved my hips, trying to get him to give me more, but instead of pushing deeper, he rubbed the silky wetness over my clit in firm little circles, his other hand sliding up the back of my neck and then fisting in my hair.

As he tightened his grip, sharp needles of pain prickled across my scalp, in perfect contrast to the pleasure he wrought between my legs. He slid two fingers all the way inside me, slowly, easily. My hands curled into claws, grasping the front of his shirt.

He began to whisper against my mouth. "There are so many things I want to do to you. I want to make you come just like this, with only my hand."

"Yes..." On tiptoe, I rode his hand as pent-up desire billowed inside me, desperate to break free. I was so close already—

"Levi," I said softly, part cry, part plea. How pathetic was it that I was about to come already? I hadn't even gotten his shirt off! But it wasn't my fault—he knew just how to touch me, just what to say, just how to work his hands and lips and tongue on my skin...it wasn't like a first time at all.

"Then I want you on that bed so I can get my mouth on you." He kissed me again, lazily, luxuriously, his tongue stroking mine, and I thought about that talented tongue on other parts of my body. His fingers worked faster, and I closed my eyes, giving in to it, to him. My legs tensed up, my fists tight in his shirt. "And then I want my cock inside you," he whispered. "I want it all."

I moaned as his mouth moved down my neck. "Levi. You *are* gonna make me come, just like this, yes, yes, yes..." My entire body shook as the orgasm peaked, and he plunged his fingers even deeper, my insides contracting around them.

Just as my legs buckled, he caught me behind the knees and under my arms, swinging me onto the bed. I propped myself up on my elbows, breathing hard as I watched his hands finish off the buttons on his shirt and shrug it off. My toes wiggled and my stomach jumped as he whipped his t-shirt over his head.

Oh God, *God*, I loved that he had a real man's body, and I don't mean ultra-ripped like a bodybuilder's, or groomed to perfection like an actor's, or glossy and flawless like a magazine spread. I mean *real*, with meat on his bones and hair on his chest and a scar on one side of his stomach. I wanted to explore every inch of that body with my hands and lips and tongue. How much time did we have left?

He pulled his wallet from his back pocket and took a condom from it, tossing it onto the bed. Then he removed the rest of his clothes and stretched out above me, and I ran my hands all over his hot bare skin. He crushed his lips to mine, his hips settling between my thighs. I felt his long, thick cock between us and put my hands on his muscular ass, pulling him closer.

"Tell me we can do this again," he said, his mouth hot on my skin as he kissed his way down my body. "I'll never get enough tonight."

"We can do this again." I arched my back and threaded my fingers in his hair as he took one hard, tingling nipple in his mouth, teasing it with his tongue. "And again, and again, and again."

"Promise?" One hand snuck between my legs, where I was wet and warm and aching for him.

"I promise. Oh God, Levi. I want you so badly." He was moving lower on my body, kissing my belly button, pressing my thighs apart. I braced myself up on my elbows again. "No, stop! You don't have to do that. You already made me come once, and we don't have time to fool around."

"Jillian." He looked up at me from between my legs, his expression serious. "Do I look like a man who's fooling around?"

"No, but—"

"Good. Because it so happens that I am taking this very…" He kissed the inside of one thigh. "Very…" His teeth grazed the other one. "Seriously." He lowered his head, and I felt the whisper of his beard against soft, sensitive skin.

"But Levi, if you want to—"

He looked up at me again. "The only thing I want to do right now is make you come with my tongue. Are you telling me you don't want that?" He cocked one eyebrow, and I gave him a helpless expression.

"I do, of course I do, but that's, like, another thing for *me*, and—"

"It's not, though. It's not for you at all, so you can just fuck right off while I do this for *me*."

Smiling, I dropped my head onto the pillow, jumping when his tongue swept up my silky wet seam, the hot pleasure of it shocking me. "Oh, God...that feels...too good to... argue with you."

He laughed as he did it again, a low rumble from the back of his throat. Then he did it a third time, one long slow sweep, making my limbs tremble, finally lingering at the top and stroking my clit with the soft, flat side of his tongue before circling it with the firm tip. "You should never argue with me when I want this, Jillian, even if I want it all the time because you taste...so...fucking...good." He paused between words to lick and suck and nibble and tease, and any thought of protest disappeared entirely as he ignited the fire inside me again, my lower body tensing up with every passing minute.

I saw red behind my closed eyes. "Levi—I'm gonna come again," I whispered.

"Fuck yes, you are. I want to feel it, right here..." He slid those long fingers deep inside me again, pressing a certain spot that had me lifting my hips off the bed, desperate for more. "And right here." He sucked my clit into his mouth, and I grabbed his head, holding him against me as I rocked my hips. Feeling his mouth on me was hot enough, but the second I looked down and *saw* his face buried in my pussy like he'd never get enough, I exploded, my head dropping back, my back arching off the bed, my mouth wide open in a silent scream, my toes pointing.

One long, low moan escaped him as my body shuddered and pulsed against his tongue and around his fingers. When the tremors finally abated, he took his mouth off me and crawled slowly up my body.

"You're amazing," I said breathlessly, reaching down to grab him under the arms and pull him up faster. "But I'm greedy. I still want more."

"Yeah?" Getting to his knees, he picked up the condom from the bed, tore it open, and rolled it on. "What do you want now?"

My core muscles clenched, aching and empty, at the sight of his thick, hard length. "I want to feel you. Every inch of you. Deep."

He braced himself over me with one arm and positioned his cock between my legs, torturing me with just the tip. "Every inch? You've got me so fucking hard right now, I'm not sure your sweet little body can take me that deep."

I wrapped my arms around his neck and my legs around his hips. "Try me."

He gave me a few more inches, a smile teasing his lips. "How's that?"

"Deeper."

He gave me a couple more. "How about here?"

Even though it felt like that was all I could take, I opened my knees wider, tried to scoot down beneath him. "Deeper, Levi. I want it to hurt."

"Oh fuck." Suddenly he slammed into me so deep and hard my eyes rolled back in my head and my feet dropped to the bed, my body fighting against the sharp twinge of pain. But he stayed there, buried to the hilt, his lips near my ear. "You shouldn't say that to me. I'll lose control."

"I want you to." Pushing past the discomfort, I ran my hands down his back and grabbed his ass, words tumbling from my mouth in shameless abandon as he began to move inside me. "I want you to lose control. I want you to fuck me like you can't hold back."

"Jesus Christ," he growled, taking my head in his hands

and grabbing two fistfuls of hair as he drove into me. "That gorgeous mouth, saying those filthy words. You're making me crazy."

"Good." I dug my nails into his flesh, daring him to lose that last thread of control, even though I gasped at the jolt of pain that rippled through me every time he hit the deepest reaches of my body. "Don't stop."

"Never. I'll fuck you as deep and hard as you want me to." His dark eyes locked with mine. "I'll even make it hurt, so it will feel that much better when I make you come again."

"Yes," I begged, writhing in pain and pleasure beneath him. "But I want you to come, too."

"For the last time, this is not about what you want from *me*, Jillian Nixon." He spoke right into my ear, his voice raw and raspy. "It's about what I want from you, and right now I want to feel that sweet little pussy come all over my cock."

He drove me into madness again, with his words and his body, and I cried out over and over as my body convulsed around his, my fingers tight on his ass. "Yes," he hissed, his jaw clenched. His eyes closed, and I watched his beautiful face twist briefly with agony then ease into pleasure as his body released the tension in surging, rhythmic thrusts inside me.

He dropped his face into my neck and kissed me, his beard tickling my skin. I wrapped my legs around him and sighed, wishing we could just melt right into each other. That our time wasn't running out. That he'd stay and we could do it all again, with a quick break for some junk food and maybe a bottle of wine. That we could fall asleep just like this afterward, and he could even stay the night.

But I knew better than to ask.

CHAPTER 10
Levi

MY HEART POUNDED hard inside my chest, but it wasn't just from exertion. It was from feeling alive—fucking bursting with it. I felt like I could scale a mountain, swim an ocean, slay a dragon. It struck me how empty sex had been during the last few years, just a release of tension and nothing more. No feeling of wanting to consume a woman's body the way I wanted to consume Jillian's, of wanting to please her for my sake as well as hers, not just to make sure the score was even. In fact, I hoped it wasn't even. I hoped it was three to one... but could I ask her without sounding like an egotistical asshole?

She sighed, and I loved the feeling of her chest rising and falling beneath mine. "As fun as the closet was, that was much, much better," she said.

"So much better." My lips brushed those pearls around her neck, and it sent blood rushing to my dick again. *Fuck. What time is it?*

"Three times better."

I picked up my head and looked down at her. "Really? Three times?"

She tilted her head, a shy smile on her lips. "You couldn't tell?"

"I was hoping. Is that...does that always happen?"

"No. *Maybe* two here and there, but honestly, that's probably because I know my own body pretty well. I know how to help myself along. But tonight..." She shivered adorably. "It was all you."

"Good." I kissed her, sending another bolt of renewed desire between my legs, where we were still connected. "I was so worried I wouldn't have enough time to take care of you."

Laughing gently, she shook her head. "You had an hour. You only needed five minutes, at least for the first one. The next two took you *maybe* another fifteen."

"It still wasn't enough. I want more."

She hesitated. "You can stay, if you want."

I closed my eyes, pushing back at the resentment. "I wish I could. But I can't."

"It's OK, Levi. Really." She squeezed me with her long, luscious legs. "We can go out again, you know. This was only our first date."

"Doesn't seem like it, does it?"

"No, it doesn't."

I kissed her forehead. "Give me a minute, OK?"

"Sure."

I got up and went into the bathroom adjacent to her bedroom, removing the condom and wrapping it in a tissue before throwing it away and washing my hands. In the mirror, I saw what a mess my hair was and tried to smooth it back a little, or else it was going to be really obvious to the sitter what I'd been up to.

When I entered her room again, she was still lying in bed on her side, a sheet pulled up to her waist. "I'm being lazy," she said, a guilty look on her face.

"You're entitled." I couldn't help staring at her a moment,

her cheeks flushed, her skin rosy gold in the lamplight, her brown hair splayed over the white pillowcase. "I wish I could be lazy with you."

She pulled back the sheet. "You can."

I hesitated for less than three seconds before getting back in bed beside her. "I can't resist you. But you have to kick me out in ten minutes."

"OK." She laid her cheek on my shoulder and put a hand on my chest. "I'm sorry. I shouldn't try to tempt you."

I kissed the top of her head. "Don't be sorry. It will be OK. If there's a meltdown, I'll handle it and I will remember that this feeling was worth it."

"Awww." She kissed my chest and threw one leg over mine. I could feel the dampness on her thighs, and my cock twitched.

Fuck. Just don't put your hand on it. I'm not sure I'm strong enough to say no.

But she didn't touch me there. Instead she brushed her fingertips back and forth over my chest. For a moment, I wished I had a body like Sebastian's—bulging with muscles, cut with lines. I was muscular in an athletic way, but I didn't have the kind of abs and arms he did.

"I love your body," she said, as if she could read my mind.

I laughed a little. "I was just thinking I wish I had more time to spend at the gym."

"What?" She picked up her head and gave me a furrowed-brow frown. "Don't be ridiculous." Settled again, she slid her hand around my ribcage and hugged me tight. "You're perfect. You're real."

"Well, thank you. You're perfect too, but actually you're *unreal*. Too beautiful."

She snorted. "Please. I think unreal would have bigger boobs and a better ass. If I wasn't so tall, I could probably wear the same clothes I wore in middle school."

"Shut the fuck up." I kissed her head again. "You have a

beautiful body. Perfect legs, perfect ass, perfect breasts, and—don't think I'm weird, but I fucking love your neck and shoulders. This necklace drove me crazy the first time I saw you in it, at the wedding, and then when I saw you had it on again tonight, I almost lost it right there at the bar." I touched the pearls on her neck, then ran my hand down her arm. "And your skin is like heaven. What the hell do you put on it anyway, to make it feel like satin? And it smells so good—like grapefruit or something, but it's so sweet."

She laughed. "Thanks. That's probably essential oil. I have an allergic reaction to most perfumes."

I inhaled deeply. "God, I love it."

Her fingers found my scar and traced it. "What's this from?"

"That is from an unfortunate run-in with a chain link fence. I was trying to climb over it and my shoelace got caught. The top of it gouged my side."

She winced. "Ouch."

"Yeah, and I fractured my wrist breaking the fall on the other side."

"Jeez. Are you accident prone?"

"Not anymore. I was a dumbass daredevil as a kid, but since I became a dad, those days are over. Now I have to watch my own daredevil at the park."

"Is he? A daredevil?"

"Yes and no." I rubbed her back as I thought about it. "He's aggressive in some ways, and he will play rough like boys do, but it takes him a while to feel comfortable joining in with other kids. He also doesn't feel pain the way most people do. So I worry about him hurting himself and not even knowing it."

She patted my side. "I should let you go home to him."

I squeezed her. She felt so good in my arms. When was the last time I wanted to hold a woman all night? "I wish I could stay."

"Another time." She sat up and looked down at me, a wry smile stretching her lips. "You might want to fix your hair before you go."

I frowned. "I thought I did."

"Think again."

I tackled her, getting her by the shoulders and throwing her onto her back. With her head at the foot of the bed, I took her wrists in my hands and pinned them above her. My hair flopped forward, making her grin.

"Be nice, little girl."

"Or else what?"

"Or else I'll take these bedsheets and tie you up, then torture you with my tongue."

She giggled. "That doesn't sound like torture."

I kissed her smug little grin. "Just you wait."

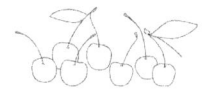

While I got dressed, Jillian used the bathroom, then threw on a t-shirt and underwear. "Give me two more minutes," she said, taking a pair of blue plaid pajama pants from her dresser drawer. "I want to send some soup home with you."

I followed her to the kitchen, which was actually on the second level of her townhouse, a long narrow space with plain maple cabinetry, stainless appliances, and beige marble countertops. She had two framed photos on the breakfast counter next to a wine rack holding six bottles of red. One photo showed her wearing a white lab coat and holding a diploma, a stethoscope around her neck, and her entire family surrounding her. The other was a close-up of Jillian with an arm around each sister, taken when they were kids.

I picked it up. "Look how cute you guys are."

"Thanks." She pulled a plastic container and matching lid

from a low cupboard, and a large blue pot from the fridge. "I think I'm about ten there. We thought we were so cool because we'd eaten red popsicles and it made us look like we were wearing lipstick."

"You're close to your family."

"Very. What about you?" She ladled soup from the blue pot into the container.

"Yes. They helped me out a lot when Scotty was a baby. Took us in. Gave me a lot of advice. As you can imagine, I was clueless."

"Most guys your age would be."

"Yeah." I set the picture down. "But it started to get a little stifling, all the advice, especially after we got the autism diagnosis."

"Is that why you moved here?" She put the blue pot back in the fridge and pressed the lid onto the container.

"That's one reason. But I also felt like it was time for us to be on our own. Scotty was about to start kindergarten, so I figured that would be a good time to do it. The move was rough on him, though—a new room in a new house, no grandma and grandpa living with us, a new neighborhood, new school…he doesn't like things to change."

"Well, I'm glad you made the move." She came over and handed me the soup. "Hope you like pumpkin."

"I do."

"I made it last night. It's Natalie's recipe. She's teaching me to cook," she said sheepishly.

"Why do you look embarrassed about that?"

She threw her hands up. "I don't know. Because I'm thirty and I should know already?"

"Fuck that. There's no deadline on learning new things."

"True."

"I love to cook, you know."

Her eyes went wide. "Really?"

"Yes. Does that surprise you?" I poked her in the side, and she giggled.

"I don't know. Maybe."

"My dad was actually the cook at my house when I grew up, so it never seemed strange to me. Plus, without another parent in the house, it's been on me to put meals on the table by myself."

"Is that enough?" She glanced at the soup, looking worried. "I should have given you extra for Scotty."

"It's plenty. I'm sure he's already eaten. His dinner is at six sharp or the world ends." I kissed her cheek. "Thank you. Next time, I'll cook for you."

"Sounds good." She put her arms around my neck. "This was fun. I hope you aren't home too late."

"I will happily suffer the consequences if I am." Wrapping my free arm around her waist, I hugged her close, inhaling her sex-and-citrus scent. "I'll call you this week."

"OK."

She walked me to the door, and after one more kiss, I forced myself to leave.

On the fifteen-minute drive home, I did nothing but think of her, every sense bombarded with memories. I could still feel her softness, taste her sweetness, smell her skin. I could still see her eyes closing, her back arching, her fingers clutching my shirt. I could hear her quiet sighs and her loud cries, my name a plea on her lips.

Fuck. My balls ached, and my cock did not seem to understand that there would be no encore tonight. I shifted uncomfortably in the driver's seat, trying to adjust myself.

But it wasn't only that I wanted to have more sex with her —although I did. (We hadn't even gotten to position two on my church list.) That feeling of lying next to her afterward, talking and laughing and touching each other…I wanted that, too. I'd never had that with anyone, and it was so easy with her. And I wanted to hear more about her—what did I really know?

I knew how she liked her martini. The name of her vibrator. That she was allergic to perfume. Drank champagne at weddings. Wore fuck-hot lingerie under her clothes. She liked red wine and popsicles, pumpkin soup and flannel pajamas, black lace and pearls.

But what was her favorite song? Her favorite color? Her favorite movie? Did she sleep on her stomach or back? Did she like e-books or paperbacks? Sand or snow? Staying up late or waking up early?

Then there were harder questions.

What was she looking for with me?

I hadn't dated anyone in years, because I wasn't good at balancing Scotty's needs with anyone else's, even my own. There was the occasional friendly fuck with a woman who did some design work with my uncle's firm, but Alison was older, divorced, and not looking for anything more than I was, which was basically just an adult human connection. (For about twenty minutes.) But when it was done, it was done. I never thought about her afterward, and I doubt she thought about me. I certainly didn't give a shit about her favorite color. And the sex was just functional. It was sort of like maintenance on your furnace or something—from time to time you needed to do it, but once it was done, you didn't think about it again until the following winter.

It was so different with Jillian. I wanted her to need me for more than just sex. I wanted to make her happy, and not just physically. I wanted to do things for her and with her. I wanted her in my life.

But how could I do it?

Seeing her during the week would be impossible with our schedules. Weekends were when I caught up with work, household chores, and made time for outings with Scotty that got him socializing in non-classroom situations. Saturday nights were our movie nights. Where would time with Jillian fit in? Was it fair to even start something with her, knowing that I'd probably end up a disappointment? What woman wants to fall for someone who can never put her first, never live with her, never promise her all the things she ultimately wants—a husband, a home, a family?

Because I couldn't. I wasn't free to make those kinds of promises.

But for the first time in eight years, I wished I were.

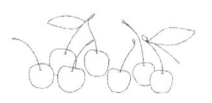

I was a little later than promised, but Scotty seemed OK with it, and happily hugged me hello and Sarah goodbye. While I warmed up the soup Jillian had sent home with me, he went back to lining up his dinosaurs on the family room rug. As I ate—the soup was delicious—I tried to engage him in conversation, asking about his time with Sarah, about swim therapy today, about his dinosaurs. But although he made noises while he played, he largely ignored my attempts at conversation, and once he told me he was too busy to talk.

When I was done eating, we went upstairs and got him ready for bed, putting on his dinosaur pajamas, brushing his teeth, reading a story, turning on his nightlight and switching off the overhead light in just that order. Even our prayers had to be recited a certain way, the list of people and things we are grateful for named in the exact same order every night. So when I added something new—"I am thankful for making new friends"— he got upset with me and told me I had to start over.

"Nope. I'm not starting over, Scotty. Prayers are how you feel at the end of the day. They don't have to be the same every night."

"But you said it wrong," he insisted, and even though he was lying down, I could see the agitation in his body in the way he started rolling from side to side, hands at his ears.

"It's not wrong, buddy. It's just something I added. We can be thankful for new things, don't you think?"

"Start over, start over," he repeated, and I sensed a meltdown coming. "You have to start over or it's not right. Start over, start over, start over."

I sighed, closing my eyes for a second. This was one of those moments where I wanted to be firm. I wanted to say *No, I don't have to start over. If I want to be fucking thankful for a new friend, you should let me say it, and stop acting like this. I love you, and I know you're doing the best you can, but stop it. Just stop.*

He began to cry, and I said nothing, just pulled back the covers and got in bed next to him. Maybe his day had been harder than I knew. Maybe his sensory input was already overwhelmed. Maybe this tiny change in the prayers sounded like an avalanche to him, where I heard only a marble bouncing down the stairs.

I didn't know. Because he couldn't tell me, and I felt ashamed of myself for wanting him to be something other than he was, even for a moment.

Just leave the prayers as they are tonight. Maybe tomorrow, you can talk about adding some new things to be grateful for, at a time when you're not trying to get him calm enough to fall asleep.

I put my arms around him, trying to quiet his restless body. "Hey, hey. It's OK. I'm sorry, I'll start again. Let's say them together."

Was I doing the right thing? Who the hell knew? Maybe I should have insisted he be more flexible. Ten fucking times a day, I second-guessed myself.

Which was another reason why it had felt so good to be in Jillian's bed tonight. No second thoughts or hesitation. I'd felt more confident, more relaxed, more *myself* than I had in years. It was like some part of me had been silenced for so long—the part that was just a man with his own needs and wants and self-interests apart from being Scotty's father—I'd forgotten he even existed (aside from the occasional furnace maintenance).

But suddenly he had a voice. Was it selfish of me to listen to it? I'd made a promise to my son, and I intended to keep it. I knew that was right.

But being with Jillian felt right too.

I couldn't walk away.

CHAPTER 11
Jillian

AFTER LEVI LEFT, I had some soup, poured some wine, and stared at the same page in the book I was reading for an hour, a silly grin on my face. Eventually, I gave up reading and got in bed, which still smelled like Levi and sex. I lay on my side, hugging my second pillow and breathing in the scent, my stomach fluttering as if I'd swallowed a flight of doves for dinner.

Moment by moment, I relived the hour we'd spent here, relishing each kiss and caress, each sigh and moan, each dirty word from his mouth and every thrust of his cock inside me.

I'd be sore tomorrow.

I didn't care.

Flopping onto my back, I smiled at the ceiling and wondered how soon we could do it again. I was still lying there, thinking about all the things I wanted to do to him next time we were together, when I heard my phone vibrate. I glanced at my clock and saw it was after midnight.

Rolling to my side, I picked up my phone, hoping it was him. It was.

Get out of my head already. I'm trying to sleep.

. . .

I grinned. **Me too.**

I'm sorry I had to leave so fast.

Don't be. I'll be sore enough as it is in the morning.

Is it bad that I'm proud of that?

No. You can be proud.

I want to see you again.

Under the covers, I wiggled my toes. **When?**

Next weekend?

Want to come over for dinner?

Yes. Thank you for the soup. I ate it all and licked the bowl.

Doesn't surprise me. You like to lick things.

Things that are delicious.

· · ·

I smiled. **I will have something delicious here for you, I promise.**

I know you will. And I'm getting hard just thinking about it. But it's my turn to make dinner. I'll bring it.

OK. What night?

Friday? Sorry it can't be sooner.

Don't be. During the week is hard for me too. I don't mind being your Girl Friday. But I wondered how much time he'd have. **How was Scotty tonight?**

Pretty good. I think he'd give me another hour on my curfew.

I laughed. **How nice of him.**

Hey. What's your favorite movie?

Of all time? Vertigo.

Hitchcock fan, huh?

. . .

YES. What's yours?

Shawshank Redemption.

Never seen it.

What? We need a movie date.

Deal. Favorite color?

Blue. Like your eyes.

Haha. Smooth.

Thank you. Now you.

Red. But not cherry red. Deeper.

You like it deep. I like that about you.

I gasped. **You are so bad.**

I know. Oh fuck hold on.

He was gone for a few minutes, and I figured Scotty had

called him. His next message confirmed it.
Hey I'm sorry. I have to go. Scotty's up.

I was disappointed, but I understood. **It's OK.**

Talk soon. Night.

Night.

I set my phone aside and turned onto my side again, hoping everything was OK with Scotty. Did Levi ever get a full night's sleep? Being a single parent had to be hard enough without throwing in all the extra issues he dealt with. And he was so devoted to his son. Clearly it would make dating difficult, if that's what we were doing—I wasn't even sure yet. But it also made him more attractive to me. Not only was he gorgeous and good in bed, he had a huge heart.

Was there room in it for me?

On Sunday evening, he called me. "Hey."

"Hi."

"How's my Girl Friday?"

I smiled. "Good. Just doing some reading."

"About what?"

"Autism research, actually."

"Oh really?"

"Yes. It's very interesting, the genetic links they're finding, what brain scans are revealing about neurological connectivity."

"Yeah, I used to read some of that stuff, but it wasn't very useful to me."

"No?"

"No. It's interesting, but there's a disconnect, you know? I'm glad they're making gains in understanding how autism looks in the brain, but that doesn't help me deal with the meltdowns on my kitchen floor."

"True," I admitted. "What does help you?"

He sighed heavily. "Whiskey."

I laughed and closed the window on my laptop. "How was your day?"

"Good. I'm on a homework break, and looking at the calendar for this week. Friday still work for you?"

"Yes. That's perfect, actually."

"Good. I'm going to get some groceries and come over at six."

"I'll supply the whiskey."

"I don't need whiskey with you. Just a way to stop time."

I smiled, but I felt a little sad too. "I wish I could do it for you. I'll see you Friday."

On Thursday night, I met Natalie and Skylar for a drink at Trattoria Stella. They were already there when I arrived, Natalie sipping on water with lemon and Skylar still perusing the wine list.

"Hi there, Mrs. Pryce," I teased, hugging her hello. "You're looking tan and refreshed. Did you have fun on your honeymoon?"

"Yes." Her eyes sparkled. "It was incredible. The beach, the sun, the sea, the food, the sex—everything."

"Sounds like it." Thrilled to find myself completely unenvious, I slipped my coat off and hung it on the back of my chair. "And how are you feeling, Nat?"

"Good. Tired, but what else is new?" She slurped on her straw. "Now tell Skylar about your date."

Skylar, sitting between us, looked at me and raised one eyebrow. "Your *date*?"

"With Pine Sol," Natalie went on before I could even get a word in. "And they had sex. Not in a closet this time."

"Jeez, Natalie. I thought you wanted *me* to tell her about it."

"And I thought you were never going to tell us secrets ever again." Skylar looked smug as she poked my shoulder. "I knew you wouldn't hold out."

"You were right. It was too good to keep in."

She gasped. "I want details. Is he as big as he looks like he would be?"

I laughed, looking over my shoulder to make sure she hadn't been overheard. "Relax. Let's order some wine first." I lowered my voice as I studied the list in front of her. "But hell yes, he is."

"Gah! I can't relax. This is too exciting!" She thumped my leg a few times.

"It is," I admitted. "I'm excited too."

She and I ordered glasses of pinot noir, which Natalie looked at longingly, and I filled Skylar in on the date. "I had three orgasms. Not even kidding."

"Three times?" Skylar's eyes bugged. "In an hour? Even I'm impressed."

"It was very impressive."

"So then what?" she went on eagerly. "Did he stay the night?"

"No. He can't really do that because of his son."

"Like, ever?" She paused with her wineglass halfway to her lips.

I shrugged. "I'm not sure. We haven't really talked about what this is yet. I mean, maybe sleepovers aren't what he's thinking for us."

My sisters stared at me a moment. "What do you mean?" Natalie asked. "You think he just wants to be friends?"

"I just *said*, I don't know." I took a big drink of wine and confessed the truth. "And I'm kind of scared to ask."

"Why?"

"Because I'm afraid of the answer," I said quietly, staring into my glass. "I really like him."

"I don't think he'd be calling and texting and making plans with you in advance if he wasn't interested in you in a more-than-friends way," Skylar said confidently. "If he just wanted a fuck-buddy, he wouldn't do all that. You'd get a text at two in the morning that says 'Hey, can I come over?'"

"But you should still talk about it with him." Natalie was firm too. "If you don't, and both of you have different ideas about what you're doing, feelings could get hurt."

I sighed. "I know. We should talk. The truth is, I'm not sure there's room in his life for a girlfriend, let alone anything beyond that."

"Why not?" Skylar asked. "Plenty of single parents date and get remarried."

"Yes, but his situation is a little different. His son, Scotty, has autism, and routine is really important to him. Levi is really sensitive to that."

"Autism," Skylar said, her brow furrowed. "OK, you're going to give me the You're Dumb and I'm a Doctor look, but is that where you don't talk? I just remember the one autistic boy in my class not speaking much, if at all. And he wouldn't make eye contact."

"No doctor look," I said, holding up my hands. "It's a fair question. Autism looks different in everyone, but no, it doesn't mean you don't talk. Sometimes there are language delays, and some kids are nonverbal, but plenty of kids with autism are very social and talkative. Some don't like eye contact, and some are fine with it."

"So what is it, then?" Natalie asked.

"Well, it's a neurological condition characterized by lots of different things to varying degrees. Often there are issues with social interaction and understanding. Some kids might have sensory issues. Some kids struggle with repetitive behaviors. Some have anxiety and/or OCD." I shook my head. "And some might have none of those things. It's really complex."

"Maybe he's like Sebastian," Skylar said hopefully. "He struggled as a kid too, but therapy really helped."

"I don't know for sure what he's like, but from what Levi has said, Scotty gets overwhelmed easily. He needs sameness to feel calm."

"Poor kid," Natalie said. "And poor Levi. That's got to be so tough, being a single parent of a child with those kinds of issues."

I nodded. "I think it is tough. And he's *such* a good dad. Totally devoted to his son."

Skylar sighed and looked off in the distance. "That's so hot. Why does that have to be so hot? It makes things difficult."

"It does," I agreed, "but it shows that, unlike a lot of other hot guys I've met, he's actually responsible and selfless. He knows how to take care of someone."

"Well, he certainly knows how to take care of you." Skylar looked at me again and wiggled her eyebrows. "So what are you thinking? I mean, what if he just wants to be friends?"

I lifted my shoulders. "Then I guess I'd be his friend. But I don't think I'd sleep with him anymore. It would be too confusing. Although…" I closed my eyes, feeling his hands on my body again. "That would be really hard. It's all I can think about."

"Ha! You fiend!" Skylar hit my shoulder. "Welcome to the club."

"Honestly, it's really ridiculous how much I think about sex with him," I said. "I've never been this way before."

"That's a good sign," said Natalie. "And you don't have to look so guilty about it. It's totally OK, even if you guys do stay just friends for a while. No need to put a label on things. I'm just saying it's good to be on the same page."

I agreed with Natalie that Levi and I should talk, but I was also reluctant to break the spell we were under. This feeling, this incredible *wanting*, and knowing I was wanted in return, felt like magic.

I didn't want to look behind the curtain just yet.

CHAPTER 12
Levi

I ARRIVED at Jillian's with groceries at quarter after six, and as I stood waiting for her to answer the door, my heart beat faster. I'd fucking *missed* her. We hadn't talked much through the week, once Sunday and once Wednesday, and I was always amazed at how quickly the time passed when we were on the phone. Half an hour felt like three minutes. Other than that there were just a few quick texts, once yesterday to ask if she ate red meat (she did), and then earlier today to make sure she had a couple ingredients I would need.

But I'd thought about her constantly, trying to reconcile my feelings for her with my responsibilities as a father. It would be so much easier if I just wanted the sex—but I didn't. I wanted more. Did she?

When she answered the door, I realized I'd been holding my breath. Or maybe the sight of her took it away.

"Hi," she said, giving me a quick kiss before reaching for one of the bags. "Let me help." She was still dressed in her work clothes, a narrow black skirt, cream-colored blouse, and black heels.

"I've got it." I held on to both bags and pushed the door shut behind me. "But you can kiss me again."

She grinned and moved closer, putting a hand on either side of my face and pressing her lips to mine. Her kiss was soft and sweet at first, but then I felt her tongue sliding along my lower lip, her mouth opening, head tilting, hands sliding into my hair. Pretty soon her body was pressed against mine and her arms were wrapped around my neck.

"Sorry," she said breathlessly. "I'm getting a little carried away."

"No complaints here," I said, "but I promised to cook for you, and in five seconds I'm not gonna give a fuck about dinner, so if you're hungry—"

"Oh, I'm hungry." She ran her hand down the front of my pants and rubbed my cock, which was quickly turning to steel. "I'm ravenous, in fact."

"Jillian—"

"Shhhhhh." She put a finger over my lips. "I'm making the rules this time."

I dropped the two bags of groceries, pushed her back to the wall, and pinned her wrists to it above her head. "I don't think so."

"I love it when you get rough with me," she whispered, like she was confessing a secret. "I always remembered that about you."

"And yet you're trying to make the rules." My calm, quiet tone was in complete contrast to the violent roar of blood through my veins. "What's that about?"

She was panting, her chest rising and falling quickly. "To provoke you. And it worked."

I shut her up with a kiss, crushing my mouth over hers and pulling her blouse from her skirt. She moaned when I slid my hands up her chest, covering both breasts and then rubbing my thumbs over her nipples. I could feel lace and wondered what it looked like. "Take your blouse off. I want to see you."

"There's a button at the back of my neck."

I found the button and undid it, lifted the blouse over her head, and let it fall.

"Like it?" she asked, her hand rubbing my cock again.

"Fuck yes, I do." I hadn't realized how much I'd missed seeing pretty, feminine things on a woman's body—or maybe it was just that I loved seeing them on Jillian. Her bra was white this time, and almost completely sheer except for a few little flowers or something embroidered on it in white thread. Her rosy pink nipples peeked through the material, begging to be licked and sucked and bitten. I pinched them, enjoying the little gasp of pleasure from her lips, the way her hand stilled on my dick.

"Leave it on this time," I told her, glancing down. "The heels too."

"I'll leave on anything you want." Her hands moved to my belt and worked quickly, then she dropped to her knees and pulled my pants down just enough to free my cock.

She took it in one hand and angled it toward her mouth, stopping to look up at me, and I can say for certain it was the first time I have ever been tempted to take a dick pic. In general, I don't think dicks are deserving of portraiture, but mine looked fucking *fantastic* next to her face.

Sorry, was that rude?

Told you I was a caveman.

Leaning forward, I braced one hand against the wall behind her. I could feel her breath on me, and nearly trembled with anticipation. I hadn't had a blow job in so fucking long—Alison and I had not traded those kinds of favors—and the fact that this was Jillian, and the lights were on, and I could watch everything, had my cock jumping in her hand like it might jerk itself off if she didn't get started. I moaned at the first long stroke of her tongue up my shaft, my other hand fisting at my side as she did it again, and again. I growled when she took the head into her mouth but didn't close her lips, just let them hover there, keeping me in agony.

She took it out again and looked up at me, a wicked gleam in her eye.

"You're killing me," I told her.

"Yes." She rubbed the tip along her jaw, under her chin, across her cheek. "Do you like it?"

"Yes. I like watching it, but I came over here to cook you dinner like a nice guy, and now all I want to do is fuck your mouth with my cock, then your pussy with my tongue."

She laughed and swirled her tongue around the tip. "Deal."

I groaned as she closed her mouth over the head and sucked a few times before sliding her lips as far along my shaft as she could take it. She kept me there for a second before pulling it out and then taking it in again, even deeper this time. I felt the tip hit the back of her throat as she began to pump her hand at the base.

"Oh, fuck," I moaned, my vocabulary suddenly reduced to one word. "*Fuck*." I slid my fingers into her hair and held myself inside her mouth as I rocked my hips in small, sharp jabs. For a second I wondered how she could even breathe, but that thought disappeared when she began to make little noises like she couldn't get enough, and my manners went the way of my vocabulary.

I grabbed her head with both hands and fought like hell against the orgasm that was threatening to choke her. Yet I thrust into her mouth too, hitting that spot in her throat, listening to her gasping breaths and greedy moans, wanting to come in her mouth so badly my body was on fire. Not yet, not yet, I begged myself. Just a little bit longer. Close your eyes or something—make this last!

But I couldn't tear my eyes away from her. Those heels, that skirt, the white straps of her bra, the dark hair spilling through my fingers, her mouth sucking me off. Jesus fuck, I need to warn her, I thought as my balls tightened up.

She knew I was close, and backed off for only a second. "Do it," she rasped. "I want it."

I had no words, even *fuck* deserted me. All I could do was growl like the beast I felt like as I tightened my hands around her head and fucked her hot, hungry mouth until I came, my cock surging and throbbing inside it.

As if that weren't enough, she swallowed and licked me as if she didn't want to waste a drop, and I was the best thing she'd ever tasted.

I dropped to my knees in front of her and took her face in my hands. "Are you sure that was OK?"

She grinned. "Positive. I hope it was more than OK, though."

"Oh, my God." I groaned and hugged her to me, burying my face in her hair. "Are you kidding me? That was fucking amazing. I'm wondering if this is a dream."

She giggled and wrapped her arms around my waist. "Nope. Just Friday."

"Fridays are awesome."

"I agree."

"I want every day to be Friday."

She spanked my ass. "Don't get carried away. Now what did you bring me to eat?"

"Oh no." I stood up, pulling her to her feet. "We had a deal."

"What?"

I yanked my pants up just enough to walk, and swept Jillian off her feet in case she tried to argue. "We made a bargain, remember? And I intend to hold up my end of it."

She swatted my chest as I carried her into her bedroom. "You can hold up any end you want later. Let's have dinner first."

"No fucking way." I tossed her onto the bed and quickly zipped up my pants. "I want something better than dinner."

In no mood to be patient, I shoved her skirt up to her

waist, pushed her knees apart and knelt down between them. She wore sheer white panties that matched the bra, and I couldn't resist leaving them on. I put my lips between her thighs, letting her feel my breath on her skin, just like she'd done to me. My mouth watered. I reached up to touch her breasts, teasing her nipples into stiff pink peaks through the thin material, pinching them gently.

She made a little sound of frustration. "Harder."

I did what she said, gratified by her satisfied moan. Keeping my fingers there, I put my mouth on her, devouring her through the sheer panties. When they were completely soaked, I yanked them down her legs.

She pulled one foot out and left them looped around her other ankle. "You're right, this is better than dinner."

"So much better." I stroked up through her center and circled her clit with my tongue. "Hotter. Sweeter." I swept my tongue from bottom to top again, weaving it from side to side, before sucking her clit. "Tastier."

Jillian brought her knees up, lifting her heels in the air. I grabbed her ankles, flicking her clit with the tip of my tongue.

"Yes," she breathed, lifting her hips. "You're so good."

"You want to come?" I asked her.

"Yes. I want you to fuck me."

My dick was hard again, and I could have, but I wanted something else. I got on the bed next to her and flipped her on top of me so her knees were on either side of my chest.

She looked down at me. "You want me on top?"

"Yeah. Of my face."

"What?" She tried to scoot down, but I pushed her up and locked my arms around her thighs, so she straddled my face, tight.

She gasped, trying to move off me. "You won't be able to breathe!"

But my arms had her pinned, so there wasn't anything she could do about it, and she fell forward, bracing her hands above my head. A moment later my tongue was pushing inside her, and within seconds she began to grind against me, unable to hold back. Loosening my hold, I put my hands on her ass, and she circled her hips. Fuck, the way she moved, the way she tasted, the way she gasped for air—I couldn't get enough. Then she sat all the way up and took her breasts in her hands, playing with her nipples, pinching them the way I had. She looked down at me, her mouth open, eyes wild with desire. It was the hottest fucking thing I'd ever seen. I moaned and she began to move faster, riding my mouth hard, her breath escaping her in anguished cries. "God, Levi—don't stop—right there—yes, yes, yes—"

Her body went still and I pulled her tighter to my face, ravaging her with my mouth. She screamed long and hard as her clit pulsed against my tongue, and I didn't stop until she begged me to.

"Please! Mercy!" she said, half laughing, half serious. She fell forward, catching herself on her hands above my head. "I can't take any more."

I helped her wiggle down my body and sat up, holding her on my lap, her knees on either side of me. Her hair was tousled, her cheeks were pink, and she couldn't catch her breath. "You OK?"

"Yes. I think so." She shivered. "That was intense."

"Good."

She pressed her lips to mine. Then she giggled. "Your face smells like my essential oil."

"I fucking love it. I can't get enough."

Tipping her head onto my shoulder, she buried her face in my neck. "I know the feeling."

CHAPTER 13

Jillian

I THREW on some jeans and a top and met him up in the kitchen, where he was unpacking the grocery bags. *This is so nice, seeing him at home in my kitchen.* My romantic history involved a few short flings, one extended disaster, and the occasional one-night hookup, but I'd never lived with anyone or gotten so comfortable with someone that he'd stayed over a lot. Watching Levi work in my kitchen gave me a little kick.

"Hope there's no ice cream in here," I said, peeking into one of the brown paper sacks.

Levi pulled out a loaf of French bread. "Nope. I like ice cream cones, but they are not beard-friendly."

"I never thought about that. You could eat it in a bowl," I suggested, grabbing the bottle of whiskey I'd bought for tonight and breaking the seal.

"What's the point of ice cream in a bowl?" He set a package wrapped in white butcher paper on the counter. "That's boring. But I will eat it with pie."

"What kind of pie do you like?"

"Jillian pie." He threw me a grin over one shoulder. "But other than that, I'm not picky."

"Well, you've already had your fill of Jillian pie for the evening, but I have—"

"Not true," he said, pulling out a package of bacon, a bag of greens, and some other vegetables. "My appetite for Jillian pie is never-ending, and it goes so well with bacon-wrapped steak bites. But go on."

I grinned and pulled two glasses from a cupboard. "I was going to say, my mother gave me a cherry pie this week. She bakes them constantly. Did I tell you I grew up on a cherry farm?"

"No. Did you really?"

"Yes, on Old Mission. Not too far from Abelard Vineyards."

"I'd love to see it sometime." He stuck a few things in the refrigerator.

My heart fluttered. "Sure. We could bring Scotty if you want."

He closed the fridge but stayed facing it, and my brain went a little haywire.

Oh shit. I said the wrong thing. I'm moving too fast. He doesn't want me to meet his son. He just wants to keep this casual. Friendly. Nonromantic.

But then what was he doing here with bacon and steak? That wasn't like coming over with a pizza and a six-pack. Bacon and steak said romantic. Bacon and steak said serious. Bacon and steak said *couple*.

He turned around and looked at me. "You want to meet Scotty?"

"Of course I do." I twisted my hands together. "If you want me to."

He walked toward me, and my stomach knotted. I couldn't read his expression at all. "Jillian. I *do* want you to meet Scotty."

"I feel like there's a 'but' there."

His jaw twitched, and he ran a hand through his hair. "I

wish there wasn't. I want this to be so much simpler than it is."

"Talk to me." I leaned back against the counter, my hands gripping the edge, feeling unprepared to deal with whatever was coming. "I can take it, Levi. I'm a big girl. If you want to keep your son separate from us, just say it. I mean, I don't even really know what 'us' is."

He reached for my hands and held them between us, staring at them. "I don't either. But I've been thinking about this all week, and I know what I'd like us to be."

"Which is?"

His eyes met mine. "I want us to be together."

"As in…romantically?"

"Yes."

Warmth flooded me, and I rose up on tiptoe. "I want that too."

"But Jillian." He squeezed my hands. "I have to be honest —I'm a seriously shitty boyfriend."

"Why do you say that?"

"Because I can't give you what you deserve."

"Which is what?"

"All of me." He shrugged as if he had a load of bricks on each shoulder. "I can't give you all of me."

"Because you have a son?"

He nodded, his dark eyes sad. "You deserve someone with more time for you. Someone who can make you his first priority. Someone who can offer you all the things you want in life."

A lump formed in my throat and I swallowed hard, the reality of what he was saying sinking in. My gaze fell to our hands. His *hands*. They were so big compared to mine. I loved how mine fit inside them—it made me feel warm and protected. I loved that he was being honest with me and not trying to string me along just because the sex was good. I loved his sense of humor and his dirty mouth and his concern about being a gentleman. And maybe it was superficial or sexist, but I loved how tall he was and the way he carried me around and took command of my body—it made me feel beautiful and feminine and cherished. And I loved the way he loved his son with all his heart—even if it meant there was less of it for me.

But what was I willing to sacrifice for it?

I met his eyes again. "Levi, I won't lie and say this is an easy decision, because I know what you're telling me. And I've been avoiding this conversation because this feels so good with you. So easy."

"It does." He squeezed my hands again. "The feelings I have for you..." He shook his head. "It's crazy. I feel like I've known you so much longer than just the last couple weeks, and ten times a day, I catch myself staring into space, lost in thoughts about you. And I don't want to ruin this, but I don't want you to hate me when I disappoint you. Because I will."

I shook my head. "Levi, stop. I could never hate you for putting your son first. I understand. He *needs* you to do that."

"He does." His eyes shone. "But what about you? I'm bad at this, Jillian. The balance. I'm afraid I'll fuck it up."

My heart ached. "You're so hard on yourself, Levi. How do you know what will happen unless we try?"

"I guess I don't know for sure. I just know that you deserve more than I can give you, and you'll realize that eventually. And yet I don't want to give you up." He kissed my hands. "I'm selfish."

"You're not selfish. I don't want to give you up either." Needing to feel his arms around me, I slipped my hands from his and twined them around his waist. He wrapped me up in his warm, solid embrace, and I laid my cheek on his chest. "I want this, Levi."

"I want it too."

I loved the way I could feel the vibrations of his low, quiet voice in his chest. "Then let's try. I struggle with balance too, between my work and my personal life. Maybe we can help each other."

He stroked my hair. "Will we ever see each other?"

"Of course we will. I don't need all of your time, and you don't need all of mine. It's about quality, not quantity. And I don't need to be your first priority, either. You're a father, and I know that comes first. But Levi…" Growing nervous again, I pulled back so I could meet his eyes. I didn't want to ask this question, but I had to. If I were twenty and didn't know myself so well and just wanted a good time, things would be different, but I was thirty and self-aware and wanted something more.

I wanted a love story. With a happily ever after.

"I do need to feel like there's the *possibility* of a future for us, at least somewhere down the road," I said, willing myself to be brave and say the next part. "If you truly feel like we can *never* get there, even taking our time and going slow, I need to know now. I don't mind being just friends, but the way I feel about you, I can't—I couldn't…keep doing what we're doing." *I'll fall in love with you. And you'll break my heart.*

He took a breath. "Jillian, a year ago, I'd have said there was no way. I thought putting Scotty first meant I had to sacrifice those things, so I never even considered it. If I ever felt alone, I told myself that was the price I had to pay to be a good father to him. But now…"

"Now?" I echoed, feeling like I was dangling off the edge of a cliff.

"Now there's you." He took my face in his hands and kissed me. "Without making specific promises, I'm up for seeing where this takes us—if you can put up with me…with us. We're sort of a package deal."

Relief and affection for him made me smile. "I'll try. Let's go slow—one step at a time." I grinned at him. "So we don't lose our balance."

He kissed me again and pulled me into his arms. "I don't deserve you, Girl Friday. But I want to."

While Levi made dinner, I mixed two Old Fashioneds. "Do you like this whiskey?" I asked, showing him the bottle. "My guy at the liquor store said it's awesome."

He looked up from his tray of bacon-wrapped steak. He'd cuffed his sleeves, which meant I could see his watch, which meant I might have drooled a little bit. "Journeyman? I love it. I'd like to visit that distillery."

"We should go sometime," I said, putting a little sugar in the bottom of each glass. "I looked it up, and it's pretty much a straight shot down ninety-four. Then we could go to Chicago!"

"Is that before or after our ski trip?"

"Hmm, we do have a lot of big plans, don't we?" I wet the sugar with some bitters and a splash of soda, swirled it around to coat the bottom, then added an ice cube. "Maybe we should start a little smaller."

"I was thinking the same earlier today," he said, sliding the tray of steak bites into the oven. "I'd like to spend a night with you somewhere."

I poured the whiskey into the glasses as my stomach flipped. "Like a sleepover?"

"Yes, a sleepover." He shut the oven and turned around, laughing. "Although I have never called it that before."

I handed him his drink. "I'd love that. Open invitation here, whenever you can work it out."

"Thanks." He took a sip and raised his eyebrows. "This is perfect. My God—she's beautiful, smart, and mixes a proper cocktail?" He clapped a hand to his chest. "I'm in love."

I knew he was teasing me, but my heart stopped just the same, and I nearly dropped my drink. "I'm glad you like it. I'll admit, I had to look it up," I said, hoping he couldn't tell how flustered I was by his words. "Is that cheating?"

"Not at all." He came closer and kissed my forehead. "You're a very good student."

"Especially when the subject is you. Guess what else I did?"

"What?" He took another drink and licked his lips.

"Rented The Shawshank Redemption so we could have our movie date."

"Did you?" He set down his glass and opened up the bag of greens. "Hey, can you grab two dinner plates for me?"

"I think I have the movie for twenty-four hours," I said, reaching for two plates in the cupboard. "But if we don't get to it tonight, we can always rent it another time."

"We might have to." He took the plates from me and set them down. "Because it's after seven already, I told my sitter I'd be home around eleven, and I want to give you at *least* two more orgasms before I go."

I giggled. "You're going to spoil me."

He picked up his drink again, tapped it against mine, and took a sip. "As much as fucking possible."

CHAPTER 14
Levi

"I'LL HELP you with the dishes," I said, bringing our plates and silverware over to the sink. There was hardly a crumb left—Jillian's appetite at the dinner table was just as voracious as it was in the bedroom, which I found delightfully sexy. It was almost funny watching her devour everything on her plate, given how thin she was.

"Don't you dare." She poured the rest of the wine in our glasses. "You cooked the entire meal. The least I can do is the dishes."

I laughed. "I'm used to doing both."

"Too bad. I'll get them done later. Come sit with me for our movie date." She set our wine on the coffee table, turned off the lights, and got on the couch, tucking her legs beneath her.

I knew what was going to happen if we got on the couch in the dark, and it didn't involve Tim Robbins and Morgan Freeman. But she looked so excited about watching my favorite movie with me, I figured I'd humor her.

We lasted ten minutes.

At that point, my hand was up her shirt, her hand was down my pants, our tongues were tangled up, I was hard, she was wet, and the only prison we gave a fuck about was our clothing. We broke free of it a lot faster than Andy and Red, whipping off shirts and dragging down jeans and flinging underwear to the floor. I brought her to orgasm with my fingers first, even though she begged me to fuck her, because I couldn't get enough of the sounds she made, the way she moved against my hand, the shape of her mouth when she came.

And it was something I could give her...there was so much I couldn't.

When her climax was over, she pushed my hand away, panting and wild-eyed. I grabbed a condom from my pants and she took it from me, tearing open the packet and sliding it over my erection with quick hands.

Fuck, that was hot. Everything about her was hot—the way she straddled my lap and lowered herself on to me slowly, like she wanted to savor every inch. The way she took me in so deep, the expression on her face a mix of rapture and pain. The way she moved her hips over mine, in rhythmic, undulating motions that had me fighting the urge to come inside a minute.

The way she accepted me for who I was, didn't judge me for my mistakes, and believed that I could make her happy.

I still didn't know how we were going to do this, and the fear of disappointing her bit at the edges of my bliss. But I was going to try harder than I ever had to make it work.

"Oh God," she whispered, her eyes locked on mine, her hands clutching my shoulders. I knew she was going to come from the way her breathing changed and the way she moved, tight and hard and fast against me, and I couldn't hold back any longer. As soon as she cried out, her eyes closing, her pussy clenching around my cock, I came long and hard and deep, my fingers digging into her hips as I thrust up inside her, my breath escaping in ragged, primal sounds.

Afterward, I wrapped my arms around her and held her

close, a shiver moving through my body. Burying my face in her neck, breathing her in, I spread my hands out on her back, feeling the bones and muscles beneath her satin skin. Somewhere underneath it all, her heart beat hard and fast against my chest, and I felt a powerful urge to possess and protect it, to offer her mine in return.

I wanted to say something to her, something to tell her how grateful I was, how swept away, how beautiful she felt in my arms. I wanted to stay here and hold her like this until that insatiable hunger burned in me again, and then I wanted to take her to bed and fill her body with mine, lose myself inside her. I wanted to make promises and keep them.

But I couldn't.

"Jillian," I whispered.

"I know," she said softly, stroking my hair. "I know."

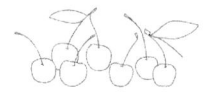

"Monica, can I talk to you about something?" My sister and I were sitting in the living room at our parents' house, drinking a beer and watching our kids and her husband Kyle play a board game on the floor. Her daughters—Emerson and Zoe, ages nine and six—were good with Scotty, and understood that he liked to play games exactly as the rules stated without any deviation. There was no letting Zoe win because she was the youngest, and there were no do-overs if you didn't get the spin you wanted.

"Sure. What's up?"

"I wanted to ask a favor."

On the hour-long drive to Charlevoix, I'd thought of nothing but Jillian, specifically the task ahead—how and when should I introduce her to Scotty? I was crazy about her, but maybe I was just crazy, period. Did she even realize what she was getting into? My life (my child) wasn't easy. And I didn't want to confuse Scotty by bringing her into our lives and then having to explain her absence if she didn't have the feelings I did, or if she decided we were too much to handle.

She and I needed more alone time together, but how could I manage that? Friday night dates were fun, but seeing her only once a week for a few hours wasn't really enough time to get to know each other—especially since we tended to spend half that time naked and sweaty. No, we needed real time together. And in order to have that, I needed to get Scotty accustomed to staying the night somewhere without me, or staying at our house overnight when I wasn't there. I couldn't ask Sarah to stay the night, so that left my parents or sister. Which one would stress Scotty out the least was anyone's guess, since none of them really understood the way his mind worked. My mother could probably come stay at the house with him, which would be preferable to having him have to sleep in a strange bed, but I'd decided to go with my sister. One, I wasn't positive how my mother would react to my leaving my son to go spend the night with a woman I'd only been dating a few weeks, and didn't want any additional guilt about it. Two, I felt more comfortable talking about it with my sister—she could get judgmental too, but it would be less embarrassing at least.

"Ask away."

"Do you think Scotty could stay overnight at your house some weekend?"

She thought for a second, tipping up her beer. "Do you think he'd do it?"

I frowned. "Honestly, I don't know. It might be...difficult, because he won't like not sleeping in his regular bed in his regular room, but maybe if we brought a few things from home, he'd handle it OK." I tried not to think about how unsettled he became simply from adding something different to the nighttime prayers. Guilt pricked at me—was this too selfish?

"I'm certainly willing to try. Do you have to travel for work?"

"No." I rubbed a hand on the back of my neck, trying to shake the feeling that I was doing something wrong. "The truth is…I met someone."

Her eyebrows went up. "Really?"

"Yeah. At that wedding a couple weeks ago."

She hit my arm. "You didn't say anything about it, you big jerk! I could have stayed longer that night."

"Well, it was a rough night with Scotty, remember, and I didn't feel right being away from home when he was so upset."

"He's not a baby anymore, Levi. And he's got to get used to doing things without you and things that are new to him and things that aren't part of his *routine* or whatever. It's for his own good and yours."

My stomach tightened. *Don't get into this now.* At least she was supportive of my dating someone. "Anyway, a Saturday night would be great. I could bring him over in the afternoon and pick him up in the morning, and of course I'd keep in touch with you the whole time."

She rolled her eyes. "Relax. I have two kids. I haven't killed either of them so far."

"I know, but Scotty is different, and if he starts to melt down, I want to know about it right away."

"Fine. Now tell me about the girl." Her eyes lit up.

I took a sip of my beer before answering. "Her name's Jillian. She's a pediatrician."

"Really? How old is she?"

"Thirty. I actually met her years ago." I filled her in on my first meeting with Jillian, leaving out the closet fuck.

Monica loved it. "How cool to run into her after all this time! And she's never been married?"

"No."

"Does she know about Scotty?"

I frowned. "Of course she does. And she wants to meet him, but...I need to get to know her better. And that's hard when I can only see her for a couple hours on Friday nights."

"I think this is great, Levi." She patted my leg. "And you don't have to feel guilty about it."

"I don't," I lied, tipping up my beer bottle so I wouldn't have to meet her eyes.

"Yes, you do. I can see it. And you're a horrible liar. But we think it's time you put yourself out there. Just because you have a son doesn't mean you have to be alone the rest of your life. You're still human."

"Who's 'we'? You and Mom?" I was annoyed, and she knew it. They always thought they knew best. And perfect Monica, who'd done everything right in her life and never gave our parents any reason to worry, had no idea what it was like to be me.

"Dad too," she said defensively. "You don't have to get angry about it. We just want to see you happy."

"I am happy." I poured the rest of my beer down my throat. "Being a good father makes me happy."

"But it can't meet every need you have," she argued. "There's more to life than being a parent. Kyle and I love the girls with all our heart, but we'd go nuts if we couldn't escape every once in a while. Do something just for us. It's healthy." She toyed with the label on her beer bottle. "Any chance this is leading somewhere big?"

I shrugged, glancing at the floor. "Too soon to tell."

"Liar." She grinned. "I know you. You wouldn't be asking me to watch Scotty overnight if you didn't think this woman was something special."

Exhaling, I looked over at the kids. "Yes. She is special. And OK, fine—I do have a feeling about us. But my situation isn't easy, so we agreed to go slow."

"It's not easy, but it's also not as hard as you're making it." She nudged my leg with her foot. "So go. Have fun. And don't feel bad about it."

"Thanks." Maybe I was being too defensive. I did have a tendency to turn everything they said into an attack. "What night works for you?"

She shrugged. "I don't care. Tonight, if you want."

My heart beat faster at the thought of spending tonight with Jillian, but I told myself to be more cautious. I'd been away from home last night at bedtime, and a second night off the routine was asking for trouble.

"No, tonight isn't good. But maybe next weekend?"

"Sure. I need to look at the calendar when I get home, but I don't think we have anything going on."

"Great." I looked at Scotty, who was telling Zoe that she didn't have her play money set out the right way. "I'll talk to him about it. If he has a good week at school, then we'll plan on it."

Later that night, after Scotty and I'd watched Jurassic Park for the tenth time this year and I'd gotten him to bed, I texted Jillian.

Hey. You awake?

Hey you. Yes. At Natalie's house painting. Well, Natalie and Sebastian are painting. Skylar and I are drinking.

I smiled. **Give me a call when you have a minute.**

• • •

My phone vibrated a moment later. "That was fast. You really don't like painting, huh?"

She laughed. "It's Miles's fault. He made this drink called a Penicillin and it's too good. I'm on my third one."

"What's in it?"

"Scotch, lemon, honey, and ginger. It's delicious. I'll have to make one for you."

"Yes, please. Sebastian is there too?"

"Yes. He's the only one painting besides Natalie."

I smiled, picturing the scene and wishing I could be there. "Of course he is. Did they have a nice trip?"

She hiccuped, and I laughed silently. "Yes. They did. I wish I could go to Mexico for a week."

"Me too. Let's fit that in after skiing and Chicago."

"Yes! Great idea. And so easily accomplished what with all our spare time." Another hiccup, and some laughter in the background, followed by shouting I couldn't decipher.

"Sounds like a good time there."

"It is. I wish you were here."

"I was just wishing the same."

She lowered her voice. "Last night was really fun. I'm so glad we talked."

"Me too. Guess what?"

Hiccup. "What?"

"I asked my sister to watch Scotty overnight next Saturday."

"You did?"

"Yes, and she said she'll do it."

"Oh my God, that's awesome!"

"What's awesome?" I heard someone yell, maybe Skylar. Then, "Everyone look at Jilly's red face! Is that from the scotch or the conversation? Who are you talking to, Jillian?"

"Oh my God. My sisters are so annoying. Hold on, I'm going into the bathroom." A minute later, I heard a bang, like a door being shut. "There," she said. "Now I can talk."

"What are they annoying you about?"

"They're teasing me about you. Apparently they can tell by looking at me today what I was up to last night."

I laughed. "Really."

"Yes. I am glowing, they said. I clearly got laid."

"Well, good. I hope."

"Yes. It is good. So tell me about Saturday. Can you stay over?"

"We'll have all night."

I heard a long squeal, ending in a hiccup.

"I'm excited!"

"Me too. What would you like to do?"

"Hmmm. Go out to dinner? Watch a movie? I never did get to watch Shawshank."

I smiled, but the memory of everything we did on her couch made my cock start to stiffen. "We could try that again." My fingers hovered near my zipper.

"I could be a good girl this time," she said coquettishly. "Keep my hands to myself."

"Jillian Nixon, don't you fucking dare."

She laughed throatily. "You know me better than that."

It made me happy to realize I did.

CHAPTER 15
Jillian

WE TALKED or texted every day that week, and my anticipation grew so intense you'd have thought I was getting married on Saturday night. By the time I was waiting to be picked up for dinner at seven, the butterflies in my stomach were so frenetic I could have taken flight. And I'd never been the kind of girl that obsessed over what she wore—I knew what worked with my body and what didn't—but it had taken me all day to decide on an outfit. I'd even consulted my sisters.

"Something sexy," said Skylar. "You want to knock him out the moment he sees you."

"Something sweet," advised Natalie. "You want him to see you as more than just a fling."

In the end I went with a little of both, pairing a sexy black pencil skirt with a soft, slouchy gray top and a great pair of heels in my favorite shade of red. I was ready ten minutes early and stood peeking out my bedroom window looking for his car. I'd set the scene in my bedroom already—candles on the dresser, clean sheets on the bed, and condoms in the nightstand.

When I saw his car pull up, my heart started to pound.

Without waiting for him to knock, I went out the door, and we met on the front walk.

"Hi," I said, drinking in the sight of him in dark jeans, a white shirt, and a charcoal jacket.

He kissed me, sending a shiver up my spine, and stepped back. "I want to scold you for not letting me collect you properly, but you looked so good running out here to meet me I can't even do it. Your legs kill me."

I smiled. "Good."

We'd decided on sushi at Red Ginger, a restaurant both of us liked, and drove there together in his car.

"I still can't believe in the last three years that we've never run into each other," I marveled on the ride there, "especially since we like a lot of the same places."

"I don't really go out that often. Scotty doesn't like hot food or sitting still for long periods of time, so eating in restaurants is somewhat challenging."

"Aha." I thought for a second. "Actually I don't either, unless I'm with my sisters or something."

"What do you normally do for dinner? You mentioned you don't cook much."

"I'm embarrassed to admit this, but a lot of nights I eat takeout or leftovers right from the container."

"Let me guess—standing at the kitchen counter."

I hid my face. "Guilty. Sometimes I make it to the couch." I held up one finger. "But I always pour my wine in a real glass. That's a hard limit for me."

He laughed. "Of course it is."

"I do want to cook more often. My mother and sister Natalie are so good at it. Sometimes they bring me what they call 'mercy meals' because they feel sorry for me."

He glanced at me. "Why should they feel sorry for you?"

"Eating dinner late and alone so often sounds sad to them, I guess?" I shrugged. "It's always been the norm for me, though."

He picked up my hand and kissed the back of it. "I'd like to change that."

I looked over at him, my mouth falling open. How was it possible he was so hot and so sweet at the same time? Didn't one usually come at the expense of the other? I'd never met a guy who was so good at both. I'd dated hot guys who couldn't *spell* monogamy, much less commit to it, and I'd met sweet guys who lacked the dirty mouth and sexual heat I wanted.

No wonder I was falling for him.

Don't let me hit the ground, I thought, staring at our hands, which rested in his lap, fingers laced. *Catch me. Please.*

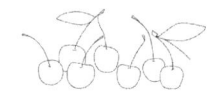

That night, after half a lemongrass martini gave me a little extra courage, I asked about his romantic history. I didn't want to pry, but I couldn't understand how any woman, career-minded or not, could abandon a guy like Levi—let alone her own son. I was devoted to my job too, but that was too steep a price for me to grasp.

"How long did you date Scotty's mom?" I tried to sound casual, but my stomach was jumping.

"About six months before she got pregnant, so about two years all told."

"Was that your longest relationship?"

He took a drink of his Manhattan and winked at me. "Is this an audition?"

Embarrassed, I dropped my eyes to my plate. "No, of course not. I'm just curious."

"Jill, I'm teasing." His fingertips touched my wrist; the shortening of my name squeezed my heart. "Yes, it was. Prior to meeting Tara, I had one relationship in college that lasted about eight months."

"What happened to her?"

"She went home for the summer and got back together with her ex-boyfriend."

"That stinks."

He shrugged. "Actually, I didn't much care. She was jealous and drove me crazy with her constant questions and accusations. And she was always begging me to tell her I loved her."

"Ah." I picked up my drink. "And did you?"

"Tell her? Yes." He sighed and took another sip. "But I didn't actually love her. And I'm such a bad liar, she probably knew it."

"Why'd you tell her if it wasn't true?"

"I was nineteen and had the emotional sensitivity of a rock; she was pretty and liked to have sex. I thought I should tell her what she wanted to hear, and didn't think it mattered that much." He winced, closing his eyes. "God, I was really an asshole. I'm an even bigger asshole for saying it out loud, aren't I?"

"No judgies," I said honestly, setting my glass down. "Who's emotionally sensitive at nineteen, anyway? I certainly wasn't."

"Maybe not, but you were a hell of a lot of fun." His twinkling eyes caught mine over the edge of his glass, and my panties melted a little.

Over sushi and crab rangoon we shared favorite memories from our childhoods, and I learned that Levi had grown up in a tight-knit family that believed in tough love, easy forgiveness, and speaking your mind.

"Sounds like my family," I said. "There's not much we hold back."

"Sometimes I wish they *would* hold back a little," he confessed. "I know they mean well, and I'm sure they're all better parents than I am, but I'm doing the best I can. And I know Scotty better than they do."

"You're doing an amazing job." I reached out and touched his sleeve. "I know you are."

He gave me a smile that warmed my insides. "Thanks."

"Are you nervous about tonight? About him being away from home, I mean?"

"Yes." He took a deep breath. "But I'm not going to think about it too much. He seemed OK when I left, and I've been dreaming about this for a week." He paused. "For eleven years, actually."

"Ha!" I stuck a piece of sushi in my mouth. "Liar."

"You'd know if I was lying. Believe me." He picked up a crab rangoon. "So tell me about your family. I don't even have to ask if you're close to your sisters. What about your parents?"

"Yes. Everyone is disgustingly close, but like your family, we are very outspoken with each other and that can grate nerves. If I never hear 'You work too much' ever again, it'll be too soon."

He smiled. "I'll try to remember that."

Over sea bass and grilled tuna we shared firsts and favorites, and I learned that his first kiss had been at age fourteen (two years before mine), he lost his virginity at sixteen, (also two years ahead of me), and his favorite thing in the world was when his son rubbed his earlobe.

"That's so cute," I said. "Like a little sign."

"It is cute. And I know he's happy when he does it, which makes me feel so good." He took a bite of tuna. "What about you? What makes you feel good?"

"Hmmm. I love laughing with my sisters. I love curling up with a good book and a glass of wine." I leaned toward him and lowered my voice. "And I feel pretty damn good when I'm naked with you."

He smiled and leaned in too. "Then you're gonna feel fucking amazing all night long."

Check, please.

Over coffee with Bailey's we described our dream vacations (both of us were torn between the mountains and the beach) and described our perfect day.

"Hmmm, no schedule. I'd definitely sleep in," he said, lifting his cup to his lips. "Then I'd make a big breakfast for Scotty and me, and maybe take him to an afternoon ball game. We'd eat a bunch of junk food and yell for our team and overpay for souvenirs. Then maybe a nap. Then I'd make dinner—Italian food, because spaghetti and meatballs are his favorite. Cold, of course. After that I'd take Scotty to the symphony. And there would be no tears, no meltdowns, no frustrations."

Listening to him tell me about his favorite things and perfect day, I could see what he meant about balance—everything was about his son. "What about *you*?" I asked. "Do *you* like classical music?"

"I do," he said, setting his cup down. "I didn't know much about it until Scotty got interested in it. But I find myself putting it on at work sometimes, or in the car."

"What's *your* favorite meal?"

"You mean besides Jillian pie?"

My cheeks warmed. "Yes. Besides that."

"I like red meat. Maybe a pan-seared rib eye with roasted potatoes."

"I'll remember that." Although I'd have to learn how to pan-fry a steak. Roasting potatoes sounded easy enough, though. "And what about a perfect day that's just for you? Would you still do the baseball game and symphony?"

"Just for me? Then no. I'd wake up with you, and we'd never get out of bed."

I laughed, my heart fluttering madly. "That sounds nice."

"And you? Perfect day?"

"Oh, I like the one you described, where we never have to get out of bed. Although we'd get hungry."

"Well, *I'd* eat Jillian pie all day."

I shook my head. "You're a fiend. But I like it."

"Good."

"OK, last question. If you had a million dollars, what would you do with it?"

"A million dollars," he mused, staring into his cup. "Honestly, I don't know. The things I want most don't cost money."

I tilted my head to one side. "What do you want?"

He didn't answer right away, and all other sounds in the restaurant seemed to fade away as he thought. "Mostly I'd like to stop feeling guilty."

"Why do you feel guilty?"

"Different reasons. But I guess what I think of most often are the promises I made to Scotty the day Tara left."

My throat got tight, and I swallowed hard. "Can you tell me about it?"

He played with the handle of his coffee cup as he spoke. "While she moved out, I took Scotty to the park and held him while I rocked back and forth on a swing, which always calmed him. I told him it was only going to be him and me from now on, and even though it would be hard sometimes, we'd be OK. I promised to take care of him, to be the best dad I could be, to give him everything I could. And I promised myself that somehow I would make up for the fact that I'd…" His voice trailed off and he took another drink of his coffee.

"You'd what?"

He set the cup down again, still staring into it. "That I'd brought a child into a fucked up relationship, that I hadn't been enough to make his mother want to stay, that I was all he had."

I took a deep breath, not at all sure I wouldn't start to weep for him there at the table.

"And I try every fucking day to live up to that. To do right by him. By everyone I care about. But I feel like it's not enough." He took a breath and exhaled, finally meeting my eyes. "I wish I were more than I am."

"Levi." I reached across the table and took his hand. "You're enough."

He smiled, although I could tell he didn't believe me, and glanced down at our hands. "I'm not, but you make me feel that way."

God, I wanted to crawl over the table and get in his lap. "I know what that's like, to feel like you're not enough," I said softly, still fighting tears. "But you are. I promise you. With me you are."

He nodded, his eyes meeting mine again. "With you I am."

The mood had shifted, the playful tone of our conversation replaced by a quiet intensity. He squeezed my hand, and I wondered if he wanted me as badly as I wanted him—needed him. And my need was different now. It wasn't only physical—I realized at that moment how he made me feel like I was enough, like I was worthy of him, worthy of love. The way he wanted me, the way he shared himself with me, the way he was willing to change things in his life to be with me...he was spending a night apart from his son for the first time in years for me. How could I show him what that meant? How could I make him see what I saw—this gorgeous, giving man who worried so much about doing right by the people he loved? I needed him to know he was more than enough.

I needed to show him love, and make him feel like he deserved it—because he did.

"Let's go," I whispered.

His dark eyes had fire in them. "I was just thinking the same."

CHAPTER 16
Jillian

I HAVE LONG LEGS, but I could barely keep up with Levi as he pulled me through the restaurant, out the door, and down the street. He drove home with one hand on the wheel, the other on my inner thigh, and I stroked him through his jeans, hardly able to sit still, every cell in my body radiating with desire.

The ride seemed to take forever, every stop sign a purgatory, every red light a hell. Finally we reached my building, and both of us unbuckled our seatbelt, jumped out of the car, and raced up the walk in five seconds flat. As I unlocked my front door, Levi stood behind me and slipped his arms around my waist, one hand sliding up to cover a breast, the other snaking down beneath the hem of my skirt. His mouth was hot on my neck as he pulled me back against him, his cock hard against my tailbone.

"Oh God," I panted as his fingers edged my panties aside and dipped inside me. "I can't concentrate. I can't get the door open."

"Do it," he ordered, "or I'm going to fuck you right here against your front door and I won't care who sees."

Finally, I got the right key and managed to turn it. As soon as we were inside the hallway, Levi pushed me back against the door, dragging my skirt up to my waist. My purse and keys hit the floor, and so did his jacket. He crushed his mouth to mine as his hand slid inside my black lace panties and my fingers frantically tore at the buttons on his shirt.

"I fucking love how wet you are," he said, plunging one finger inside me, then two. He pushed them in deep. "I want my cock right there. I want to bury myself inside you so deep it hurts, just the way you like it."

"I want it," I hissed, pulling his shirt from his pants and unbuckling his belt. "Now." But before I could unzip his pants and get my hands on him, he dropped to his knees in front of me and fastened his mouth on my pussy through the lace, and I grabbed two fistfuls of his hair.

When my panties were thoroughly soaked inside and out, he yanked them down my legs and off my feet. Then he put his mouth on me again, the flat of his tongue stroking my clit as his fingers slid inside me.

"Levi, please," I begged. "I want you inside me. I want your cock."

"Not until you come like this." I felt his breath on me and then a few light flicks with the tip of his tongue. "Then you can have all the cock you want."

Two minutes later, I was screaming his name, my hands clutching his hair, my head thumping back against the door as my clit throbbed against his tongue. I barely had time to catch my breath before he stood up and whipped my top over my head, reached behind me and unhooked my bra, and slipped it off my shoulders.

He left the red heels on.

Our mouths hot and panting against each other's, we tore at his clothing until my hallway was littered with every stitch he'd been wearing tonight. I watched him roll on the condom before turning around and bracing two hands against the door. "Like this," I whispered. "Like the first time."

He stood behind me, teasing my ass with the head of his dick. "The only thing that will be like the first time is the way we're standing. Everything else will be much, much better. Now spread your gorgeous legs for me, and let me show you how."

I opened my legs wider for him and held my breath as he slid inside me, so deep he pushed me up onto my toes. "Yes," I whispered as he reached around and rubbed my clit with his fingertips, not too hard or fast, but in steady, rhythmic circles that made me sigh. His other hand moved up my stomach to cover one breast, my nipple hard against his palm.

"I fucking love it when you beg for my cock. It makes this moment, when I first get inside you, that much sweeter." Buried deep, he held himself there and kissed the back of my neck, sending chills down my spine. His mouth traveled down one shoulder, and I turned my head to meet his lips with mine. Our kiss was languid and sensual, our mouths soft, tongues searching.

He began to rock into me, slow and deep, his fingers between my legs moving a little faster, pressing a little firmer. "I want this all the fucking time, Jillian. I want my mouth on you, my hands on you. I want my cock inside you, making you come. It makes me feel so fucking good."

"I love it," I said on a sigh. "I love what you do to me." *And I love that being inside me is your respite from everything, your sanctuary.*

He teased my nipple with his fingers, sending sparks of lust straight to my core, and I felt him grow even thicker inside me. "Fuck, I get so hard for you."

"I feel it," I said, wincing as he thrust harder, went deeper. "And I think about it—all the time."

"You think about my hard cock all the time?" He stopped moving for a second. "Goddamn, that's hot."

I laughed, a little deliriously, then gasped when he jabbed into me again with even more force. "Yes. I think about how big you are, how thick, how hard. I think about the way you fuck me, how you make me come so fast, and I have to touch myself, but all I want is the real thing."

"And I think about this sweet little pussy," he whispered, rubbing my clit even harder. "The way it tastes, the way it feels, the way you get so wet for me. Every night when I'm in bed alone, I want to fuck you so badly it hurts. I fuck my hand just to relieve the tension, but it's not nearly good enough."

Thinking about him jerking off to me in bed at night was so hot I nearly exploded. I took my hands off the door and reached back, grabbing his neck. "*This* is what I want. You're everything I want."

His mouth was right at my ear as he thrust deep inside me. "Come for me, love. Let me feel it."

Oh God, Levi. Call me love and I'll do anything you say. An orgasm is the least of it.

But since you asked…

Hanging on to his neck for dear life, I arched my back as he fucked me, crying out as the climax erupted, my legs shaking and weak, my insides pulsing around him.

Afterward, I fell forward against the door, flattening my palms above my head, and he grabbed my hips, holding me steady as he drove into me hard and fast. "God, I love your back," he said, his voice raw. "I love your arms and your neck and your ass. I love your legs—oh fuck." He groaned as I brought my feet together, making myself tighter for him. "You have no idea what you do to me. I'm losing my *fucking* mind. If you knew—if you knew—" His words turned to short, snarling rasps of breath that matched the ferocity of his movement. His fingers dug into my hips as he began to moan, his body going still as his cock throbbed inside me.

"Yes. Come for me, love," I breathed over one shoulder, repeating his words so he would know I felt what he did, so he would know he wasn't crazy, so he'd know he wasn't alone.

So he'd know he was enough.

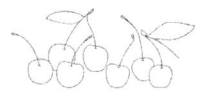

Levi used the bathroom next to my bedroom, and I threw his white shirt on and went up to the kitchen to get some water. It smelled like him, which sent a tingle up my spine, and I put my face in the collar, breathing in his scent.

While I was up there, I cleaned up a little in the guest bathroom and wondered if he wanted to come up and watch a movie or something or if he wanted to go to bed. It was only about ten-thirty, which I was both happy and sad about—it meant we still had about twelve hours, but it also meant that we *only* had about twelve hours. Our night together had barely gotten started and I was already sorry it had to end. When could we do this again? Would it be another week? Longer? He probably couldn't ask his sister to take Scotty overnight that often.

The difficulties in dating a single father were suddenly even more real.

Don't ask. Don't say anything. He feels bad enough about that. He'll think he's disappointing you.

Levi came up the stairs wearing just his jeans as I was pulling two bottles of water from the fridge. His bare chest and tousled hair and handsome face made the butterflies in my stomach start up again, and I smiled as I handed him a water. "I like seeing you here."

He smiled. "I like seeing you in my shirt."

"I love it. It smells like you." I sniffed the collar again. "Would it be too adolescent of me to ask you if I can keep it to sleep with?"

He laughed as he uncapped the water. "Then I'm keeping your underwear that's on the floor down there."

I giggled and swallowed half the bottle of water. "What would you like to do? Watch a movie or something?"

"I'm fine with anything." He tipped back the water and drank as much as I had.

"Did you check in with your sister? Everything OK?"

"I did, and no message. I assume everything is fine." Worry creased his forehead. "It was sort of…a rough week at school."

"I'm sorry to hear that." He didn't look entirely pleased that his sister hadn't let him know how things were going. "If you want to call her, it's OK."

He put the cap on the bottle and set it down. "Come here." I set my water aside too, and he pulled me close, wrapping his arms around me and leaning back against the counter. "Part of me does want to call her, but another part says to leave him be. If there was a problem, she'd call. I want tonight to be about you."

I hugged his torso, pressing close. In our bare feet, the top of my head nestled under his chin. "It's not just about me. It's about us."

He kissed my head. "It is about us. We need this."

With one light on above the range, the kitchen was dark and intimate, the only sound the hum of the fridge. We stayed in the cozy embrace for a moment, neither of us moving.

I couldn't stop thinking about what he'd told me at the restaurant—about feeling guilty, about the promises he'd made to his son, about feeling like he wasn't enough. Although it made me sad for him, I was happy he'd opened up to me that way, that he trusted me with his feelings. It helped me understand him so much better, especially his reluctance to enter into a relationship. Any time and attention diverted from his son must feel like a betrayal. But he had to know that it wasn't, right? Otherwise, how were we going to make this work?

I pressed my lips to his chest, wishing I could make everything better for him.

"Hey," he said.

I pulled back a little and looked up at him. "What?"

"Am I insane?"

I smiled. "I don't think so. Why?"

"Because I'm standing here in your kitchen thinking crazy things."

"Like what?"

"Like how much I loved making dinner for you the other night. And what I can make you for breakfast in the morning. And when can I see you in *my* kitchen. And when can we spend another night together. When can we spend two nights together?"

I giggled, squeezing him tight. *He feels the same way!* "We haven't even spent *one* night together yet."

"I know, that's why I'm telling you it's insane. But I also know one night with you won't be enough." He kissed me softly. "I want all your nights, Jillian."

"You can have them," I whispered, my pulse racing.

"But I can't. I *can't*. And I'm resentful of that." He closed his eyes. "And here's where the guilt gets me."

"Shhhh." Running my hands over his skin, I pressed kisses everywhere my lips could reach—his mouth, his jaw, his cheek, his throat, his chest. "No guilt. Let's not worry about anything beyond being here together tonight, OK?" I looked up at him, my breath catching. "This is what we have, and it's all I need."

He took my face in his hands. "You're so beautiful. And sweet. You could have so much more than I can give you."

"No more of that. I just want you, Levi." My hand slid down the front of his jeans. "Tell me I have you."

"You have me." He crushed his mouth to mine so hard our teeth clicked, his tongue sliding between my lips. His hands moved into my hair, and his breathing was ragged and heavy. Turning us so that my back was against the counter, he put his hands on my waist and lifted me onto it.

I opened my knees and reached for the button on his jeans as he kissed a hot, fiery path down my neck. When I had his pants undone, I shoved them down and reached inside for his cock. It sprang up like I'd flipped a switch, growing hot and hard and thick in my hand. I slipped the solid flesh through my fingers as he unbuttoned the shirt I wore and put his hands on the sides of my ribcage, his thumbs brushing over my nipples. They stiffened and tingled at his touch, and he groaned against my throat as I teased the head of his cock with my fingers. How was it possible I was aching for him to fill me again already?

"Inside me," I panted.

"I have to go get a condom from my jacket. My wallet's in my pocket." His breath tickled my neck.

"No!"

He picked his head up and looked at me. "What?"

"Don't go," I said, stroking him softly, desperate to feel that hot, velvety skin inside me with nothing between us. Maybe I couldn't give him all my nights, but I could give him this. "I'm on the pill. It's OK."

He hesitated. "Are you sure you trust it?"

I understood his concern for risk—he'd already dealt with one surprise pregnancy in his life. But I was diligent about taking my pill. "Yes. I promise it's safe. I want to feel you this way. I want to be that close to you. Let me."

"I want it too." He reached between my legs and moaned as he slipped a finger easily inside me. "I want it so fucking badly."

A moment later, he was pulling me closer to the edge of the counter and positioning the tip of his cock between my legs. He teased me a little first, stroking it up through my center, brushing it over my clit. Both of us watched as he slid inside me.

"Oh fuck," he whispered, his eyes closing.

I couldn't speak, I was so mesmerized by the sight of his body slipping inside mine, by the thought that there was nothing between us. Running my hands up his chest, I locked them behind his neck and our mouths came together. He moved his hands to my ass and held me steady as he moved in and out, the rhythm slow and steady, the friction hot and tight.

Eventually he moved one hand between us, his thumb rubbing my clit. "That feels so good," I whispered against his lips, desire pulling tight in my belly. "You know exactly how to touch me. You know just what my body wants."

He drove into me faster and harder, and I locked my legs around him, pointing my toes as my orgasm peaked. I yelled his name, over and over again, writhing and clinging and clawing at him like I was drowning and he was dry land. Slipping his hands beneath my ass, he lifted me off the counter and bounced me up and down his long, hard shaft. I cried out every time he let me all the down, his cock stabbing deep. He turned and put my back against the refrigerator, pounding into me so hard the entire thing shook. Then somehow he slipped his arms beneath my legs so my knees were slung over his elbows, my body open even wider to him.

"I'm gonna come so fucking hard inside you," he growled.

"Yes!" I panted, wild with the thought, bursting with the desire to ease something within him. "I want it, I want everything. Give it to me."

With one final violent thrust, he groaned long and hard, burying himself deep within me, his cock throbbing again and again and again. I clung to his neck, our lips barely touching, sharing a breath between us.

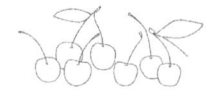

We decided to take a shower, not so much because we felt dirty but because we realized we probably needed a break from sex but still wanted to be naked and touching each other. A shower was a good excuse. Levi threw on a shirt and ran out to the car to grab the bag he'd packed while I ran the water, joining me a few minutes later.

We washed each other's hair—I had to stand on tiptoe for that—soaped each other up, and probably touched every single inch of each other's skin, but not necessarily in a sexual way. It was sweet and tender and romantic the way he knelt down in front of me, the way his hands moved over my limbs, the way his lips brushed the backs of my knees, each vertebra of my spine, the nape of my neck.

"So do you sing in the shower?" I asked him as he sudsed up my hair.

"Not usually." He grinned wryly. "Scotty doesn't like the noise. Every time I try to do it, he begs me to stop."

I laughed. "Seriously? I finally found something you're not good at?"

"You did. I can carry a lot of things, but a tune is not one of them. I think he cried last time I tried to sing to him. He hates when I wash his hair too."

"Now *that* I know you're good at." I smiled and closed my eyes as his fingertips rubbed my scalp. "You can wash mine any time you want. If I cry, it's because it feels so good."

We dried each other off, hung up our towels, and I grabbed a wide-tooth comb from a drawer. "Want to comb my hair too?"

"Sure."

I turned around and faced the mirror, and he stood behind me, patiently combing through my shoulder-length dark hair. "So gentle," I said.

He caught my eye in the mirror and cocked one brow, bringing that flutter back. "When I have to be."

Oh, damn. The reminder that he was rough sometimes turned the flutter into an urge. I fidgeted as he finished up, admiring his strong, masculine body in the mirror. When he finally set the comb down, I turned to face him. "Ready for bed?"

"Yes. Just need a minute to brush my teeth."

"Me too. And take a pill."

His eyes went wide. "Yes. Please take that pill."

I pulled the case from my makeup bag and held it up. "No worries. Hey, this is kind of like a little vacation."

He kissed the top of my head. "That's exactly what it's like."

We finished getting ready for bed, and I lit the candles in my room while he checked his phone one last time. I loved that he felt comfortable enough to walk around naked in front of me. I loved that we were going to bed together. I loved everything about tonight.

"All good?" I asked, tucking the lighter back in my nightstand drawer.

"I guess. No word from her." He looked a little concerned but shrugged.

I ran my hands up his arms and rose up on my toes to whisper in his ear. "Want to naked cuddle with me?"

He made a noise that was half-laugh, half-groan, and I felt his cock twitch against my thigh as he pulled me close, walking me backward toward the bed. "Yes, I want to naked cuddle with you. I want to naked everything with you. All the time."

He kissed me, catching me behind my back and crawling

onto the bed. I locked my arms around his neck as we slid between the sheets, kissing and clinging, and he rolled over so I was on top. "Mmmm," I murmured, bringing my legs astride his hips. "I'm never going to want you to leave."

"I wish I didn't have to." His tone was serious.

Oh, fuck. I shouldn't have said that, even to tease him. Now he feels bad. "Let's not think about that. We still have all night." I sat up and he took my hands, kissing them before lacing our fingers together above his chest.

"I wasn't looking for this," he said quietly, candlelight flickering in his eyes.

"For what?"

"To fall in love."

My breath caught and I couldn't move or speak or even blink. He kept our hands twined together, focusing on them as he went on.

"It wasn't anything I thought I wanted or needed or deserved."

"Levi," I whispered, my heart aching for him. "Everyone deserves love."

"I didn't want my son," he continued before I could say anything else. "I didn't want to be a father."

He was quiet for a second and I nearly rushed to defend him, but something told me to stay silent and merely listen. He'd bared his body; now he was baring his heart and soul, and I wanted them as much as I wanted the physical.

"I wished, before he was born, that he wouldn't exist. I thought he was a mistake, and I told Tara I would support her if she decided not to go through with the pregnancy." He swallowed hard. "Every day, I'm sorry for that. Every single day."

My throat squeezed so tight I couldn't have spoken even if I wanted to. *This is why*, I thought. *This is where his guilt comes from, and it's rooted so deep, twined so inextricably with his love for his son.*

"The day he was born, the moment I saw him for the first time, I was overcome by this powerful longing to protect him, this overwhelming love I'd never felt for anyone or anything before. But it was matched by this...*shame* that I hadn't wanted him." He looked up at me. "I've never told anyone this before. I hate the words."

"But that's not you anymore. You were so young, Levi. And it was so unexpected. Anyone would need time to adjust. It all changed once you saw him, right?"

He nodded. "I held him in my arms and cried, apologizing silently, over and over again. I swore to be a good father."

"You are, love," I whispered fiercely. "You are."

"I'm trying." He met my eyes again. "And I'll try to be what you deserve too. But I'm worried I can't be both."

"Levi, stop. You can love us both, I promise. You don't have to choose." I leaned over and kissed him, softly at first, feeling his cock begin to swell between my legs. I rocked my hips over him, stroking between his lips with my tongue, feeling his hands slide up my back. "I told you—you're enough...although I can't seem to *get* enough." I sat up and put my fingers in my mouth, and his jaw dropped as I reached between my legs and rubbed myself.

"Jesus Christ." His eyes were wide, and his dick jumped beneath me.

I knelt over him and he took it in his hand, placing the tip between my legs. I lowered myself slowly, enjoying every inch of hot, bare skin sliding inside me. When I rested on his hips, my body filled with him, I braced my hands above his shoulders and leaned down to brush my lips over his, feeling him grow even bigger and harder inside me.

"Listen to me," I said. "Yes, this took us by surprise. Yes, the situation is difficult. Yes, we could walk away. But I don't want to, Levi. I love you. And if you love me, then let's make it work."

"I do love you. That I know. But I don't know when I can do this again," he said, his hands rubbing my back. "Stay with you like this. And that kills me."

I started to move over him, whispering in his ear. "Then let's make every second count."

CHAPTER 17
Levi

I TOLD HER, and she still wanted me. I told her everything—and here she was, saying she loved me, taking me inside her, wrapping me up in her softness. How did she know exactly what I needed? How was it possible she wanted to give it to me? This beautiful woman, who loved like an angel and fucked like a porn star...what had I ever done to deserve her?

Stop fucking questioning it. For fuck's sake, she's riding your cock like Calamity Jane on crack—just enjoy it!

And that's when my phone went off.

No. Oh fuck. Please, no.

Jillian stopped moving, her hands falling from where she'd been holding her hair on top of her head. Her breath coming fast, she looked over to the dresser, where I'd set my phone. It was vibrating, the screen lit up.

She looked back at me. "Want to get it?"

No, I don't want to get it. I want you to keep fucking me like you were. It's the best thing I've ever watched, and I'm about to flood your body like the levees broke. "Give me one second."

She swung her leg over me and got off my dick, which

was immediately cold and angry with me. I went over to the dresser and checked the call—it was my sister.

My stomach clenched. "Hello?"

"Hey. I'm so sorry to call you."

"That's OK, what's up?" But in the background I could hear what was up—a massive meltdown.

"It's Scotty. He's upset about the nightlight."

"Oh, fuck." I tipped my forehead into my hands. How could I have forgotten to pack the nightlight? And after a tough week, too. *Fucking idiot!*

"He says he has to have it to sleep?"

I swallowed, so angry with myself I wanted to punch my reflection in the mirror over Jillian's dresser. "He does."

"I've tried everything—other nightlights, leaving the hall light on, even leaving the bedroom light on, but nothing was right. This is the problem with letting him be so particular about things all the time."

My temper flared, but I took a deep breath and counted to five. "Let's not get into that now. Has he slept at all?"

"I don't think so. But he didn't really start to break down until about ten or so."

I grabbed my watch. "Ten! Monica, it's twelve thirty! Why didn't you call me?" God, I was an asshole. I *knew* why she hadn't called me.

"Because I was trying to let you have a night to yourself, Levi! I'm sorry!"

I exhaled, closing my eyes. "No, I'm sorry. I appreciate your trying to help." And would it really have been any better if she'd called sooner? I'd have missed out on half the time I'd spent with Jillian. Maybe we wouldn't have had the kitchen sex or the shower together. Maybe she wouldn't have told me she loved me.

"I wasn't going to call at all, but you said if it really got bad, you wanted to know."

"No, you did the right thing." I set my watch down and pinched the bridge of my nose. "Can he talk?"

"I don't know. Let me try. Hey, Scotty? Your dad's on the phone. Want to talk to him? Come on, it'll make you feel better. Want to say hi?"

I took a deep breath, picturing the scene. Scotty balled up in a corner somewhere, hands over his ears, crying inconsolably, rocking back and forth. *Don't get mad. It's not his fault. It's yours—you forgot the nightlight, asshole. You were so excited about your nonstop all-night fuckfest, you forgot one of the essential things he needs to go to bed. And if you're really honest with yourself, you'd admit that after the kind of week he had at school, an overnight at Monica's wasn't the right decision for him.*

"He won't talk," Monica said. "I'm sorry."

"That's OK. I'll come get him."

"OK," she said. "I wish I knew how to handle this better, but it's so late, and the girls are trying to sleep, and we have to get up for church tomorrow…"

"Monica, it's fine. I know. I'll be there as fast as I can." I looked around for my bag. "Tell him I'm on my way, and he'll be able to sleep in his own bed tonight."

"I will. See you in a few."

"Bye." I ended the call, set my phone on the dresser, and rubbed my face. "Fuck."

"Bad news?"

I turned around and saw her sitting up in bed, her arms wrapped around her knees. "Yeah. I fucking forgot to pack the damn nightlight. He needs it to sleep."

She nodded. "Poor little guy."

"Jillian." I sighed. I didn't even have time to finish what we'd started, and my dick was at half-mast anyway. "I'm sorry."

"It's OK, Levi."

"No, it's not. But there isn't anything I can do about it." I spotted my bag on the floor near the foot of the bed and grabbed some clothes, throwing them on with jerky movements. "And I'm mad about this, so I feel even worse."

"It's OK to feel mad."

"No, it's not."

"You're mad at Scotty? Or yourself?"

I paused, buttoning up my shirt. "Both," I admitted. "And I feel like the biggest asshole in the world for saying that, but I'm angry at both of us."

"You're not an asshole. You're human."

I tugged on socks and stepped into my shoes, bending to lace them up. "Well, I feel like an asshole, because even though part of me knows I deserve all the blame for this, and I should hug him and comfort him and tell him it's all my fault, there's another part of me that's like *why can't you just fucking fall asleep with the hall light on?*" I straightened up and shook my head. "But I know why he can't." I looked around for my coat. "And I'm frustrated that there's nothing I can do about it."

"Well, maybe you could try doing the nightlight and the hall light for a while? Then do one or the other? So he gets comfortable with different things?"

"Maybe," I said stiffly. I don't know why her comment made me bristle a little. She was only trying to help. And she was a pediatrician, for fuck's sake. It's not like she didn't have a clue about kids. But I was always irked when people who didn't know Scotty tried to give me advice. "But I doubt it would work. He's really set in his ways."

"OK," she said easily. "Sorry if I upset you."

I hadn't realized it was obvious I was bothered. Now I felt like an even bigger dick. "You didn't. I'm sorry." Softening my tone, I slung my bag over my shoulder and went to the side of the bed where she sat. "I'm just frustrated. For many reasons."

She nodded slowly. "I get it."

"Jillian." Setting my bag down, I sat at her feet and put my hands on top of them. They were chilly, and I wanted nothing more than to get naked again, wrap myself around her, and tuck us in under the sheets. But that wasn't an option. "I wanted to wake up with you so fucking badly."

"Me too," she said. "Next time."

"Next time." Was she wondering, like I was, when that would be? And if we'd actually get to see it through? I wanted to say *I promise*, but I couldn't. I'd never be able to promise her anything. The weight of that reality made my limbs heavy and my chest ache.

"You better go." She tucked her hair behind her ears and gave me a tiny smile. "He's waiting for you. He needs his daddy."

I nodded and said what I had to, even though I had to rip the raw words from my throat. "Jillian. I want you to give this some thought. These kinds of things...they're going to happen. I can't promise they won't, and I can't prevent them."

"You don't have to—"

"Listen to me. Please. I love you, but I will understand completely if you don't want this in the morning."

She looked at me for a moment, then got to her knees. Wrapping her arms around me, she laid her head on my shoulder. "I love you, too. And I don't give up easily, Levi."

I kissed the top of her head, love and gratitude for her swelling in my chest. "I'm glad to hear that. I'll call you tomorrow, OK?"

She sat back. "I'll walk you out."

After throwing on a robe, she saw me to the door and gave me a quick hug and kiss on the cheek. When I tried to kiss her lips and linger there, she gave me a gentle shove on the chest and laughed. "You better go. Or I'll never let you leave."

One last kiss on her forehead and I went out the door.

On the way to my sister's house, I kept thinking about her,

about everything we'd done, everything we'd said, everything I felt. As amazing as the night had been, I didn't want our relationship to be nothing but these short, intense bursts. I wanted more, but I didn't know how to get it.

Yes, you do—you have to stop trying to be two people. You can't be Dad here and Levi there and expect to keep everyone happy. You're just going to end up feeling more guilty all the time. You have to bring her into your life as it exists, into Scotty's life. You have to let her in.

I rubbed a hand over my beard, wondering if that was really the answer. Wasn't it too soon to introduce her to my son? What if she got to know him and thought he was too much of a challenge? What if she didn't understand him? What if she saw the way I had to live and realized she couldn't handle it? Or thought I was dealing with him wrong, like my family sometimes said?

It's too soon. I should wait.

For that matter, was it too soon to be so in love with her? Was there a schedule for these things? I was so used to doing things a certain way—my life at work and at home was governed by calendars, plans, lists, charts, deadlines, routines. I was an architect, for fuck's sake. You don't build a house without a foolproof design first. But...it felt liberating to have this other thing happening in my life, something impulsive and extraordinary, something instinctual and unstoppable. When I was with her, I felt so *alive*.

Yet it was frightening too. I'd never been in love like this before. Without experience or wisdom or a plan to guide me, how did I know if what I was doing was right for my son? Or for Jillian?

I was just feeling my way.

It was scary as fuck.

Scotty fell asleep briefly in the car on the way home, but he woke up when the car stopped and refused to go back to sleep in his bed, even though all his usual comforts were there. He'd gotten himself too worked up to feel calm, and I had to lie down with him in my bed with my arms wrapped around him like a baby simply to get him to stop moving. When his body and mind finally were settled, he played with my ear as he drifted off and I felt bad again for being angry about tonight. He didn't ask that much of me, and he struggled to feel good about himself in so many ways. School this week had not gone well...he threw his pencil again during a math test, refused to do a writing assignment after getting frustrated with corrections, cried twice, and shut down once. He actually wet himself on Thursday morning (the day of the test) in an attempt to miss the bus, but I'd cleaned him up and driven him to school. He'd seemed happy enough at swim therapy and during dinner Friday evening, so I'd hoped Saturday night would be fine, but I'd been wrong.

You should have canceled tonight. You said you'd only do it if he had a good enough week, and you knew in your heart he hadn't. You convinced yourself he'd be fine just so you could get what you wanted, and that's fucking selfish and mean.

Fuck! My stomach churned. *Had* I been mean to make him sleep away from home so I could wake up with Jillian? Did it serve me right that it wouldn't happen? Maybe this was the universe telling me to be thankful for what I had and not look for anything else.

I hoped not...I loved her. I needed her.

But maybe that was selfish too.

CHAPTER 18
Jillian

I WENT BACK TO BED, missing the warmth of Levi's body next to mine, the sound of his voice in my ear, the press of his lips against my skin. The scent of him clung to my sheets, so I did too, gathering them up in my arms and snuggling them as if they could snuggle back.

It was a poor substitute.

I tried my hardest not to resent the fact that he had to leave, but it was difficult. I'd been so excited about having the whole night together. It wasn't that I was angry with anyone —I completely understood and didn't blame Scotty, Levi, or his sister—so maybe resentment isn't what I felt. Maybe it was plain old disappointment. Sadness. A little envy for any girl who got to spend every night in the arms of the person she loved. I just wanted one night. One.

Quit being selfish. So you didn't get exactly what you wanted. So what? You had a lot more time than you've ever had together, and like you said—it's about quality, not quantity. Think of all the things he said to you, the way he opened his heart. That's worth something. That's worth everything, isn't it?

I wanted it to be, and I believed that he loved me, but I couldn't shake this nagging fear that he was going to decide I wasn't worth the hassle of trying to juggle everything in his life to fit me into it. Like he said, he hadn't been looking for love, hadn't needed it or wanted it. Why should I think I'd be enough to change that?

I slept fitfully and woke up to the sound of rain against my window. The clock said it was only eight thirty, so I tried going back to sleep, but I couldn't. Eventually I gave up on sleep and made coffee, deciding to get a jump-start on my day.

Around nine thirty, I was sitting at the breakfast counter with my laptop open when my phone rang.

"Hello?"

"Good morning, beautiful."

"Good morning." Hearing his voice warmed my insides, and I couldn't help smiling. "How are you?"

"Tired. How are you?"

"Good, a little tired. How's Scotty?"

"It was a rough night. But he was up at six thirty like nothing happened."

"Wow. That's early. And you did all that driving last night, no wonder you're tired."

"All the *what* I did last night?"

I laughed. "Exactly."

"I miss you."

"I miss you too." My eyes strayed from the counter over to the fridge, and my stomach whooshed. "Are you going to church?"

"Oh, yes. We don't vary the schedule around here simply because Daddy got no sleep. The world might end."

"Poor Daddy. Maybe you can get a nap in later."

He sighed. "I'll try. But there's homework and laundry and other stuff too."

"I wish I could help you." I looked around at my condo, which was beautifully furnished and always clean, but often felt empty and too quiet on weekends.

"Me too. What are you up to today?"

"Some chores. A little paperwork. Maybe grocery shopping. Dinner at my parents' house later."

"With everyone?"

"Yes." *I wish you could come too.*

"Say hello for me."

"Maybe one of these Sundays, you could join us. You and Scotty."

"Maybe." But he didn't sound that hopeful. "I better get us out the door. Don't want to be late for Mass." He lowered his voice. "Bad enough I'm showing my face there after everything I did to you last night."

I laughed. "I'm looking at my refrigerator right now."

"Is there a dent in it?"

"Probably several."

He groaned. "I better go, or I'm going to walk into church with a very large erection."

"It *is* large. Even larger than Magik Mike."

He laughed. "You just made my day."

"Good."

I hung up feeling better.

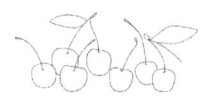

"I'm dying," Skylar said, dropping onto the couch next to me. She shrugged out of her coat and dropped her bag to the floor. "I have to hear about last night."

"I promised Natalie I'd wait for her."

"Where is she?"

"In the kitchen, helping Mom. Did you even go in and say hello yet?"

"No. Natalie!" Skylar yelled.

Sighing, I closed the magazine I'd been looking at and set it aside. "Where's Sebastian?"

"He and Miles are helping Dad move some equipment into the barn."

Natalie appeared in the family room doorway. "What?"

"Get in here," Skylar said. "I want to hear about Jilly's night, and she won't tell me without you."

Natalie's face looked pained. "OK, give me one minute. I have to get the potatoes in the oven." She darted back into the kitchen, yelling over her shoulder. "Don't start without me!"

"So was it amazing?" Skylar raised her sculpted brows.

I sighed in response.

"I knew it!" she squealed, clapping her hands. "I swear to God, the moment I saw you two together…"

"Hey, you promised!" Natalie scurried in and sat on the floor in front of us.

"Relax, I only asked her if it was amazing and all she did was this." Skylar imitated my lovelorn sigh, making it much more dramatic, almost tragic.

Natalie laughed and looked at me. "That good, huh?"

"Yeah. I mean, it's always good, but last night was different."

"What was different?" Skylar wanted to know.

"We talked a lot. He really opened up to me."

Skylar swooned and fell back. "I love when those big, strong types get all talky and vulnerable. It's so hot."

"It was," I said. "But it was kind of sad, too."

"Why was it sad?" Natalie asked.

"He's just really hard on himself," I said, careful not to reveal things Levi had told me in confidence. "In all things. He feels bad for not being able see me more often. He wonders if he's making the right choices for Scotty. He regrets things from the past. He's convinced he's going to fail at trying to balance being a dad and a boyfriend, and he thinks I deserve more than he can give."

"Wow. What did you say?" Skylar leaned forward.

"I told him I want him, and I understand I can't be his first priority. I told him I can be patient, and we can go slow."

"And what did he say?" Natalie was rapt.

"He said he loved me."

Skylar squealed and leaned back, kicking her feet, and Natalie's jaw practically hit the floor. "So much for going slow!"

"Oh my God, I'm dying." Skylar sat up again. "And then what?"

"I told him I felt the same, and then there was more sex." I paused. "In a bed this time."

"Where was it before?" Natalie asked.

"Uh, in the hallway at the front door. In the kitchen."

"The kitchen?" Skylar blinked.

I nodded. "On the counter and against the fridge."

She fanned her face. "Oh my God. This is insanely hot."

"Yes…until he had to leave right in the middle of the bedroom episode to go pick up his son."

Her hand stopped mid-fan. "What?"

I shrugged. "His sister called. Scotty wasn't sleeping and wanted to come home."

"So he *left*?"

"He had to. It's not like Scotty was being difficult for no reason. He was really upset."

"What about you?" Natalie asked. "Were you upset?"

"I was, but then I realized I was being selfish. I knew going into last night there was a chance that might happen. And we did have an amazing night…it just ended sooner than we wanted. He was as upset as I was. Maybe more."

"Wow." Natalie leaned back on her hands. "That's tough. Like, this could keep happening."

I nodded, feeling my fun mood dissipate a little. "It could."

"So now what?" Skylar asked, crossing her arms. "What's

the next step? Do you just keep going on dates once a week?" Her expression told me what she thought of that idea.

"I don't know," I admitted. "We haven't made any other plans. It's hard because getting away is so tough for him."

"Well then, you should go there. Hang out with him at home. Meet Scotty," Skylar said firmly.

I lifted my shoulders. "I've offered, so we'll see. I think he's nervous about it. I'm nervous about it."

"Of course you are," Natalie said. "It's more pressure than meeting someone's parents. This is a person you'd have to live with, if things worked out. There's a lot to consider."

I held up my hands. "Whoa. Don't jinx me. We have strong feelings for each other, but it's only been a month. And I do think there's merit in going slow." Deep breath. "I just want to keep going forward. Somehow."

Late that night, so late I was already in bed with the lights out, he called me again.

"Hello?"

"Hey." His voice was low and hushed.

"Hey."

"Did I wake you?"

"No. I'm in bed, but I wasn't asleep yet."

"Thinking?"

"Yeah."

"About what?"

"About you. About last night. Truthfully, it's been hard to think about anything else all day."

"I'm so sorry about how it ended."

"That isn't what I meant, silly." I rolled onto my side. "I was thinking about it in a good way."

"I know. I'm still sorry."

"Stop apologizing. One interrupted night isn't the end of the world. It was bad luck. We can give it some time and try again."

"Sure. I've been thinking about it today too…and it really was my fault."

"What was?"

"The meltdown. Not only did I forget to pack the nightlight, but he'd had a really tough week at school. I should've known going off the routine was a bad idea."

"Math again?"

"Among other things, but yes—he has a lot of anxiety about math tests, even though he can have the tests read to him, and he gets extra time."

"I used to get nervous about math tests too. Not that my anxiety is anything like Scotty's," I said quickly, "but I remember the nervous feeling. And you know what my dad did?"

"What?"

I laughed at the memory, which I hadn't thought about in years. "He gave me a lucky stone."

"A what?"

"A lucky stone—at least he claimed it was lucky. It was this Petoskey stone he'd found on the beach. He polished it for me, and I'd keep it in my pocket, then take it out and put it on my desk during a test. Or hold it in my left hand."

"How old were you?"

"Maybe second or third grade?"

"I'm trying to picture you at Scotty's age. What did you look like?"

I giggled. "Tall. Skinny. One shoe always untied."

"Adorable. So did the rock work?"

"It did. I totally believed him that it was lucky, and I remember feeling much more confident about tests when I had it in my hand. Got any lucky stones lying around?"

He laughed softly. "I'll have to look. Anything is worth a try."

"I agree. And really, don't feel bad about last night. If you're going to think about it, think about the good parts."

"There were lots of those."

"There were." My whole body tingled, and I hugged my knees to my chest.

"Can I see you this weekend?"

"Of course." I crossed my fingers and ankles. *Invite me to your house. Let me meet your son.*

"I need to check with my regular sitter, but would Friday work?"

"Sure. That's actually my birthday."

"Get the fuck out. It is?"

I laughed. "Yes. I definitely wouldn't invent a birthday. Who wants to keep getting older?"

"We have to celebrate. I want to take you somewhere nice. Are you sure Friday night is open? Your family doesn't want you on your birthday?"

"I'm celebrating with family on Sunday. Friday's yours if you want it. I actually took the entire day off."

"Did you really?"

"Yes." I took a breath. "You know, if you can't get your sitter, I could come to your house or something…" I left it dangling, hoping he'd grab on.

"Maybe. We'll see. Wouldn't be much of a date that way. And by that I mean there wouldn't be any birthday sex. I'd be very, very sad about that. And it isn't even *my* birthday."

I had to laugh. "OK, well, let me know. I only wanted you to know I'm up for that."

"I know you are, and I appreciate it." He paused. "I love you."

I hugged my knees. "I love you too."

"Night."

"Night."

Setting my phone on my nightstand, I curled up again under the covers. I was a little disappointed he hadn't offered to introduce me to Scotty yet, but I had to trust he'd know the right time. We were in love, yes, but it still felt young and fragile. Maybe more time was best.

CHAPTER 19

Levi

I HAD a surprise visitor the next day at work.

"Knock, knock, darling."

But she didn't really knock. She just came right in.

"Mom. Hi. What are you doing here?"

"I was doing some shopping down this way and thought I'd stop by." She tucked her silvery bob behind one ear. She'd gone completely gray in her thirties, so any day now I was expecting to wake up with a beard and head full of white, but so far it was only a few strays here and there.

"Come in." I gestured to the chairs in front of my desk. Since leaving my uncle's firm, I worked for myself and rented office space in a building downtown. Working from home sounds good in theory, but I did it for a while and found it hard to separate home from work—I found it much easier to get shit done in both environments when I wasn't tempted to avoid work in one by taking up a chore in the other.

"I was wondering if you had time for lunch, actually." She raised her eyebrows at me hopefully.

I frowned at the work on my desk and rubbed the back of my neck. "I don't know, Mom. I have a lot of things to get done before a meeting at Scotty's school at two."

"Oh? About the IEP?"

"Yes. Among other things."

"Well, let's grab a quick bite and you can fill me in. I like to know how things are going with him, and we haven't had a chance to talk much. You're so busy these days."

Fucking Mom Guilt. Nothing worse. "I know, Mom. Sorry, I just don't have a lot of spare time."

"I'm not blaming you, darling," she said breezily. "I merely want to know how you're doing."

I fought off the groan building in the pit of my stomach and turned it into more of an exasperated sigh. "I wish you would have called first. I could have planned for lunch with you."

"You'd have turned me down. I know you." She arched a brow at me, then smiled cajolingly. "Come on. Humor your old ma. I won't be around forever, you know."

I rolled my eyes. She might have just turned sixty, but she was as healthy and active as someone half her age. "OK. A quick bite."

She beamed. "Thank you. Shall we go now or do you need to finish something up?"

"We can go now." I closed my laptop. "I'll pick up my dry-cleaning too."

"I could have done that for you today." She was saying it to be nice, but somehow I felt it as another scolding—like I should have *told* her I had dry-cleaning to be picked up.

"I didn't know you were coming down, Mom. Remember?"

"I know, but if you need help with things at home, I'm happy to do it," she said, leading the way out of my office, through the little lobby area I shared with an accountant and an attorney. "The drive isn't that far, and I'd love to see you and Scotty more often."

I shut my office door and followed her out, taking deep breaths. *She's not saying this to criticize you. She's simply offering to help.* "I know, and I appreciate it. I'll let you know if I need anything."

We walked to a nearby diner and were seated at a small table near the window. After looking at the menu, I ordered a grilled chicken sandwich and she ordered a Reuben. After my iced tea and her Diet Coke arrived, she put her elbows on the table and propped her chin in her hands.

"So tell me what's new. How is Scotty? At the birthday dinner, he seemed very preoccupied with his electronics."

"His iPad. He earns breaks with it when he does what he's supposed to."

"Don't you think he should do what he's supposed to just because? Won't he always expect a reward for behaving properly if you keep doing this?"

I stiffened. "If this lunch is about criticizing my parenting, it's over."

She held up her hands. "It's not, it's not. I'm sorry. You know best."

"I do."

"I only worry that as he gets older, it will get tougher on him. The school and his peers aren't going to treat him like a baby."

"I don't treat him like a baby, Mom. I treat him like he needs to be treated to get through his day and feel good about himself."

"OK, darling, don't get upset. Without seeing you two every day like I used to, I don't know the situation. Tell me about the IEP."

I filled her in on things at school, and she appeared genuinely concerned. "He wet himself? On purpose?"

"Yes. Hoping that it would delay going to school, so he could miss the math test."

"Oh, the poor thing. I hope he doesn't do that at school. The kids would be so cruel."

"I worry about that too," I admitted. "But I can't control

how other people react to him. I'm trying to help by getting him a few more accommodations at school, but it's an uphill battle. And I hate those meetings."

"Why?"

"Because the focus is always on what he's not doing, or what he's doing wrong. He has a lot of gifts, and he's so smart. Why can't they figure out a way to help him learn based on what he does *well*? Why force a kid to take a test the same way as every other kid when, neurologically, he is not like those kids?"

"What would help?"

"More time. A separate room without any noise or distractions for testing. Allowing him to give verbal answers."

"I thought you wanted him in a regular classroom."

"I do. I'm talking about having a safe space at school where he can go if he needs it. Maybe an aide for at least part of the day."

"I see." She lifted her shoulders. "That sounds reasonable."

"You'd think."

Our sandwiches arrived, and she waited until the server had refilled our drinks and left before saying anything else.

"OK, I can't take it anymore. Tell me about her."

For a second, I blanked. But one look at her eager expression, and I realized. Fucking Monica. I picked up one half of my sandwich. "Her name is Jillian Nixon. She's a pediatrician."

"Is she related to Dale and Bunny Nixon?"

"No clue. But I don't think so. She grew up on a cherry farm on Old Mission."

"Hm. Maybe a different family, then. I think Dale was originally from downstate." She looked a little disappointed, then flapped a hand before picking up her sandwich. "Oh well. So tell me more. Monica mentioned you met her at a wedding?"

"Yes." I gave her a sanitized version of our meeting eleven years ago and told her we'd run into each other—sort of literally—at Sebastian's wedding.

"The lawyer?"

"Yes. His wife is Jillian's sister."

"How nice." She smiled and touched her lips with her napkin. "So you've been seeing her about a month?"

"About that."

"And it's going well?"

"It is."

I said nothing further, and she sighed dramatically. "For heaven's sake, Levi. You're killing me."

"How so?"

"Because this is the first woman you've talked about in years, and I'm thrilled for you, and you won't give me more than the vital stats and two-word answers."

I swallowed a bite. "It's new."

"Another two words. Can I at least have four please?"

Taking another bite, I chewed and thought. "I like her a lot. There, that's five."

Another sigh. She put her reuben down, a hurt expression on her face. "You're punishing me. I get it."

"Do you?" Haha, another two words. I kind of liked this game.

"Yes. You moved out because I was all up in your business, as Monica tells me, and now you've shut me out completely. Am I really that bad?"

I popped the final piece of my sandwich in my mouth and thought about how to answer that. "Sometimes."

"Is that really why you moved out?"

"Monica said that?"

"Only because I was griping about never seeing you. She said you've been busy and told me you'd been seeing someone. I was shocked that I had no idea. And hurt. I want to be in your life, Levi. And Scotty's life."

"I know, Mom. And I want you to be in it. But you have to stop telling me I'm doing everything wrong."

She put a hand on her chest. "I never said you're doing everything wrong!"

"Well, that's how you make me feel. Look, I know you think I screwed up and got someone pregnant."

"Levi!" She sat back, her expression stunned, maybe even hurt. "I have never said that to you."

"I guess I just felt it then. Like Monica did everything right—college, marriage, children—and I was the fuckup."

"That is not me talking." She crossed her arms and lifted her chin. "My grandchildren are the light of my life and every one of them was destined to enter this world and be loved to pieces by me, whether they were a surprise or not. And your dad and I did not raise any fuckups."

I had to smile at hearing her use that word, but it was short-lived. "You criticized me so much as Scotty got older that it made me feel that way. Like you thought I couldn't possibly be mature or smart enough to handle parenting a child on my own."

"Not once did I think that. All parents criticize their children's parenting skills! It's our right as grandparents!"

I considered that. "Maybe I was extra sensitive, then. I already felt bad enough that Scotty was going to grow up without a mother, and as he grew and it was clear he wasn't a typical kid, I felt even less sure of myself."

My mother leaned forward and spoke softer. "I could see that, Levi. So I tried to help the best way I could. I managed to raise two beautiful, smart, amazing people. I thought I had something to offer you."

"You did," I said. "You offered me and Scotty a home and helped me take care of him when he was a baby. I needed that, and I'm so grateful. But I got to a point where I really wanted to find my way on my own, and I couldn't do that living in your house."

Her shoulders slumped a bit. "I see your point. It's hard not to mother your child just because he's an adult, especially when he lives with you. I guess I saw you struggling and couldn't resist trying to make it all better."

"You can't." My tone was firm.

"Back to two words, huh?"

I cracked a tiny smile.

"I saw that," she teased. Sighing, she sat up straight again. "OK. So no more criticizing. I will listen when you need to talk and try my very hardest to let you do things your way and not say a word, even if I disagree."

"Thank you. I appreciate that."

"And in return," she went on smoothly, "please tell me more about Jillian. Monica said she hasn't met Scotty?"

"Not yet." I focused on the other half of my sandwich.

"I think that's wise, really I do."

I looked at her to see if she was being facetious, but her expression was earnest. "I think you two need time to get to know each other before you bring her into his life."

"I agree."

"You don't want to introduce her too soon and confuse Scotty about who she is, especially if it doesn't work out. And for her sake, you don't want to make it seem like you're simply looking for a replacement mother."

"She would never think that. And it couldn't be further from the truth."

"Plus you need time alone together. Romantic time," she said authoritatively. "Just because one of you has a child doesn't mean you shouldn't treat her to a proper courtship."

I almost laughed. *Yes, that's exactly what I was doing against her refrigerator Saturday night. Treating her to a proper courtship.* "What was that about promising not to meddle?"

He face went blank as she picked up her Diet Coke. "I never said anything about not meddling. No mother in her right mind would ever promise not to meddle. I promised not to *criticize* so much."

"Oh."

"And anyway, I hope you'll like this meddling, because I want to do something for you."

"What's that?"

She grinned. "How about if Dad and I come down and stay with Scotty for a weekend? Or even a night? Don't get mad, but Monica told me what happened Saturday night. I felt terrible for you."

I groaned, setting my sandwich down. "Fucking Monica."

"Well, you know she can't keep a secret, darling. You can't lie and she can't keep a secret. That's always been the way you two are."

I sucked up some iced tea, wondering if it was too early for some whiskey.

"Anyway," she went on breezily. "What do you think of my offer? I promise to do everything exactly the way you want me to. Scotty can stick to his regular routine in his normal environment, your dad and I get some quality time with him, and you get alone time with your lady friend."

My lady friend. Jillian would love that one.

Should I do it? God, I was so tempted. If she meant what she said, and she'd stick to Scotty's routine without any "improvements" or surprises, he might be OK. Staying at Monica's had been a change in routine and a change in environment. This had the potential to go a lot smoother. Maybe I'd try it for a night, and if it went well, we could do a weekend eventually.

"OK, Mom. I'll take you up on the offer."

She clapped her hands together. "Good!"

"But you have to do it exactly like you said. Follow the routine to the letter. And call me at the first sign of a meltdown."

She held up three fingers. "Scout's honor."

"In that case, what's your weekend like?"

"I'm all yours."

"Friday night would be great. It's her birthday."

"How nice! Take her somewhere wonderful. Maybe Chateau Grand Traverse. Or one of the new wineries! You could have dinner at one of the tasting rooms." She noticed my expression. "Does that eye roll mean I'm meddling?"

"Yes. I can handle the date details if you can handle Scotty."

"I can."

"Good. If you come down in the early afternoon, you could take him to swim therapy after school. He really loves it."

Her eyes got misty. "Oh, I'd love that. I'm so happy, Levi. This is perfect."

Nothing was perfect, but an entire night with Jillian sounded pretty close. I couldn't wait to tell her.

CHAPTER 20

Jillian

WHEN I CHECKED my phone Monday after work, I noticed I'd missed a call from Levi. He hadn't left a voicemail, but he'd texted. **Give me a call when you get a moment. Good news.**

What kind of good news? I wondered. Maybe he'd talked to his sitter and she was available Friday. I would be happy if that was the case, but part of me kind of hoped she wouldn't be able to watch Scotty, and Levi would ask me to come over instead of canceling the date. I didn't need anything elaborate for my birthday, and getting to meet his son would have been a wonderful gift. But I didn't want to pressure him.

I called him back on the drive home.

"Hey you," he said when he answered.

"Hi."

"How was your day?"

"Good. Yours?"

"Good. I had lunch with my mother."

"Oh yeah? Was that planned?"

"No, it was an ambush. She pretended to miss me and said she just wanted some time with me, but really she'd heard about you from my sister and wanted the scoop."

I laughed. "That sounds like something my mom would do. Or my sisters. How'd it go?"

"It was good, actually. I tried to get out of it at first, but she guilted me into going, and then once we were there, I ended up saying some things to her I probably should have said a while ago."

"Really? Like what?"

"Nothing earth-shattering, but I let her know that her criticism of my parenting choices wasn't appreciated. And I'd be glad to spend more time with her if she agreed to stop doing it."

"Good for you. It's hard to stand up to your parents, even as an adult."

"Yeah, I think she understood where I was coming from. And honestly, a lot of what I took as criticism or felt as censure might have been typical mom advice I was just extra sensitive to, because I already felt like I had no idea what I was doing."

"That's possible."

"I'd always felt like the bad kid growing up, because Monica was so perfect and never got in any trouble, so when I got Tara pregnant I kind of assumed they viewed it as my biggest fuckup ever."

As ridiculous as it sounds, the phrase *I got Tara pregnant* spiked a rush of jealousy so fierce, my heart rate sped up. Had he said when Tara got pregnant, I don't think I'd have reacted that way, but somehow the *I got* made me think of him actually having sex with her. Creating a child inside her. Watching that child grow within her. Being present at his birth. Experiencing with her all the wonderful and miserable things new parents experience—hearing him cry for the first time, changing diapers, feeding him, giving baths, taking him to his checkups. Every day I saw bleary-eyed, adoring new parents in the office. He'd already done all that with someone. It's not like I hadn't known it before, but I felt an ache in my gut all the same.

I tried to clear my head. "Wow. Did you say that to her?"

"I did, actually. And she swore it wasn't true."

"Good."

"She also promised to do less criticizing and more listening, and she offered to come down with my dad and stay overnight with Scotty at the house so you and I can have some time alone together."

"She did?"

"Yes. She called it treating you to a proper courtship."

I winced. "Oh, God. That's embarrassing."

"What the hell are you talking about?"

"It's weird that your mom knows we have sex!"

"Well, considering I have a son, I'm pretty sure she already knows I have sex."

"I'm talking about me. You can do no wrong, you're her son, but I don't want her to think I'm promiscuous before she even meets me."

"But after she meets you, it's OK?"

I groaned. "No."

"Listen, stop worrying. She will love you when she meets you. Trust me."

I wondered when that would be. "OK."

"So let's talk about your birthday. Can I pick you up a little early? Like around two?"

"Uh, sure. What's the plan?"

"It's a surprise."

"Really?"

"Yes. Pack an overnight bag."

My heart pumped faster again, for a good reason this time. "OK. What should I wear?"

"You always look gorgeous. Anything you want—but if it shows your legs or neck or shoulders, be warned I won't be able to keep my hands off you."

I smiled. "Got it. I can't wait."

On Friday morning, I treated myself to a massage and facial before heading home to shower and pack a bag for the night. I still had no idea where we were going or what we were doing, but I really didn't care—I was happy that we'd finally have our night together. In the back of my mind was the fear that he'd get the call and have to go home, but there was no sense dwelling on that. Part of loving him was accepting that he was always a father first, and I could do that. It made having all his attention that much sweeter when I had it.

The day was sunny but cool, so I dressed in fitted jeans, boots, and a slouchy sweater that Skylar had gotten me for Christmas last year. It was soft and cream-colored, and its draped cowl neck fell off one shoulder, which I thought Levi would like. Underneath it I wore a camisole but no bra, something I could do that my full-chested sisters could not. It was a small perk, and didn't make up for being denied their luscious curves, but it was still a perk.

In case I needed something dressier tonight, I threw a dress that packed well and a pair of heels into my bag, along with a deliciously sexy bra and panty set in a deep maroon color. For tomorrow, I put in another top I could wear with jeans, plus extra socks and underwear.

Yes, I was a Girl Scout.

Finally, I tossed in my hairbrush and makeup bag, making sure to double-check that I had my birth control pills inside it. While I was waiting for Levi's knock, I wondered if Tara had been on the pill. He'd never said exactly how the pregnancy had happened. Natalie had gotten pregnant accidentally because she'd messed up taking her pills, so I knew it was possible. Was it something I could ask casually about? I wasn't sure. He seemed open on the subject of his past, but I didn't want him to think I was obsessing over it. Because I wasn't.

At five after two, I heard the knock and threw my bag over my shoulder.

When I opened the door, the sight of him left me momentarily breathless. God, I loved that feeling. It was one of the best parts about falling in love.

He wore jeans too, and a fitted dark blue button-down with a light brown jacket.

"Hey, happy birthday." He kissed me and caught me in his arms, lifting me right off my feet. "Mmmm, you even smell like a cake."

I smiled, burying my face in his neck. "Thanks."

"Can I have a piece?"

"Now?" I laughed as he set me down.

"I guess I could wait." He sighed. "But it won't be easy." Picking up the bag I'd dropped at my feet, he took my hand and led me to the car. He opened the passenger door for me, then put the bag in the back. I took off my coat and tossed it into the back seat, and he did the same with his jacket before getting behind the wheel.

"I'm so curious," I said. "What are we doing?"

He gave me a crooked smile and patted my knee. "It's my sister who can't keep secrets."

"You won't even give me a clue?" I asked as he buckled his seatbelt and started the car.

"Nope." He backed out of the parking space and threw the car in drive. "But I will let you control the music."

I eyed the satellite radio panel. "Then I'm going to torture you the whole ride to wherever we're going."

"With what?"

"With 90s on 9." I pressed a few buttons and turned it up. "And I hope it's Spice Girls the entire time!"

He groaned as I threw myself a little party in the front seat, dancing and singing like I was twelve years old again.

When the song ended, I took pity on him and turned it down. "Still no clue?" We were headed south out of town; that was all I could tell.

He shook his head. "Nope."

I put my hand on his leg and slid it up his thigh. "Please?"

He smiled but said nothing.

I brushed my hand over the crotch of his jeans. "Pleeeeeeease. I'll be so nice to you while you're driving."

He glanced at me. "How nice?"

"*So* nice." I stroked him a little harder through the denim, which was tight against the bulge in his pants.

"Hmmmmm. This is a very tempting offer."

"Isn't it? It will feel so good," I cooed. "And it's been so long—almost a whole week—since I've touched you like this."

He groaned. "Tell me about it."

"Did you have to do it yourself?" I asked, a lilt in my voice. I slipped the button of his jeans through the hole.

He glanced at me and shook his head like he couldn't believe me, a slow smile tipping his lips up. "You're so bad."

"Did you?"

"Yeah. I did. Every night."

I giggled as I dragged the zipper down. "You're worse than me. I only did it twice."

"I had a lot of material to work with after Saturday night. Oh fuck," he breathed as I slid my hand inside his boxer briefs. "You shouldn't even say that stuff to me while I'm driving, let alone touch my dick that way."

"Why not?" I freed his growing erection from his pants and swirled my fingers over the tip. "Doesn't it feel good?"

"It feels too good."

I stilled my hand. "Want me to stop?"

He took a deep breath and exhaled as we turned onto the

highway. "Fuck no. Tell me about what you did. It will be a good exercise in control for me."

"Well, once was in the shower."

"Yeah?"

"Yes." I continued teasing the head of his cock, my touch light and playful. "And I wasn't planning on doing it because it was in the morning before work, but then I remembered you in my shower, and I pictured your body with water streaming down your arms and chest and torso. I imagined getting my hands on your wet skin, and you getting your hands on mine, and before I knew it, I had my hand between my legs."

Levi took another deep, deep breath.

"I thought about watching your cock get hard, how hot that would be. I pictured it getting bigger and thicker, imagined how it would feel in my fist, in my mouth, sliding inside me."

He reached over and ran his hand up the inside of my thigh. "God, I wish you'd worn a skirt. I want to feel your pussy right now so fucking badly."

"I'm wet, just like I was in the shower." My voice was breathy and soft. His dick was hot and hard in my hand. "I told myself I didn't have time to fool around, but I couldn't stop."

"Fucking hell." Leaning toward me slightly, he undid the button and zipper on my jeans. "I don't care who sees. I have to touch you."

Under ordinary circumstances, I'd probably have zipped up my pants and crossed my legs. I was somewhat daring in bed, but public sex was not my thing. But fuck—it was my birthday.

And Levi was no ordinary man.

Plus, we sat up sort of high in the SUV, the windows were slightly tinted, and this stretch of highway wasn't that crowded at two thirty in the afternoon. So instead of demurring, I slid them down a little, surprising myself—and shocking the hell out of Levi.

"Oh God. Oh Jesus." He moaned as he slipped his fingers between my legs and found me warm and wet, exactly like I'd said. "Keep talking."

I put my hand down his jeans again. "I started to fantasize that my fingers were the tip of your cock, and you wanted to get me off just like that—rubbing the tip against me."

As I talked, he used his fingertips on me like I'd done in the shower, probably not with as much artistry as he'd have liked but with my jeans only at my knees and his hand at an angle, he didn't have a lot of room for finesse. Then there was the whole driving on the highway thing.

Still.

I felt the orgasm building and tried to move my hips to give him better access. If there was any lingering trepidation about being on the road, it vanished with the climb. "I kept saying no, you should stop, I'll be late for work, but you just kept rubbing me harder and faster. You told me you wouldn't stop until I came, and that even if you had to keep me there in the shower all day, you wouldn't care."

"Fuck no, I wouldn't."

"And it was so good, so good…" It was so good I couldn't even talk anymore. I wrapped my hand around his cock and squeezed, my breath coming in sharp, quick pants, my hips thrusting against his fingers. "Levi, yes, yes, yes…"

I moaned hard as my clit throbbed against his fingers, completely oblivious to our surroundings. When I finally opened my eyes and grabbed his wrist, stopping him from touching my sensitive nerves, I gasped. "Oh, God. We're in the car."

"Yes, we are. And that was the best fucking thing that's ever happened in my car. Ever."

I looked around and didn't see any gawkers or hear any sirens, so I figured we were good…and I could keep going.

Taking my hand off him only long enough to pull up my jeans, I angled my body toward his and resumed talking.

"Want to hear about the second time?"

"Uh. Yeah." He flexed both hands on the wheel. "But I'm so fucking hard right now, I'm afraid of coming all over my clothes. So you have to be gentle."

I smiled. "Didn't you pack other clothes?"

"Not another dress shirt."

"I won't mind if you wear the same thing twice," I whispered, sliding my hand up and down his hot, thick shaft. "And I won't tell anyone why."

He closed his eyes for a fraction of a second and shook his head. "Jesus Christ. OK, you can talk, but I am not allowed to come."

"If you say so," I said, starting with light, sweeping strokes that made him groan. A few beads of liquid desire wet my fingertips.

"Fuck, fuck. What are you doing to me?"

"I'll tell you exactly." Tucking one leg beneath myself, I gave him some slow, steady pulls. "The second time I got myself off this week, I was in bed. And I was thinking about being on top of you. How hard you were. I could feel it between my legs, and I wanted it inside me." I circled the tip of his dick with my thumb and fingers and dragged my hand down gradually. "I slid down your cock nice and easy, just like that. You had me so wet. I was aching for you to fill me."

Levi's jaw was clenched tight. "I can see you," he said with quiet intensity. "So fucking hot."

"I took you in so deep it hurt—it always hurts a little—but I love it. I love the way my body hugs yours so tight, every inch of you." Squeezing a little tighter, I moved my hand up and down his shaft, wishing I could get my mouth on him too. Actually, I wished I could straddle him and finish what we'd started that night, but I didn't think that would be too safe in a moving car on US-131. The hand job would have to do.

For now, anyway.

"And I missed you there so much I had to get my vibrator out."

"Yeah?"

"Mmhm. I was nice and wet just from thinking about you, so I put it inside me and pretended it was you."

"Wait, wait. Did you ride it like you rode me? I need the whole picture."

I smiled. He was such a man, wanting the complete visual. "I did. It was a little tricky, but I got on my knees and put it between my legs, then I lowered myself onto it like I did when you were there. Right in the middle of my bed."

"Did it feel good?" he asked between pants.

"It wasn't even close to the real thing, but yes, it did." I picked up the pace and pressure with my hand. "I remembered the way you felt as I slid up and down your cock, so hot and hard and wet with my pussy."

"Oh, God," he said through clenched teeth. "You're totally gonna do this, aren't you?"

"Want me to stop, love? I will. We can save your nice shirt. Or," I suggested, jerking him even harder, "you can come all over it. Drench it, like I wanted you to drench me, like I drenched my toy. I came so hard thinking about fucking your cock, riding it and yelling your name, I—"

"Fuck!" Levi's dick throbbed in my hand, and he exploded all over his dark blue shirt—and I mean *exploded*, thick streams shooting as high as his shoulder.

It was a serious thing, an orgasm, but I felt like laughing the second he stopped desecrating his poor dress shirt. *Oh God. Look at him.*

Breathing hard, Levi looked down to check the damage. "Wow. That's, ah…"

"Impressive." I took my hand off him and bit my lip. "Got any napkins in here?"

He glanced at me. "Are you laughing at me?"

I tried to keep a straight face. Tried like eighty percent hard, maybe even ninety. "No."

"Christ, you're as bad a liar as I am." He grimaced but he was half-laughing too. "Check the glovebox. I might have something in there."

I opened the glovebox. Maps. A sunglasses case. A plastic dinosaur. "Nope. No napkins."

"Fuuuuuck." Levi looked down at his shirt, and his dismayed expression was so funny to me, I completely dissolved into giggles.

"Thanks a lot," he said wryly. "This is all your fault, you know. Here I am taking you out on a nice, classy outing, *courting you properly*, and you caused a big mess. Are you even the least bit sorry?"

"No. Oh my God, that shirt…" I put my hands over my stomach, which hurt from laughter. "It's everywhere. It was like dynamite or something."

"It was all you."

"Um, I'm not sure I want the blame for that splatter-painted shirt."

He gave me a menacing look. "Looking for birthday spankings early, little girl?"

I gasped. "You wouldn't."

He smiled and kept his focus on the road.

CHAPTER 21
Levi

THE LOOK on her face when I threatened to spank her was hilarious—part scared, part intrigued, part wondering if I was teasing her.

I wasn't. I had plans for tonight.

But fucking hell. What was I going to wear? I had a couple extra t-shirts in my bag, which would actually be fine for food and drinks at the Journeyman Distillery, but she didn't know that.

I decided to play with her a little. "I need a new shirt. We'll have to find somewhere to buy one."

"Seriously? Let me look in my bag. Maybe I have some tissues." She scooped up her purse from the floor and set it in her lap.

"Tissues? I need a shop-vac for this shirt. Fuck tissues."

"Oh, come on. Here." She took a girly little packet of Kleenex from her bag and pulled one out, fluffing it up. "Let me try."

"I can do it." I reached for the tissue, but she held it away from me.

"I'll do it. It was my fault, like you said."

She bit her lip like she was concentrating hard, but

swiping at the jizz on my shirt with one piece of Kleenex was like trying to soak up Lake Michigan with a cotton ball.

"Maybe I need two," she said, and her expression was so adorably serious, I wanted to fucking pull over just to make out with her. Tell her I loved her face. Tell her how goddamn happy I was right now, ruined shirt and all. When had I last fooled around like this with a woman?

"Forget it, babe. I'll buy a new shirt. It's fine. I'm sure the place we're going isn't *that* dressy."

"Oh. OK." She took a couple more swipes at my shirt with a clean tissue but eventually gave up. "I feel bad now."

"No, don't feel bad. Are you kidding me?" I took her hand and kissed the back of it, held it in my lap. "That was awesome."

A few miles down the road, I saw what I was looking for—a sign for a gas station that catered to truckers and road trippers. "I'm gonna get gas."

I exited the highway and pulled into the station. Before getting out of the car, I ditched the blue shirt and tossed it into the back seat, glad I was wearing an undershirt with no holes or pit stains. I had plenty of those, but since I'd been seeing Jillian I'd actually invested in some new ones. She wore such beautiful underwear, I figured the least I could do was wear t-shirts without yellow underarms. *Look at that, less of a caveman already. Mom would call her a good influence.*

I liked that.

After pumping gas, I poked my head into the car, willing myself to keep a straight face. "I'm gonna run into the store and see if they have a shirt. Want anything?"

"No." She cocked her head, pressing her lips together. "You're going to look for a shirt at the gas station? Don't you want to look for a nicer store?" She looked over her shoulders, like maybe there was a Nordstrom hiding behind the Quick Save BP.

"No. It's fine. I'm sure there's something in there."

SOME SORT OF LOVE (JILLIAN AND LEVI) 195

Five minutes later, I came out wearing a light blue t-shirt that said MOTHER TRUCKER on it. Jillian stared as I got in the car. "That's the shirt you bought for tonight?"

"Yeah. Like it? It's badass, right? I was tempted by the one that said 'My Girl Is Dirtier Than My Truck' but I thought that might not be nice enough for where we're going."

"Um, it's fun." She chewed her lip all the way back to the highway. "Is…is the place where we're going really nice? I feel bad about your dress shirt."

"I guess you'll find out." I couldn't even meet her worried eyes. I could tell she thought maybe I really was a caveman and I was going to wear a shirt that said MOTHER TRUCKER into a fancy restaurant, but I loved the look on her face too much to tell her the truth.

I loved everything about her.

She saw the sign before we actually arrived. I knew right when she figured it out because she gasped, clapped her hands, and stomped her feet. "Journeyman!"

I grinned. "You guessed it."

"I love it! I'm excited!" She slapped my shoulder. "You should have told me!"

"I like surprises. And I don't get to give them much."

We pulled into the parking lot a few minutes after six, and Jillian was bouncing up and down in the front seat like—well, like a birthday girl. I think she was glad when I threw my jacket on over my new t-shirt, although she was too nice to say so.

We went into the distillery and took the tour, admiring the former factory's nineteenth century maple floors, the brass, stainless steel and oak equipment, and the passion and precision with which the makers created their product. Later we sat at the concrete bar tasting whiskey and marveling that the original owner of the factory, who'd made his fortune manufacturing featherbone corsets, had been a prohibitionist. We raised our glasses.

"To EK Warren, misguided fool," I said. "Although I think you'd look good in a corset."

She laughed and we tipped back the shots. "Ah, that's good," she said. "I like that sign over there—I'd rather be someone's shot of whiskey than everyone's cup of tea."

I looked where she was pointing. "I like that too." Dropping a kiss on her shoulder, I added, "You're my shot of whiskey, cup of tea, slice of pie *and* scoop of ice cream."

She gave me a coy smile. "I thought you didn't eat ice cream."

I whispered in her ear. "I do when it's yours."

The expression on her face was better than a million dollars. Making her happy felt so fucking good.

We shared the crisp pork belly appetizer, a plate of roasted vegetables, and the whiskey barbecue chicken, and we drank a little more whiskey than we probably should have. Every time she looked at my shirt, she burst out laughing, and I threatened to wear it the first time I met her parents—or better yet, buy the one about the dirty girl.

"I am dirty," she whispered as we wandered through the parking lot, hand in hand. "I can't believe I did that in the car. I've never done that before."

"Good." I walked her to the passenger side of my car and backed her into it. "A car virgin. I like it." I kissed her, finally. It felt like I'd been waiting all day.

"A car virgin," she said, her hands running up my chest inside my jacket. "But not a closet virgin."

"Nope." I kissed my way down her neck. "I took care of that when I had the chance."

"Did you ever do it in a closet with anyone else?"

I picked my head up and tried to think.

"You don't *know*?"

"I was not a well-behaved or responsible person for many years, Jillian. If you want the real answer, I have to think."

She shook her head. "OK, forget it. I liked what you were doing before better."

"Me too." I put my lips and tongue on her throat again, tasting her sweetness—vanilla tonight. And something flowery. Lavender? "You smell so fucking good. I have to get my mouth on all of you."

"No argument here. Where are we staying tonight?"

"A bed and breakfast. It's not far."

"A bed and breakfast!" She took my face in her hands and kissed me. "You're so mother trucking romantic, I can't stand it. Let's go."

We pulled up at the bed and breakfast, a big nineteenth century Victorian home that was called A Night to Remember.

Jillian giggled at the sign hanging out front. "I like the name."

"That's why I chose it."

She got out of the car and admired the house while I went to the back and unloaded our bags. "It's beautiful," she said. "When do you think it was built?"

I studied it for a moment. It was dark, but I could make

out the lines and materials well enough. "Probably the eighteen seventies." My knowledge of historical architecture wasn't all that comprehensive, but because of the area where I lived and worked, I did have some familiarity with different Victorian styles. This one was French-inspired, with a mansard roof and shutters on the windows, its bricks painted a light yellow.

"I love it." She threw her arms around me. "This is so nice, Levi. No one's ever given me such a great birthday surprise."

I kissed the top of her head. "Let's go in."

The owners of the house, Bob and Jenny, a couple in retirement age with matching pear-shaped bodies and welcoming smiles, greeted us at the door as if they'd been waiting for us. It was my first inclination that this might not be quite as private as I'd like. Here we were entering this lovely old home, the owners graciously giving us a tour, inviting us to sit on the antique furniture, sip cordials in the parlor, or drink tea off grandmother's china, and all I could think of was taking Jillian upstairs and spanking her ass before fucking her senseless.

Clearly I hadn't thought this all the way through.

We were shown our room, which was large with high ceilings, a fireplace, and an antique queen-size bed. Jillian spun around, a huge smile on her face, and I was happy I'd chosen this place. *Hope you have earplugs, Bob and Jenny. Or you're gonna be up all night.*

I locked the bedroom door after they left and took off my jacket and the trucker t-shirt. Jillian took her bag, went into our private bathroom, and came out five minutes later wearing the sexiest fucking lingerie I'd ever seen. It was dark red and strappy and lacy and sheer and rendered me completely speechless.

"You like it?" she asked, hands behind her back.

"I fucking love it. It's not even my birthday." I went over to her and ran my hands down her arms, up her chest, brushing my thumbs over her nipples. They perked up, and I kept rubbing them lightly. Jillian's eyes closed and she swayed toward me. I lowered my lips to where they just barely touched hers but didn't kiss her.

"You're teasing me," she whispered.

I smiled. "Ready for your present?"

She nodded. "Sure."

I pulled it out of my bag and handed it to her. She took it over to the bed, which squeaked when she sat down on it. Looking up at me in alarm, she bounced on it a few times, and the squeaking continued, even louder. "Holy shit, Levi," she whispered frantically.

I grinned. "Hey. What can we do? It's an old bed. Open your gift."

She began to unwrap the package, and I suddenly felt nervous.

"It's nothing big."

"Stop it. You didn't have to get me anything—you arranged this whole night for me." She took the lid off the box and gasped when she saw the framed photo. "Oh my God."

"Do you like it?"

"I love it." She lifted it out of the box and held it up. "I haven't even seen wedding photos yet—how did you get this?"

The picture was of Jillian and her sisters, Skylar in the middle, an informal shot taken sometime after the ceremony. It was a close-up, and they'd leaned in toward each other, arms around waists, matching blue eyes and huge smiles. "I contacted Sebastian this week, and he put me in touch with Skylar. She'd just gotten digital proofs and sent me this one. I thought you'd like it for your counter."

"Yes!" She put a hand over her heart. "It's perfect, because I don't have a recent one. And it's beautiful—look how happy we are."

"You do look happy. And I know how important family is to you."

"It is." She looked up at me. "You're important to me, too, Levi. Thank you so much for doing all this for me." She set the photo aside and stood up, wrapping her arms around me. "I'm so happy tonight."

I smiled and hugged her back, wishing more than anything I could make her happy like this all the time. Here, in this beautiful room, only the two of us, it almost felt possible. But it wasn't real life—it had all been planned and arranged, everything from the distillery tour to the bed and breakfast reservation to childcare. If I asked her right now to run away with me, she'd probably say yes, because she'd think it could be like this all the time. But it couldn't...*I* couldn't. She didn't know what she was giving up to be with me.

Her hands were sliding up my back, her lips along my throat. "I love you so much," she whispered.

I slid my fingers into her hair and kissed her ravenously, possessively. She lifted my shirt over my head and unbuttoned my jeans, but I couldn't bear to take the beautiful lingerie off her yet. When I was completely naked, I caught her behind the knees and shoulders and laid her on the bed, stretching out above her.

It groaned under our weight, and she smiled. "Oh, dear."

"I don't care," I said, kissing my way down her body. "Let's keep them up all night."

I'd planned on spanking her, teasing her, tormenting her—making her "pay" for being such a bad girl in the car. But I didn't feel that way now. I simply wanted to worship her, adore her, devote myself entirely to her pleasure in bed the way I couldn't in real life. Once we left this place tomorrow, I couldn't give her all of me.

But tonight I could.

And I didn't give a fuck about the noise.

She sighed and moaned as I undressed her, then devoured her breasts one at a time. When one hard nipple was under my tongue or between my teeth, the other was between my fingers. She arched and gasped, whimpering as I fucked her with my fingers, and then my tongue, and then used them both on her at the same time, my mouth sucking greedily at her clit as her pussy tightened and throbbed. And she cried out when I slid my cock inside her, my name on her lips, my hands in her hair, my body rocking into hers with deep, powerful strokes.

But nothing was louder than that fucking bed—it whined and groaned and creaked and squeaked, louder and quicker, perfectly matching the rhythm of my hips as momentum built. It went finally, blissfully silent when we came together, the climax paralyzing every muscle in my body, my awareness centered only on the pulse shared between us.

If we hadn't been so carried away, we probably would have laughed.

Instead she cried, tears dripping from the corners of her eyes as she clung to me, her hands pulling me in tighter to her, as if she couldn't get close enough. And I understood her tears, fought hard against my own.

I brushed her temples with my fingertips, kissed them, tasted the salty sweetness of her tears. Resting my forehead on hers, I whispered her name like a prayer, desperately wishing I could have this, have *her*, every single day of my life.

But something inside me wouldn't believe it was possible.

CHAPTER 22
Jillian

WE WENT FROM THE BED—WHICH screamed louder than I did—to a chair by the fireplace to a rug on the floor, and only when the clock said three-thirty did we fall back into bed, happy and exhausted and laughing that we'd probably kept everyone else up too.

"No more bed and breakfasts for us," Levi said, pulling my back against his chest, his knees tucked into mine.

I giggled. "At least not until we're old and don't care about sex anymore."

"Bite your tongue. I will never be too old to care about sex with you. When I'm ninety, if you're still around, I'll be trying to get in your pants."

"Of course I'll be around." I snuggled back against him, trying not to let my feelings get ruffled by the comment. *He's teasing. It was a joke.*

"Good." He kissed my head once more and we fell asleep, our breathing synced like I wished our lives could be.

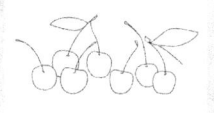

We woke up so late we missed breakfast, but I didn't care. Waking up next to Levi was even more amazing than I thought it would be. He lay on his back with his arms around me, and I cuddled up against his side, one leg thrown over him, one palm on his stomach, my cheek pressed to his chest. I felt warm and peaceful. Happy. Loved.

"Probably better we don't have to face anyone down there anyway," he said.

I squeezed my eyes shut. "We wouldn't even have to introduce ourselves. They all know our names because they heard us shouting them all night long."

"Totally." His hands stroked up and down my back. "And they'd be angry because they didn't get any sleep."

I burrowed in closer. "Let's never leave. This is like a dream."

"I don't want to go back to real life yet either."

"Maybe they'd let us stay all day."

He sighed. "I wish I could."

"Hey." I picked up my head and looked at him. "We can have this feeling in real life, you know. There's nothing magic about this room."

"No? Felt like it."

"No. The magic is you and me together, and we could have that anywhere."

"You're right, sorry. I'm being grumpy about everything I have to get done today. Come back."

He tugged me back down, and I nestled against him again. "Why don't you let me help you out today?" I asked. "I'd be happy to do something for you."

"You sound like my mom."

I wrinkled my nose. "Ew. That is not romantic."

"Sorry. I didn't mean that you remind me of her, just that she's always wanting to do things for me. She thinks I'm incompetent or something."

I sat up again. "It's not the same, Levi. I don't want to do things for you—and maybe she doesn't either—because I think you're incapable of doing them yourself. I'm trying to help you. Accepting help from someone who cares about you doesn't mean you couldn't do it all yourself; it means that you're willing to let someone share the burden who *wants* to."

"I don't want to burden you with anything, Jillian. It's bad enough that I can only see you once a week. I'm not going to ask you to do my fucking laundry."

I stared at him. "I don't understand. Are you never going to let me into your regular, everyday life because you think I won't find it romantic? I'm thirty-one years old, Levi. I get that life isn't all sunshine and rainbows. Relationships aren't always whiskey and sex. There are good times and bad. Beautiful things and ugly things. Rib eye steaks and fast food hamburgers. It's not either, or. I don't expect you to be perfect all the time."

"Shhhh, hey, come here. Don't get upset." His tone contrite, he reached for me again, pulled me down. "I know what you're saying. I promise I do. I just…" He squeezed my arm. "I just want this for a little longer, OK? I want it to be only us, whiskey and sex. Beautiful things. We said we'd take it slow, right?"

Immediately I felt bad for pushing. "I'm sorry." I threw my leg over him again. "I know we said we should go slow. I just love you and want to be close."

"Me too." His voice went husky, his hand covered one breast, and his cock stirred beneath my inner thigh. "What do you think about getting close in the shower before we get dressed?"

I slipped a hand between his legs. "I'm all for it."

"God, I couldn't even look Bob in the eye at checkout," I said as we drove back to Traverse City. "And Jenny's face was *so* red!"

"I know." Levi laughed as he switched to the left lane. "We gave them a night to remember, that's for sure."

I groaned, slapping my hands over my hot cheeks. "I think you were right. Hotels from now on."

"Definitely." Levi patted my leg and then left his hand there, steering with the other.

I looked out the window as the scenery rolled by, happy we'd had such a great night together, and grateful for all the birthday surprises, but something nipped at the edges of my contentment. I felt closer to him than ever before, and yet I still felt this reluctance on his part to really let me in. Even though I know we said we'd go slow, it was hard not to feel a little hurt that he didn't want me to meet his family yet. Especially his son. I understood the need to be cautious, but from what he'd said this morning, it seemed like he wanted to keep me separate from his home life for the foreseeable future, while we enjoyed the beautiful things. But for how long?

And I was glad that he'd smoothed things over with his mom and that Scotty had been fine last night, but that would make it even easier for him to lead two lives—one where he was with me, and one where he was Dad.

I wanted to know both sides of him.

Why wouldn't he let me?

In the weeks leading up to Thanksgiving, I became Levi's Girl Friday again, and we'd have our one incredible night together —twice he was able to stay over—and I'd go Saturday through

SOME SORT OF LOVE (JILLIAN AND LEVI) 207

Thursday missing him and wishing he was ready to take the next step. My feelings for him grew stronger, and he told me he loved me every single day. I believed him, but I also grew increasingly nervous that while our feelings continued to grow, our level of commitment had somehow stagnated. It was always us alone, and once we'd met up with Skylar and Sebastian for dinner, but he'd yet to introduce me to his son, and when I invited him to Sunday dinner at my parents' house, he always had a reason why it wouldn't work. More than once, I'd offered to come to his house on a Friday night, but he never wanted me to, and his reason was usually sexual.

"I know, it's totally selfish of me," he'd said tonight in my bed. "But I can't bear the thought of having to go another week without being this close to you. Without getting my mouth on you. Without making you come." Then he'd moved down my body and buried his face between my legs, making it impossible to argue with him.

I know. It was selfish of me.

Because I did want the sex every week. I craved it. I loved our phone conversations and our texts too—I'd never been emotionally needy or clingy, and my job kept me so busy during the week, the days went quickly. But there had to be more, didn't there? Maybe I was the only one who wanted it. Maybe he didn't see the future for us that I did.

I decided to ask.

As he pulled on his jeans and t-shirt, I lay on my side watching him, my hands tucked under my head. "Hey."

He looked at me. "Hey." Then he came over and planted a kiss on my shoulder. "You look way too good lying there. It's tempting me to stay."

"I was hoping we could talk about that."

"Sorry my mom couldn't do the overnight this weekend. I was hoping for it too."

"That's not what I meant."

He glanced at me before pulling his sweater on and sitting to tug on socks and shoes. "Oh? What's up?"

Be brave. Be brave. Be brave. "I feel like you don't want me to meet Scotty."

He sat up straight. "That's ridiculous. You know I do."

"It's been two months, Levi. When?"

"Soon. I don't want to rush it, Jill. He's had so much trouble with school this fall, and then with me going away overnight..." He ran a hand through his hair. "Plus, I like keeping our time together sort of sacred. Private. Romantic. Don't you?"

"Of course." I frowned. He was hard to argue with. "But being a father is such a huge part of your identity. And I hear you talk about it a lot, but I feel like I'm not allowed in to that huge part of your life. I just want to know why...is it because you don't think this will last? And you don't want to introduce me to Scotty because you're planning on leaving me when the sex gets old or something?"

"Of course not." Immediately he pulled me up against him, gathering me in his arms. "I love you so much. And I'm sorry if I've hurt your feelings by not introducing you to Scotty yet. I just...it's a big deal, Jillian. It's not something I take lightly."

"I completely understand that," I said, fighting tears. "But *you're* not something *I* take lightly. I miss you when we're apart all week long."

He exhaled, resting his chin on my head. "Somehow, in my mind, it's easier to balance being a good father and being in a relationship with you if I keep it separate. No confusion for me, for Scotty, or for you. When I'm at home with him, I'm Dad, and when I'm with you, I can completely devote myself to you. It's a respite for me."

I nodded. Hadn't I known that already? Hadn't I, in fact, relished the idea of being his respite, his escape from everything that made him feel as if he wasn't enough? Now I was adding to that, and maybe he'd leave me because of it.

Don't ruin this with your stupid insecurity. He loves you and you love him. Let that be enough for now.

"I understand." I sniffed. Took a shuddery breath. "I'll try to be more patient."

He kissed my head. "And I'll think some more about the introduction."

"Thanks."

We kissed each other languorously, his arms wrapped around me, and some of the tension and fear and unanswered questions melted away.

But some remained.

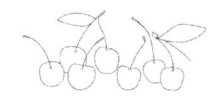

On Thanksgiving, which I spent at my parents' house with my family and he spent in Charlevoix with his, my sisters wanted to know how things were going. The three of us stood in the kitchen, Natalie making stuffing, Skylar peeling potatoes, and me slicing the ends off green beans. Our mother had gotten the turkey in the oven earlier and had gone up to take a shower, and our dad was watching football in the family room with Miles and Sebastian.

"It's going fine," I said, forcing a casual tone. "He's at his mom's house today."

"No plans to meet his son yet?" Natalie asked. Her ultrasound had recently revealed she was having a son, and both she and Miles were over the moon. Skylar was still insisting it could be a girl, and refused to believe she'd been wrong.

"Nothing concrete," I admitted. "But I keep telling him I'd like to."

They exchanged a look.

"What?" I said, looking back and forth between them.

Skylar cleared her throat. "We're only hoping you don't get hurt. He seems really into you, and it's obvious you're into him, but it feels like he's asking you to be his side dish."

My cheeks burned. "That's not true. You have no idea what it's like to be him and have to balance being a full-time single parent, work a full-time job, and have a relationship."

She held up both hands. "You're right. I don't."

"He's doing the best he can," I snapped.

"Easy," said Natalie. "Skylar didn't mean to attack Levi. We think he's great. We only mentioned being worried because we can't imagine being in a relationship with someone you love where you only see that person once a week."

"It's hard," I admitted. "I don't love that part of it." And I knew I shouldn't jump down their throats for seeing the same things I did and asking the same questions. But I couldn't help but defend him.

"As long as you two are communicating, that's the main thing," Skylar said. "Fuck what we say or anyone else. I'm sorry if I hurt your feelings."

Her apology was what brought a few tears. "It's OK. The truth is, I want more than he's giving me too, but I feel like I can't ask for it."

"Why not?" Natalie was indignant.

"Because I'm scared he'll leave." The tears spilled over. "We made this agreement when we first got together two months ago or whatever, that we'd go slow and be cautious. I said I understood not being his first priority, and he warned me he could never give me all of himself. I still get that."

"But what?" Skylar rubbed my arm. "I feel like there's a but coming."

"That sounded dirty," Natalie whispered.

I laughed ruefully, grabbing a tissue from a box on the

counter. "The *but* is that I want more. I'm OK not having *all*, but I want more than he's giving."

"Do you think he's capable of giving more?" Skylar asked.

"Yes," I said firmly, swiping at my nose. "But he's stubborn. And convinced he has to balance things this certain way, with me on one side and his son on the other. He feels safer that way, I guess."

"I don't get it," Skylar said. "Safer how?"

I hesitated. I didn't want to betray Levi's confidence by revealing the things he'd told me, but I also needed some advice. "I think he's afraid. The night he first told me he loved me, he admitted that he was scared he couldn't love us both enough. As if he only had so much love to give, and by giving some to me, it meant less for his son. Maybe he's thinking if he really lets me in, he's a bad father."

"That's ridiculous." Natalie put a hand on her belly. "Showing his son that he loves someone and lets himself be loved is a wonderful thing."

"It is," I agreed, "but he has a lot of guilt over not wanting a baby before his son was born. Part of him still feels like he has to make up for that."

"But where does that leave you?" Skylar pressed.

I sighed. "It leaves me wondering what I originally wondered. Is there a place for me in his life or not? But…I'm scared to ask. I love him now. What if the answer is *not*?"

"OK, I know I'm the baby sister here," said Natalie, "but I have to say from experience, staying in a relationship where you're not happy just because you're scared of what will happen when you ask the hard questions is a *bad* idea."

"I second that." Skylar held up one hand. "In addition, there have to be truthful answers. If Sebastian had been honest with me about his relapse when it started instead of waiting until the breaking point, it could have saved us a lot of pain."

I tossed my tissue in the trash and washed my hands. "So you think I should say something more?"

"Yes," they said together.

"But what? I've already said that I want to meet his son, and I'm ready. It's Levi who isn't. Do I say *do it or else*?" Groaning, I tipped my forehead into my hands. "I don't want to issue any ultimatums. That is so not me."

"I don't think you have to put it that way," Natalie said. "But I do think you're worth more than you're getting. I wish you believed that."

"Me too," said Skylar.

I nodded, feeling the tears threaten again. I had a decision to make. Could I be content with what I had with him for now and trust that it would grow to be more over time? Or should I ask for more, believing I was worth it, and risk losing him?

CHAPTER 23
Levi

I SPENT all of Thanksgiving Day worrying.

I arrived at my parents' with a pie that Jillian had given me to bring, a cherry pie her mother had baked.

"How sweet," my mother said, taking it out of the box and leaning in to smell it. I had the urge to do that too, thinking it would smell like Jillian.

Jesus. I was messed up.

"When do we get to meet the famous Jillian?" my mother asked, setting the pie on the counter. "You could have brought her tonight, you know. Did you invite her, like I asked?"

"She's with her family," I said, avoiding the question. Later, at the table, I fretted so much I could hardly eat.

Jillian was getting restless. I could feel it. And she had every right to be. It was wrong of me to keep her from meeting Scotty. She loved me and she wanted to be part of my whole life, not just my Girl Friday anymore. Could I blame her?

I didn't like it either. From Saturday through Thursday, I thought of her every other minute. So many times I caught myself wanting to bring up her name to Scotty, so it wouldn't be such a shock to bring her into our life as someone who was important to me but completely unknown to him. A gradual approach would be better.

And she would be so great with him, wouldn't she? She'd understand his mind and his quirks and his sweetness better than anyone could, not only because she loved and understood me, but because she was a pediatrician, which meant she'd dedicated years of her life to helping kids feel better. What more could I ask for?

She'd been totally right about the lucky stone idea. After the Thursday math test debacle last month when he'd wet himself in the attempt to get out of school, I'd purchased a satiny smooth Petoskey stone for him at a gift shop and told him it was a lucky rock. He kept it in his pocket at school, and when he felt anxious about a test or an assignment, he'd take it out and hold it in his hand or put it on his desk where he could see it.

When I'd thanked her for the idea and told her she was brilliant, she'd blushed and said how happy she was to be of help.

So why the fuck was I so scared of taking the final step and letting her all the way in?

I'd made a thousand excuses in my head—it was too soon, it wouldn't be right for Scotty, it would take away from our alone time, she was only saying she wanted to meet him to be polite, my family would criticize me, Scotty might act up...

But the truth was, I was scared.

And I hated myself for it.

But I couldn't wrap my head around the fact that she wanted me that much. That she'd be willing to stay once she saw that some days, I was barely holding things together. That she'd be willing to love a child that wasn't hers for me, when I hadn't been enough to make even his own mother stay.

I hadn't loved Tara, so her leaving didn't hurt me, but her abandonment of Scotty had scarred me in a different way.

There were times in the last eight years when he'd needed a father *and* a mother, when I'd needed someone with whom I could share the beautiful, painful honor of bringing him up in this world, someone who understood the blame I placed on myself when things didn't go well for him, the way he could break my heart and put it back together again.

I hadn't counted on falling so hard for Jillian. What if Scotty took to her and she didn't take to him? What if she did but decided she couldn't handle the way we had to live? What if letting her in only meant revealing to her all my weaknesses?

What if she left? Then what?

When Tara left, it had been hard, but it hadn't broken me. I'd been solely concerned with my son.

If Jillian left, it would break me.

And maybe I would deserve it for my shortcomings.

I couldn't put it off forever. But I had to protect myself a little longer.

CHAPTER 24

Jillian

THE WEEK AFTER THANKSGIVING, Levi and I made a date to do some Christmas shopping at the mall and have dinner. I knew it was pointless to ask, but I did anyway.

"Does Scotty want to come along? We could go out for Italian after."

"No. He doesn't do well at the mall. Too many sounds, smells, noises. It's overwhelming for him."

"OK."

The week after that, Scotty was sick and Levi didn't feel it would be right to leave him. "Poor thing," I said. "What does he have?"

"Just a virus, I guess. We saw the doctor this morning. He's pretty miserable."

"Why don't I bring you both some dinner? I don't have to stay. I can see you for a minute and bring you something to eat so you don't have to cook."

"You're sweet to offer, but no. I wouldn't want you to get sick."

"I'm a pediatrician, Levi. I'm around sick kids day in and day out."

"I know, but it's OK. If my mom comes down tomorrow, maybe we can have coffee or something."

My stomach churned. "Sure. Whatever you want."

We hung up, and I was so worked up that I went to the gym and got on the treadmill, walking fast and hard for forty solid minutes, huffing and puffing, my anger boiling inside me.

This was not OK. It was one thing to accept being less than the top priority in his life; it was another to accept being treated as if I were frivolous, insignificant, good for a laugh or a fuck, but not essential.

This wasn't asking too much. I saw that clearly. I wasn't asking for a ring. I wasn't asking to live together. I wasn't even asking for a promise that those things would happen. I was asking for a chance. I was asking to be given the opportunity to love them both.

To deny me that at this point was unfair.

My sisters were right. Levi was right.

I deserved more.

I loved him with all my heart, but I couldn't go on feeling like this—like I wasn't enough.

Of all people, he had to understand that.

He texted me the following morning. It was Saturday, the first week of December, and I was spending the morning catching up on housework.

Hey, beautiful. I miss you.

. . .

I miss you too. How's Scotty?

He's OK. Still has a fever. I'm so sorry about yesterday.

I understand.

My mom said she'd come down later. Can I see you?

Yes. I'd like to talk.

It took him a while to reply. I knew it would. Was he nervous?
OK. Should I come over?

Well, it's not like you let me come to your house. **Sure. Time?**

How about 5?

That works.

Good. I can't wait to see you. Love you.

Love you too.

. . .

I spent the rest of the day scrubbing toilets and sinks, the shower tiles, and the kitchen floor. I vacuumed the carpet, swept the downstairs hall, and cleaned off windows and mirrors. I changed the sheets on my bed, washed a load of towels, and paid bills. The entire time I worked, I thought about what I was going to say to him, and what his reaction might be.

Would he get defensive? Angry? Sad?

Would he admit I was right but refuse to budge?

Would he try to sweet-talk me into waiting a little longer?

Would he put those hands on me in a way that would decimate all my carefully constructed arguments, render me completely defenseless against him?

Maybe I should tie him up. Put a bag over his head. Stick him in the closet and talk to him through the closed door.

If I saw him, heard his voice, felt his touch, it would be so much harder to stand up for myself.

But I had to.

By the time I was in the shower, I knew exactly what I wanted to say to him. I wouldn't accuse or criticize. I wouldn't yell or cry. I would calmly but firmly explain why I felt it was time for us to take the next step, tell him how much I loved him, and ask for the chance to love Scotty too.

He'd see that I was serious, that I was understanding, that I wasn't expecting him to be perfect, just to be fair. I didn't need *everything*, but I needed more. And I was worth it.

Needless to say, it didn't exactly go as planned.

He knocked at twenty after five, and I opened the door to a blustery cold breeze and an apology.

"Hey, I'm sorry I'm late." He grabbed me in a hug. "I had

trouble getting out the door."

"That's OK." I wrapped my arms around him, and we stood still for a minute, chest to chest, my head tucked under his chin. It felt so good that my resolve wavered.

"God, I missed you last night." He kissed my head. "I've missed you all week."

"Me too, Levi." I pulled back. "That's why I want to talk. Come on upstairs."

He nodded, but I could see the anxiety in his expression.

I led the way up the stairs and went into the kitchen. "Can I get you anything?" I asked. "A drink? Some coffee? Something to eat?"

"No thanks." He took off his coat and hung it on the back of a counter stool. "Is everything OK? You're making me nervous."

On the other side of the breakfast counter from him—which wasn't an accident—I took a breath. "I don't know if everything is OK. I need you to tell me."

"What do you mean?"

I tucked my hair behind my ears. "For the last month, I've been asking to meet Scotty, and you keep putting it off. I'm starting to feel like you're delaying the introduction because you don't have the feelings I do about us."

"That's not true," he said, coming around the counter and taking my hands. "Jillian, I love you. I'm crazy about you. You know I am. I just want you all to myself for a while."

Tears filled my eyes, and I knew my plan to remain calm and rational was futile. "I do think you love me, Levi. If I didn't, this would be so much easier. We could call it quits, and I'd go nurse my broken heart."

"Jill—"

"I think you love me and you're just afraid."

His brow furrowed. "What are you talking about?"

"You're using your son as an excuse not to let me into your life because you're scared."

He dropped my hands. "What the fuck, Jillian? I've told you why I haven't introduced you yet."

"I know. And those reasons made sense for a time. But if you really feel about me the way you say you do—if you really love me—you'd let me into his life too, because he's everything to you. You'd give me the chance to love you both."

"You said you understood," he said, his jaw clenching, fingers flexing. "You knew from the beginning I had to put his needs first."

"Stop blaming him!" I shouted. "This isn't about Scotty's needs, and you know it! This is about you being unwilling to let me in because you're scared of something—and I don't even know what! Do you think I won't be patient with him? Do you think I might not love you if I see you make a mistake? Do you think I'll try to be his mother? Or *your* mother?" I put a hand on my chest. "I'm not interested in criticizing you or judging you for the parenting choices you make. I want to be part of your life on a real level, not just a romantic interlude."

Levi let me finish, but I could see his hands curling at his sides like they did when he felt attacked and on the defensive. Those fucking hands—I couldn't even look at them. They never failed to arouse me, and that was the last thing I needed to feel right now.

"I told you," he said, his tone bitter, "I told you from the start I couldn't be what you wanted. I told you I couldn't give all of me."

"I don't *need* all of you in that way," I said, wiping my eyes. God, was he not *listening*? "I don't need all your time or attention or love. But I want to *see* all of you. I want to *know* all of you. I want to *love* all of you. Why won't you let me?"

"I don't know, OK? I don't fucking know!" He shook his head, his eyes closing. "I knew it. I knew I couldn't do this right. I told you I was bad at balance."

"You don't need better balance!" I threw my hands up. "Don't you understand? You need to stop being one person over here and another over there! You only need to be one man, one whole man, and realize that you have enough love for both of us! It's not a zero-sum game!"

He struggled for words and retreated back into self-doubt. "Jillian, I love you. I love you more than I've ever loved any woman, but I don't know how to do what you're asking. I knew I'd be a disappointment to you. I've always said you deserve more than I could give you."

I shook my head. "I don't deserve more than you *can* give me, Levi. I deserve more than you're *willing* to give me. And you know what? A few months ago, maybe I'd have been content to live like this, loving you from the outside. Looking in. But you gave me a taste of what it feels like to feel worthy of being loved, to feel like I'm enough. I want more of that."

He sighed, his dark eyes sad, but his chin rising stubbornly. "So that's it? You're walking away?"

My throat closed as his walls went up. "If I have to. Let me in, Levi. Let me in, or let me go."

His breath left him in an angry huff. "I always knew you would go."

I crossed my arms and called his bluff. "Are you forcing me to leave now because you're afraid I'll leave later?" And then it dawned on me, the source of the fear. God, how had I not seen it sooner? "I'm not Tara, Levi. Stop letting fear of the future and guilt from the past prevent you from being happy. You've done it long enough!"

He reacted as if I'd slapped him, his eyes blazing with anger, his lips compressing to a thin line, his back snapping straight—and I knew I'd touched a nerve. *Oh fuck. I shouldn't have said that.*

"Say something!" I yelled, my heart hammering. *I'm losing him. I'm losing him.*

But he said nothing. He backed away from me, grabbed

his jacket from the back of the stool, and took off down the stairs.

A few seconds later, I heard my front door slam.

"Fuck you, you coward!" I screamed, my hands squeezing into fists too. I stood there seething for a moment, then burst into tears, weeping into my hands while I leaned against the breakfast counter for support, right next to the framed picture of my sisters and me that he'd given me for my birthday.

How had they done it? How had they figured love out and made it work? Had I fucked up? Should I have been more understanding? More patient? More flexible?

I ran down the stairs to my bedroom and threw myself on the bed, sobbing into my pillow for an hour. When I was completely cried out, I blew my nose and put drops in my eyes. Then I picked up my phone and called Skylar.

"Hello?"

"Hey. Are you busy?"

"Jillian? What's wrong? Where are you?"

I took a shaky breath. "I'm at home. But I need to talk."

"Let me call you right back."

We hung up and I called Natalie. "Can I come over?" I asked her.

"Of course! Are you OK?"

"No. I'll be there in ten."

By the time Skylar called me back, I was on my way out the door. "I had to check with Mia and see if I could get off a little early," she said breathlessly, as if she were hurrying somewhere on foot. "She said it was fine. I'll be there in twenty minutes."

"Go to Natalie's house," I told her. "I need you both right now."

"Done. I'll see you there."

I hung up, taking measured deep breaths and telling myself I would be OK, even if I lost Levi.

I still had family. I still had love.

CHAPTER 25
Jillian

ON THE TEN-MINUTE drive to Natalie and Miles's adorable house, complete with white picket fence, a nursery upstairs, and a sign hanging on the front door that said Love Lives Here, I kept telling myself I'd done the right thing. I'd fought back tears the whole time, but as soon as I saw that fucking sign, I lost it. Natalie opened the door to find me wailing on her porch, and she opened her arms.

I went into them, crying into her shoulder like I was the baby sister needing comfort for once. Miles appeared and shut the door behind me, then rubbed my back. "How about a drink, Jilly?"

"OK." I sniffed, picking up my head. "Got any whiskey?"

"I sure do. On the rocks?"

"Perfect." I sighed, my shoulders releasing some tension. "I need a tissue."

We filed into the kitchen, which smelled delicious, like when my mom used to make homemade chicken pot pie. It was a smell that reminded me of home, of family, of happiness. Would I ever have those things? I blew my nose, willing myself not to start crying over fucking chicken pot pie.

Miles brought me the whiskey a moment later, and Natalie

rubbed my shoulder. "You look terrible. Your eyes are all puffy."

"I know. I feel terrible."

"Should we go into the family room?"

I nodded. "OK. Skylar's on her way."

"Good. Miles, will you check the pies and see if the crust is golden brown yet? If they are, please take them out and turn the oven off."

"Sure thing."

"Thanks, babe."

I will not be jealous, I vowed. *I will not, I will not, I will not. This is just a bad night.*

In the family room, I dropped onto the couch and Natalie sat beside me. I couldn't resist putting a hand over her belly. It was hard and round, about the size of half a basketball. "How are you feeling?"

"Good. He's moving around in there a lot today."

"Yeah?" That cheered me up a little, and I left my hand there. Took a sip of whiskey. A few seconds later, I felt it—that tiny little thump of life within her. I grinned. "Awww. There he is. Hi, baby."

She smiled too. "He says hi back."

"Any favorite names yet?"

She rolled her eyes. "Well, I have favorites and Miles has favorites, but if you're asking do we agree on any names, the answer is no."

I laughed, sniffling again. "What do you like?"

"I like James, Alexander, or Colin."

"What about Miles?"

"Miles likes Gotham, Optimus, and Huck."

"Huck?" I nearly choked on my whiskey.

"Oh, yes," she said with a straight face. "Short for Huckleberry."

"Miles wants to name his son Huckleberry Haas?" I shook my head, laughing. "That's hilarious. And kind of awful."

"Are you kidding? It's totally awful, and somehow he thinks Gotham Haas is a nice compromise."

"Oh, God." I lifted the glass to my lips as I heard Miles greeting Skylar in the kitchen. *This is what I need—a little whiskey, a little laughter, a little sisterhood.*

"Hey." Skylar rushed in and dropped down on the other side of me, placing a hand on my shoulder. "How are you?"

"I'm OK. But…" I shook my head, fighting off tears. "I think I broke it off with Levi."

"You think?" Skylar's brows went up.

"Yeah. I decided to do the right thing and be honest. Ask him why he's holding back. Tell him I want and deserve more."

"Did he disagree?"

"No," I said, my eyes filling. "He didn't. He basically just said, 'I knew this would happen' and stormed out."

"What?" Natalie squawked. "What an asshole!"

"I know, but…he said he loved me too. He said he's never loved any woman the way he loves me."

"Then what's the problem?" Skylar crossed her arms. "I don't get it."

"He also said he doesn't know how to be what I want. He said he knows I deserve more."

"Forcing you to make the decision to end it, so he could say 'See? I told you you'd leave.'" Skylar harrumphed, crossing her arms. "Passive aggressive bullshit. Sebastian tried to pull this same thing. He was scared as all get out to open himself up to being hurt, so he built up this wall of stubborn resistance and refused to let me in until I had to be the one to say 'I love you but I can't do this.'"

"Yes!" I exclaimed, throwing one hand up. "That's it exactly. I asked him flat out if he was forcing me to walk out now so he could avoid the pain of being abandoned later on, since he's *so sure* that's what would happen."

"God, that's so sad," Natalie said quietly. "I mean, I don't think he's right, but it's really sad to feel like you don't deserve love, to be so scared that you have to push it away."

"It is sad." Skylar's voice was soft, and she laid a hand on my shoulder. "But I had to say it, and so did you, Jilly. You did the right thing."

The lump in my throat grew. "I'm not so sure I did. I..." Swallowing hard, I confessed what really had me terrified. "I hit him where it hurt the most. All this time, I felt like this guilt, this self-doubt, stemmed from his love for his child, but I think there's a deeper source. I think when his son's mother abandoned them, he blamed himself. Like if he'd been a better man, she might have stayed." I squeezed my eyes shut. "He fucking told me as much, almost in those exact words, the night he first told me he loved me. But I didn't realize—because he wasn't in love with her—how bad the wound was. And then I made it bleed tonight."

"What? How?" Natalie asked.

"I accused him of being afraid of a future with me because he's scared I'll leave them like she did."

"Oooh." Skylar winced. "That had to be tough."

"It was. I think that's what made him walk out."

Natalie put her hand on my knee. "But not because it wasn't true, Jilly. Because it *was*."

"I agree," Skylar said. "You had to use the hard words. If Levi is stubborn, like Sebastian was, they have to hear it that way. They have to confront their fears. They have to live with them."

"Can I say something?" At the sound of Miles's voice from the entrance to the family room, we all turned.

"Sure," I said. "Come on in."

He shuffled in and plopped down on the floor at Natalie's feet, setting his drink on an end table. "I never had the things in my life that Sebastian or Levi had to deal with. No OCD or anxiety, no child." He glanced at Natalie's bump. "But I did have a hell of a hard time seeing how I could change my life to be with Natalie. I thought there was no way I could do it. I thought I wasn't capable of doing it. Even though I loved her and she knew it, I still needed to hear the hard words from her telling me it's not enough to just love someone. You have to work for it. You have to let it ruin you a little."

I sniffed. "We've definitely done that tonight. At least I did."

"Then give him some time. Seriously," he said, pushing his glasses up his nose. "I think he needs to let this sink in. He'll realize his life is better with you in it, and he'll do anything it takes to get you back."

"Geez, Miles," Skylar said wryly. "When did you get to be such an expert?"

"Since your sister schooled me." He shook his head. "I'd never had a woman turn me down or make me wait before, but that time between telling Natalie I loved her and her accepting my proposal was the longest, like, five minutes of my life."

Natalie threw a pillow at him.

"Thanks," I said, taking a deep breath. "I do think I did the right thing. I'm just scared I'm walking away from the love of my life."

"Oh, honey." Skylar put her arms around me and tipped her head onto my shoulder. "Sometimes we have to."

CHAPTER 26
Levi

I STORMED out of Jillian's house, mad as fuck and scared as hell. From the heavy sound of my feet on the pavement, you'd have thought I had conviction about what I was doing, but I didn't. God, why did I have to be so fucking stubborn? Why couldn't I just admit to her that yes, I was scared, of course I was. Why couldn't I just tell her she was right, tell her I wanted her in my life and Scotty's life, that I wanted to build a life *together*? Why did I have to be such a fucking defensive asshole just because she *got* me?

Shouldn't I be happy about that? Shouldn't I feel good that there was another human being on this earth who knew the way my mind worked and still loved me? Who tolerated my dirty jokes and caveman habits and insatiable sexual appetite? Who knew the man I was, knew I *wasn't* the man I wished I could be, and told me I was enough?

What the fuck was wrong with me?

I got in the car and hit the steering wheel with the heel of my hand hard. Twice. Then three more times. Fuck! Fuck! Fuck! Should I go back up there? Apologize? Give her the chance to love us both, like she said? My eyes watered and I shut them tight. She probably could love us both. She had that much love in her. I reached for the door handle.

My phone buzzed on the seat beside me, and I looked at it in surprise. I hadn't even realized it wasn't on me, I'd been so anxious to see her. When I picked it up, I saw right away that I'd missed a call and three texts.

Scotty doesn't seem right to me. Gave Motrin but can you call?

He spiked a fever. 103. Please call or come home.

Motrin not working. Fever up to 104.5.

Dropping the phone in my lap, I started the engine and tore out of the parking lot, tires screeching. As soon as I got on the road home, I picked it up, hit voicemail and heard my mother's voice.

"Levi, Scotty had a seizure. I called 911 and the ambulance is taking him to the hospital. Don't panic, he seems OK but sleepy. Please call when you get this or come to the hospital. I wish you had given me Jillian's number."

My heart was pounding, adrenaline coursing through my veins. *My son, my son, my son.* I hit the gas hard, blew a stop sign, and sped like a madman all the way to the hospital. I parked in the emergency room parking lot and ran at full speed into the lobby. *If anything happens to him, it's your fault!* screamed a voice inside me. *Your head isn't in the right place, hasn't been in the right place for weeks!*

At the desk, I showed my identification and was given Scotty's location. A nurse hurried me through two huge automatic swinging doors and showed me into a long rectangular room where patient beds were sectioned off by curtains. Scotty was in the last one on the left, lying on his back, sleeping soundly and looking pale, but breathing. "Scotty," I croaked, my throat raw and tight.

"He's doing fine," said my mother, who sat in a chair at his side.

I didn't believe her. I wanted to throw off the blankets and examine every inch of him. Wake him up and see for myself that he could focus and talk and smile and laugh and play dinosaurs and listen to music and tell me hundreds of useless baseball statistics. I'd sit and listen to him talk about them for hours, in fact. I wanted to hear him ask for his yellow spoon, his iPad, his dinosaur pajamas. I wanted him to rub my ear, make me smile, hold my hand.

I wanted him to forgive me. Tell me he was OK. Tell me *we* were OK.

My mother was saying my name, but I didn't respond to her. I lowered myself onto my son's bed and stretched out on my side, putting an arm over his middle—careful not to hold him too tight—and let the tears fall silently, sorry for everything.

They kept Scotty for observation for a few hours and then let us go. He seemed himself, just tired and even less talkative than usual, not hungry or thirsty, and not asking for anything. When we got home, I helped him into his pajamas and put him to bed, lying with him until he fell asleep, playing with his ear. *You scared me, Scotty. I'd never forgive myself if anything happened to you, and I'm so sorry this happened and so angry at myself for not being here. I never should have left you while you were sick. I was selfish to think of myself, to put my feelings ahead of yours. You've been doing so well lately, much better in school, and it makes me happy to see you content. You're the most important thing in the world to me, and I need to concentrate on you, not me. You're what matters, and I love you so much.*

I willfully pushed Jillian out of my mind, even though I'd been dying to call her ever since I got the word from the doctors that Scotty had had a febrile seizure. From what I'd learned at the hospital, this kind of seizure was not harmful in the long-term, and he'd mostly need only rest and the usual care. But was that the truth? Were they not telling me everything? Jillian would be honest—she was good at that. And she was good at reassuring me.

But I didn't call her.

Instead I went downstairs, where my mother was putting together some dinner for us, although I wasn't hungry.

"Is he asleep?" she asked, glancing over at me.

"Yes." I sighed and sank into a chair at the island, rubbing a hand over my beard. *Jillian, I wish you were here.* As soon as I had the thought I was mad at myself.

"And how are you?"

"Miserable."

"Why?"

"Because I wasn't here," I snapped, taking my anger out on her. "Don't you want to scold me about that?"

"Why would I do that?"

"Because my son was sick and I left him here to go see my girlfriend. You even said on your voicemail that I should have given you Jillian's number. And I should have. I also should have taken my phone into her house with me. Actually, I shouldn't have even been away from the house! But I fucked up. Again. And my child had a seizure."

She stopped what she was doing and put a hand over mine. "Levi, darling, you're being too hard on yourself. Scotty would have had the seizure whether you'd been here or not. He had a high fever. And even if you'd given me Jillian's number, I don't think you'd have gotten to the hospital any quicker. You were there only about twenty minutes after we were."

I gritted my teeth. "I still should have been here. A good father would have been here."

"For heaven's sake, Levi," she said, going back to her stir-fry on the stove. "Being a good father doesn't mean never doing anything for yourself. What are you teaching Scotty that way? That being a good parent means you sacrifice your own happiness for someone else's? That you can't have a personal life? That you can't be a whole person with your own needs?"

"Well, doesn't it?" I asked, feeling like I was right back where I started with her, and everything I did was wrong.

"No," she said firmly. "Being a good father does not come at the expense of being a happy, well-adjusted person."

"Well, I don't know how to do that," I said bitterly. "I never have."

"Nonsense," said my mother. She didn't even look at me. "You're just stubborn as a mule and don't want to let anyone help you. You said you have a girlfriend?" she went on before I could argue back. "Where is she? Who is she? Not only do I not have her number, I don't know a damn thing about her. Does she even exist?" She looked at me over one shoulder, arching a brow. "Are you gay?"

"For fuck's sake, Mom."

She threw up one hand and shook the pan with the other. "What? There's nothing wrong with it. Betsy Hillerman's son is gay, you know. The attractive one. The dermatologist. I could introduce you."

"Mom. I'm not gay."

"Well, you can't blame me for wondering. You're thirty-two, Levi. And you haven't had a companion to speak of since Scotty was born. That's not healthy. Either you're gay, you're not human, or you're lonely and suffering and telling yourself you deserve it." She looked back at me again. "And I think we both know which one it is."

I rubbed my eyes, exhausted all of a sudden. "I give up. I don't know what to do."

"Well, I don't either," she said, turning off the heat under the pan. "But if you want the gay dermatologist's number, let me know. He's *very* attractive."

I sighed. Heavily. "You mentioned that."

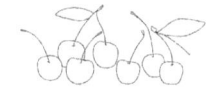

Later that night, after a lot of arguing with myself, I called her. I half-expected it to go to voicemail—I wouldn't want to talk to me if I were her—but she answered. *That's because she's not a fucking six foot four chicken like you are.*

"Hi," I said.

"Hi."

"I'm really sorry about today."

Nothing.

"I feel bad about the way I left."

Nothing.

Can you blame her? You're not adding anything new to the conversation. You're not offering her anything. Tell her what's going on with you. And be honest, asshole.

"I...it's been a rough night. Scotty had a seizure while I was at your place."

She gasped. "Oh my God! Is he OK?"

"He's fine."

"A febrile seizure?"

"Yes."

"Did he go to the ER?"

"Yes. My mom couldn't reach me because my phone was in the car, and she didn't have your number—which I feel horribly guilty about—but she called an ambulance. When I got to my car, I heard the message."

"I'm so sorry, Levi. That can be scary."

"It was. But he's home sleeping now."

"Good."

Silence.

I opened my mouth.

Silence.

I closed my eyes.

Silence.

I clenched my fist.

"Well, I should go," she said woodenly. "I'm very sorry to hear about the seizure, and thank you for calling."

"Jillian, wait." I took a deep breath. "I'm sorry. I felt so horrible when I left you tonight, and then this thing with Scotty happened and it made me question everything even more. I just…I need some time to think, OK? I already miss you, and I know I've probably fucked things up too much already, but would it be too much to ask for some time? I need to make sure my head is in the right place."

"I don't know, Levi. I want to say yes, but I don't really get the sense that you're ready to put your fears aside. It's easier to put *me* aside. And I feel like you just want time to wallow in your guilt some more. Beat yourself up."

God, she knew me so well. Too well.

She took my silence as confirmation she was right. "Goodbye, Levi."

"Jillian, wait—I love you."

I held my breath.

"I love you too," she said, and I could tell she was crying. "It wouldn't hurt so much if I didn't. But time is not going to make a difference here. I'm done waiting on the outside."

I couldn't think of anything to say.

And she hung up.

CHAPTER 27
Levi

I WAS MISERABLE. Food tasted terrible. Sleep was even more elusive. Clock hands crawled. I caught Scotty's virus and sneezed, coughed, and sniffled my way through, feeling like I deserved it. My mother brought me soup and helped out with Scotty while I lay on the couch watching horrible television and contemplating my wretched existence.

Even when I was physically healthy again I felt sick. Achey, listless, unmotivated to do anything for myself. I kept the daily routine going for Scotty's sake but couldn't bring myself to do anything extra. I didn't go to the gym, didn't call Jillian, didn't even wear my new t-shirts. I wore the ugly, gray, stained ones and said ridiculous, self-pitying things to myself like, *now your underwear matches your soul.*

Even Scotty knew something was off, and this is a kid who struggles with affective cues. Two weeks after I'd last spoken to Jillian, Scotty and I were lying on the floor with pillows watching Up, one of his favorite movies, when he leaned over and rubbed my ear. Moved by the gesture, I took his hand in mine and kissed it.

"You have to smile," he said. "Why didn't you smile?"

My throat got tight. "I'm sad, Scotty."

"Because Ellie died?"

"No, because I lost a friend. She...she's *my* Ellie. She didn't die, but I feel like I lost her."

"But adventure is out there! The wilderness must be explored!"

That made me smile, if a little sadly, because I knew he wasn't simply repeating the line for fun. Scotty recognized that, like Carl in the movie, I was missing someone, and parroting Russell's lines was his way of communicating that he understood and wanted me to feel better. It might also have been his way of telling me to go look for her.

"Thanks, Scotty. I do want to explore the wilderness. But it can be scary."

"What can be scary?"

I took a deep breath. "Love. To love someone like Carl and Ellie loved each other. You have to be brave."

"We come to love not by finding a perfect person, but by learning to see an imperfect person perfectly," he quoted.

I smiled, a real one this time. "Thanks, buddy. I'll try to remember that."

That night I went to bed with those words still on my mind. It was almost like Scotty was telling me it wasn't about bravery...it was about acceptance.

Fucking genius, my kid.

The following Tuesday morning, my mother called to tell me she was coming down and wanted to see Scotty, if he was free after school. I told her she could take him to play therapy and get his dinner if she'd like, and she jumped at the chance.

"Thanks," I said. "That will give me some time to go to the gym and maybe catch up with a friend." I was getting much better about letting her help out and not feeling it was an indictment on my parenting.

"How nice. Jillian?" she asked nosily.

"No. A guy friend."

She said nothing for a moment.

"Just a friend, Mom. I'm not gay."

"OK, OK," she said briskly. "You know I don't care either way, I'm only interested in your life. I want you to be happy."

I closed my eyes. "Yes, Mom. I know."

When we hung up, I texted Sebastian. **Can you grab a beer after work?**

Sure. Time and place?

Jolly Pumpkin at 7 work for you?

See you there.

I'd asked Sebastian to meet me because I needed advice, and he was the closest guy friend I had these days. Plus he was married to Jillian's sister and might have some insight as to what I could do to make things right.

He was there when I arrived, sitting with Natalie Nixon's fiancé Miles at the bar, and I shook both their hands before sitting next to Sebastian.

"Hope you don't mind my joining you," Miles said. "I had to get out of the house. Working from home can be a little stifling."

"I hear you. I did it for a while too." I ordered a beer and took off my coat.

"So what's new?" I asked Sebastian. "I haven't talked to you for a couple weeks. Thanks again for putting me in touch with Skylar about the photo. It was perfect."

"You're welcome. I heard she loved it."

"She did."

"I'm glad. Jillian is a great girl."

"She is, but I..." I sighed, running a hand over my beard. "I fucked up."

Neither of them said anything while our beers were set in front of us. Once the bartender was gone, Sebastian asked, "How so?"

I gave them the bare bones of what happened, and it was amazing to me how much clarity came from telling someone else the story. As the words poured out, it was almost like being able to take a step back, see things from her point of view, or even an outsider's, understand my fear and defensiveness better, and put them in perspective.

"Wow," Sebastian said, taking a drink of beer. "So she said no to giving you more time? That doesn't sound like her."

"I think it was the way I asked. She wasn't convinced I would use the time to work through anything. But I have—I just don't know what to do now." I closed my eyes and exhaled. "I need advice."

Sebastian recoiled. "Oh Jesus. I'm the last person who should give relationship advice."

"Why not? You and Skylar have a great relationship."

"Yeah, but that's because of her. I tried to sabotage it a thousand times before I realized how lucky I was that she understood me and accepted me, and that I had to stop trying to drive her away."

"Why did you try to drive her away?" I asked.

"Fear. Plain and simple."

"I did the same," put in Miles. "I was such a dick to

Natalie after I realized I had feelings for her. Just because that was easier than facing them and upending my life."

I nodded, understanding. "That's it exactly. And I'm so fucking tired of being afraid. I love her. I want her in my life. In Scotty's life."

"Then go get her," said Sebastian.

"I don't even know if she'll have me. I might have missed my chance. She said she was done waiting."

He ran a hand through his hair. "Yeah, Skylar says that shit to me to sometimes too. It's because they know we need to hear it in order to quit fucking around and get our shit together."

"Agreed," said Miles. "I actually know for a fact that Jillian's fucking crazy about you. I shouldn't say this, but she came over to the house last Saturday night and she was a mess."

"Fuck." I rubbed the back of my neck. "That's the day we fought. She called me out on my bullshit and I was a stubborn asshole."

"Yeah, she admitted she was harsh. She was all kinds of fucked up about it. But she loves you. And she wants you, trust me. Not on any terms though—she was clear about that. She wants the real thing."

"She deserves it." I grimaced. "So what do I do now?"

"Something that will show her you know you were wrong, you're ready to give her what she wants, and you understand what's important to her," said Miles. "Then you have to figure out a fucking amazing way to do it. Impress her."

"How do you know all this?" I shook my head. "You're like an expert."

He grinned and tipped back his glass again. "'Cause I had to do it too."

I thought about it for a minute as I took a few sips of my

beer. "Her job is important to her, but I think family is the closest thing to her heart."

"I think you're right," said Sebastian. "The Nixons are a tight bunch. But they're great, too. You'll love them."

My insides warmed as I thought about the Nixons letting me and Scotty into their clan. It would be good for both of us. Suddenly it made even more sense, her feelings about being on the inside of my life. When you come from a close family like hers, you want that for yourself. "Any ideas for a fucking amazing way to impress her?"

Sebastian went silent.

"Actually," Miles said, his eyes lighting up, "I do have an idea. I happen to know that the entire Nixon family will be at a party at Abelard Vineyards on Christmas Eve. And *no one* knows this, but something pretty fucking cool is going to take place. I think it would mean a lot to her that you were there that night."

"Really?" Sebastian looked at Miles.

"Really." Miles gave him a warning look. "But you can't say a word. Natalie would fucking kill me."

"I won't."

"Christmas Eve, huh?" An idea was taking shape in my brain. "I think I could be there."

"Good." Miles raised his beer. "Cheers, brothers."

CHAPTER 28
Levi

CHRISTMAS EVE WAS five days away, but there was no way I could wait that long before contacting Jillian. One, I missed her too fucking much, and patience where she's concerned had never been a virtue of mine; and two, I didn't want her to suffer anymore. If she was half as miserable as I was, she was barely getting through a day.

I called her the day after I met Sebastian and Miles at the bar. It went to voicemail.

"Hey, beautiful. I miss you so much, and I hope you're doing OK. I know I have not behaved well and don't deserve another chance, but if you can meet me this week for coffee or a drink or dinner—anything—I'd love to see you. Let me know."

I pressed end, feeling like I hadn't said the right things to convince her, but what could I do? I wasn't a poet, I had no singing voice, no magic words—I was just an imperfect guy hoping the perfect girl would love him.

She called me back after work that night.

"Hi," she said when I answered. "I got your message."

"Hey." The sound of her voice made my heart beat faster. "I'm so glad you called."

"I wasn't going to."

"I wouldn't have blamed you." I set a plate of (cold) chicken, frozen peas, a warm—not hot—dinner roll, and a slice of cantaloupe on the island for Scotty. "Come and eat," I called to him where he was playing on the family room rug.

"Oh, are you having dinner?" she said. "Just call me later."

"No! I mean, yes, of course I will, if you want, but have you thought about my invitation?"

"I'm...still thinking."

My spirits flagged a little. "I understand. Anything I can say to persuade you to say yes? I'll say it."

"I don't know. I miss you, and I want to see you, but... what's different this time, Levi?"

"Everything," I promised. It suddenly occurred to me that my invitation on her voicemail hadn't made that clear. I'd just invited her out like I used to. "In fact, I want to amend my earlier offer. Instead of coffee or a drink, why don't you come over for dinner Friday night?"

"To your *house*?"

"Yes. I want to introduce you to Scotty."

She sighed. "Levi, you know I'd love that, but I'm not doing it if this is just what you think I want to hear."

"It's not," I said. "In fact, it's not for you at all, it's for me. You know how selfish I am." I heard her laugh, and it made me smile.

"OK, then...OK. I'll come over Friday."

"Great. I've been talking about you a little."

"You *have*?"

I smiled even bigger at the shock in her voice. "Yeah. He looked a little worried when I said you were a doctor—he doesn't love checkups—so don't wear the white coat."

She laughed. "I'll be sure to leave that behind. Can I bring anything?"

"Nope. Just your company."

"What time?"

"Is six OK?"

"Yes, I'll come right from work."

"Perfect. Can't wait to see you."

"Same. I miss you. And I can't wait to meet Scotty."

We hung up, and I felt better than I had in a month. I could do this. I looked over at Scotty, who was carefully scooping his frozen peas onto his yellow spoon, a few spilling off the plate, and felt a rush of love for him, too. Neither of us were perfect, but we tried.

Sometimes that's all you can do.

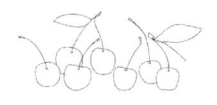

I called my mother that night too. As I'd suspected, it didn't go over well that I wouldn't be at their house on Christmas Eve until I hinted at something bigger than just the holiday.

"I understand that you have to make things up to her, but why does it have to be on Christmas Eve? That's for family."

"That's the point, Mom."

"But those people aren't your family."

"But I'm hoping they will be."

She gasped. "What? What does that mean?"

"It means that I'm serious about her, and I have to show her that I want her to be in my life, and I want to be in hers."

"Well, what about Scotty? Why don't you bring him here to spend the night with us while you go to her party, and then you can come up here afterward to sleep and you both wake up here on Christmas morning. Just like it used to be!" she said brightly, as if she'd found the perfect solution.

"No, Mom. I don't want what used to be. I want to make new traditions. I want to be with Scotty and Jillian on Christmas Eve, and wake up with Scotty in our house."

She sighed, a big, dramatic Mom Sigh. "Fine," she said. "I understand. You'll still come for brunch Christmas Day though, right?"

"We'll be there. Would it be OK to bring Jillian?"

"Of course!" She perked right up. "We'd love to have her!"

"Good. We'll see you then."

In the days leading up to Friday, I spoke about Jillian to Scotty. He listened, I think, but whenever he'd ask about her, he'd refer to her as Ellie, no matter how many times I reminded him her name was Jillian. It was sort of sweet, and very Scotty, so after a while I gave up correcting him and figured it would work itself out on its own—or maybe it wouldn't. Maybe he'd call her Ellie for the rest of her life. Somehow, I knew she'd be OK with that, because it meant Scotty recognized that we loved each other.

As long as he didn't start calling me Carl.

CHAPTER 29
Jillian

I HADN'T BEEN this nervous since my board exams. Walking up the front steps of Levi's house, my knees knocked, my hands shook, and my stomach flip-flopped like a fish out of water. At the front door, I took a second to stand still, breathing slowly and deeply. On the count of three, I knocked.

Levi pulled the door open, and I barely had a chance to look at him before he grabbed me and pulled me to his chest, hugging me so tight I could hardly breathe.

"It's so good to see you," he said in my ear. "I missed you so much."

"I missed you too." I wrapped my arms around his waist and breathed him in. This felt so good. Was he really ready to move forward, get past his fears? God, I hoped so. I knew it wouldn't be easy, but all I needed to hear was that he was willing to try.

"You're freezing," he said, rubbing his hands up and down my back.

"It is pretty cold. I think we're going to get some snow too. But I'm fine."

He released me, kissing me hard on the lips before taking my hand. "Come on in. There's someone I want you to meet."

My heart hammered in my chest as he walked me from the front entrance through a small formal dining room into a family room that was open to the kitchen. For a guy's house, it was decorated nicely—art on the walls, beautiful finishes like granite counters and polished wood floors, fabrics and paint colors that complemented each other in warm neutrals. I don't know why it surprised me, since he was an architect and had an eye for design, but he was always referring to himself as such a caveman. What kind of caveman has throw pillows on the couch and candles on the dining room table?

"Hey, Scotty. Come here." Levi held on to my hand as Scotty got off the floor where he'd been playing and came over to us.

My heart ached, and I squeezed Levi's hand. He was so sweet. Huge, dark eyes like his dad's, the same thick, tousled brown hair, those adorable ears that stuck out a little. He didn't quite meet my eyes, but that was OK.

"Hello," he said, holding out his hand.

"Hello." I dropped Levi's hand and took his son's, leaning down. "I'm Jillian. Nice to meet you, Scotty."

"Nice to meet you, Scotty," he repeated.

Levi and I exchanged a smile. "I hear you like baseball. I do too."

"Babe Ruth hit sixty home runs in 1927," he told me, twirling his hand in his hair.

"Wow," I said. "That's impressive. Is he your favorite player?"

"Who do you like on the Tigers, Scotty?" Levi prompted. "Who do we want to go see hit a home run at Comerica Park?"

"Miguel Cabrera has 408 career home runs," Scotty said.

"I like Martinez," I told him.

"J.D. Martinez. Eighty-five career home runs, thirty-eight last season."

"You know your stuff." I smiled at him. "Very impressive."

"What do you say, Scotty?" Levi asked.

"What do you say, Scotty?" he repeated.

"You say thank you." Levi's voice was firm but kind.

"Thank you."

"You're welcome." I met Levi's eyes and saw they were shining.

"Can I get you something to drink, Jillian?"

"Whatever you're having."

"Can I have my iPad?" Scotty asked hopefully.

"Sure, buddy." Levi ruffled his hair. "Go check off swim therapy on your chart and then grab it."

Levi poured some wine for us, and I sat at the island while he prepared dinner. Watching him move easily in his kitchen, managing several tasks at once, turned me on so much I had to cross my legs. *Put those thoughts away*, I told myself. *That is not why you're here, and it's not happening tonight.* But part of me understood why Levi always wanted to meet out or at my house—when we only got to see each other once a week, we wanted to do more than look.

But this was a different kind of night.

It was the kind of night that made me feel good in other ways—I felt a part of something. I felt the love between Levi and his son. I felt the effort Levi was making to show me there was a place for me in his life, a place for the love we shared. And I felt even more respect and admiration for him as a father, understood better the weight that being Scotty's only parent placed on him, as well as the joy it brought him.

When dinner was over, I insisted on helping with the dishes, and when they were loaded and the food put away, Levi told Scotty he could have some extra playtime while he showed me the house.

My heart beat faster at the thought of being alone with him, even though I knew we couldn't have sex.

Which was why I got the wind knocked out of me when Levi shut his bedroom door behind us and caged me against it, crushing his lips to mine.

I gave up on breathing and kissed him back, my body straining against his.

"I fucking want you so badly right now," he whispered. "You have no idea."

"Uh, yes I do," I said as he wedged one thigh between my legs. "Believe me."

"I'm sorry we have to wait."

"It's OK, really."

"God, Jillian." He shook his head, his eyes serious. "Tell me we're OK. Tell me I didn't fuck this up. I'm so sorry."

"We're OK," I said. "This is what I wanted. To know what it was like to be here with you."

He let my arms drop and gathered me against him. "I love you here with me. With us. I thought being a good father meant I had to deny this part of myself, but it wasn't true. I had to accept it, without fear or reservation. I want Scotty to see what love looks like, all kinds of love."

I locked my hands behind his back. "Scotty is so sweet."

"He is. He's also having a very good day. A good week, actually. It does get harder than this."

I slapped him lightly on the butt. "Such a pessimist."

"I'm serious. You need to know that."

"I know. I'm teasing you. And it's OK—we all have good days and bad. Nothing and no one is perfect."

"I love you." He kissed my head.

"I love you too."

When it got close to nine, I saw that Scotty was getting tired and knew how important it was that he get to bed at the regular time. Levi helped me with my coat, threw his on as well, and walked me to my car. Snowflakes were starting to fall.

"So what will you do for Christmas?" he asked. "Do you go to your mom's?"

"Usually," I said, shivering. "Ooh, it's cold. But this year we're going to a party at the winery where Skylar works on Christmas Eve, and then to my mom's on Christmas Day for dinner. What about you? Heading up to Charlevoix?"

He nodded and wrapped his arms around me to keep me warm. "Yes," he said, dropping a kiss on the tip of my nose. "And you are invited to come to brunch there on Christmas morning."

"Really?"

He laughed. "I love how that lit you up."

"Well, that's exciting for me, to meet your family. I want you to meet mine, too. You and Scotty."

"That would be nice," he said.

"Could you…could you maybe stop by the winery on Christmas Eve?" I asked hopefully. "It would be so nice to see you that night."

"I wish I could," he said, "but I think my mother would kill me. Now you better go, before you get frostbite out here."

"OK." I tried not to feel too disappointed. Being invited to Christmas Day brunch was amazing, and I couldn't wait to tell my sisters.

We kissed goodnight, and he opened the car door for me. "Drive carefully, OK? I'll talk to you tomorrow."

Life got a little hectic in the days before Christmas, and we didn't get another chance to see each other before he had to leave for Charlevoix, although we spoke every day. He called me on his way up.

"Are you getting ready for the party?" he asked.

"Yes," I said, hunting around for the right earrings for my dress. "I wish you were coming with me." It was our first Christmas Eve as a couple, and we had to spend it apart. I was trying not to feel sad about that.

"I know. I'm sorry. My mom is all insistent that Christmas Eve is for family."

That made my heart ache a little. "I get it."

"Well, listen. I better go. Roads aren't great and it's getting dark. You have fun tonight and call me in the morning when you're heading out. You have directions and the address, right?"

"Yes. Drive carefully, please," I begged, worried about him on the dark, snowy highways.

"I will. Love you. Merry Christmas."

"Love you, too. Merry Christmas."

I hung up and finished getting ready, trying to focus on all the good things in my life, not on how much I'd miss him tonight. But it was hard.

Christmas Eve was for family, his mother insisted. I didn't disagree, and I loved my family fiercely. But I wanted him in it.

Was that crazy?

CHAPTER 30
Levi

I SET the phone down and smiled. Pulling off the white lie about tonight hadn't been easy, since I was so bad at deception, but every time I thought about her face when she saw Scotty and me at the party tonight, it gave me the strength to keep up the act. *At least she couldn't see my face today*, I thought, which hadn't been straight at all during our conversation. It had been much harder the other night when I'd had to turn down her invitation in person.

I felt a twinge of guilt thinking about the comment I'd made regarding family but decided it would make her that much happier when she saw that family to me included everyone I loved most—and that meant her.

I hummed a holiday tune as I went to collect Scotty from his room for his shower. "Ready, bud?"

"Yes," he said, putting his hands over his ears. "But Dad. Stop singing."

I grinned. "You got it."

"Where are you going?" he asked as I drove through the snowy dark up the highway on Old Mission peninsula.

"We are going to a Christmas party."

"At Grandma's house?"

"No, at a new place."

"This is a snowstorm." Worry made his voice shake a little.

"Don't worry, I'm driving nice and slow, see? It's not bad. And there will be treats there." I'd double-checked with Sebastian that it was OK for Scotty and me to be there, and he said Skylar was thrilled and wouldn't say a word to Jillian about it. I'd also asked about how many people would attend, and while he wasn't positive, he didn't think it would be more than thirty.

Miles had told him to let me know I should arrive by eight, so I tried to leave extra time for the drive, knowing the roads would be slow. We pulled up at the winery at about five to eight, and I felt exceedingly proud of myself for being on time. With a quick *thank you, God* for letting Scotty have a good day today, I got out of the car, took Scotty's hand, and hustled up the front steps.

CHAPTER 31

Jillian

THE WINERY LOOKED BEAUTIFUL, the tasting room decked with candles, white lights and holly, mistletoe hanging in every archway, and a huge evergreen tree in one corner, hung with French-themed ornaments and colored bulbs, a fleur-de-lis at the top. Instrumental carols played on hidden speakers, the wine flowed, and the food was delicious. Instead of tables and chairs, as there had been for the rehearsal dinner, the room was staged with cozy couches and chairs in conversational groupings to encourage mingling, but I noticed that the area in front of the fireplace had been cleared. Maybe they didn't want anyone sitting too close to the fire, which crackled and popped, giving the room a warm glow.

The guest list was intimate: just my family, the Fourniers, the families of a few Abelard employees and two families who were visiting the Fourniers for the holidays. I got chatting with one of the wives, a lovely woman with strawberry blonde hair and flawless porcelain skin, whose name was Erin. She told me she had grown up across the street from Mia Fournier, and they'd remained best friends. The third in their trio, a gorgeous brunette named Coco, was at the party as well. She spent almost the entire evening chasing around three young sons with dark eyes and mischievous grins.

"Coco was Mia's roommate in college," Erin said, taking a sip of her water. She was pregnant with her second child; her handsome husband Charlie, a cop, was walking around with their adorable blonde one-year-old daughter on his hip. "The three of us are really close, so this is so nice to spend time together up here."

"How often do you get up to see her?" I asked. I couldn't imagine moving away from my sisters.

She smiled. "Not as much as we'd like, but that might change. Coco's husband, Nick, is opening a restaurant up here." She gestured toward an attractive, dark-haired guy who was chatting with Natalie and Miles.

"Really? That's great."

"What about you? Are you married?"

For once, the question didn't bother me at all. "Not yet. I'm dating someone," I said shyly, looking into my wineglass, "but he couldn't be here tonight."

"Oh, that's too bad."

"Yeah, he has an eight-year-old son, and they always go to Grandma's on Christmas."

"Totally get it," Erin said. "Charlie has a daughter from a previous marriage too."

"Really?" I stood up taller. "Was it…hard to make that work? When you got married, I mean?"

"Well, yes and no. His daughter Madison is wonderful, but we still had to go slow and make sure she was comfortable with everything. We're lucky that Charlie has a good relationship with Madison's mother. That made things easier."

"I bet. I guess I'm lucky there, since there is no mother in the picture at all. Levi is a full-time single dad."

"That might make it a little easier," Erin said. "At least

politically." She grinned ruefully. "But I imagine it makes finding alone time difficult."

I grinned back. "Uh, yeah. A bit."

"But you know what? If he's bringing you into his life, and his son's life, that means he thinks you're really special. He must be serious about you."

I blushed, my eyes dropping again. "I hope so. I wish he was here tonight."

"I can tell."

And then the most amazing thing happened.

I looked up and saw him coming toward me over Erin's shoulder. In his black suit. Tall and gorgeous, holding Scotty's hand, a hint of a smile on his face. I saw him…was it real?

"Oh my God. He's here. He's *here*."

Erin looked over her shoulder and then back at me. "In the black suit? With the beard and the broad shoulders?"

I blinked. "Yeah. This is crazy. But that's him and his son."

She touched my shoulder. "I love it. Merry Christmas."

"Merry Christmas," I said, meeting her eyes, still in a daze. What was he *doing* here?

I set my wineglass down on a nearby table and started walking toward him, and we met halfway. I grabbed his free hand and threw the other one around his neck, and he lifted me right off my feet. Against my chest, his rumbled with laughter. "Hey, beautiful."

"Hi," I said, tearing up. "Oh my God, what are you doing here?" I released him and stood back to greet the boy at his side. "Hey, Scotty. How are you?"

"How are you?" he asked, not quite meeting my eyes.

"We came to see you," Levi said, squeezing my hand. "You look gorgeous."

"Thank you. You both look great too." I took in father and son in matching black suits, white dress shirts, and dark ties, and grinned. "Quite a pair you make."

"Thanks."

"But what about your mom? What about your family?"

He leaned in and kissed my cheek. "You're family to me, and this is where I want to be."

I hugged him tight again. "I love you so much," I whispered.

"I love you too," he said. "This is everything I want."

I was so happy I didn't even know what to do with myself. "Are you hungry? Thirsty? You have to meet my parents! Is it too noisy?" I glanced at Scotty.

Just then the music faded, and a female voice rang out at the front of the room.

"May I have your attention, please."

Levi and I turned toward the fireplace and saw Mia Fournier addressing the room. "We're so glad you're all here tonight. It means so much to be able to share the holidays with the people you love."

"Hear, hear!" someone shouted, and I felt another tug on my hand.

"Tonight is extra special," Mia went on, her eyes sparkling. "Something is about to take place, something that will remind us that aside from all the gifts and the lights and the snow and the food and the wine, this is a season about love."

At first I thought she was going to make a toast, so I was surprised when she said, "Could Jillian Nixon and Skylar Pryce please come forward?"

"What on earth…" I muttered, glancing at Levi.

"Come on up here, ladies," Mia called.

"Go on," he said, his eyes sparkling, like he was in on a joke.

Confused, I made my way to the fireplace at the same time as Skylar, who looked equally perplexed.

Mia smiled at us before reaching into a box I hadn't noticed at her feet. She pulled out two small bouquets of winter white flowers and evergreens and handed them to us.

We exchanged a frantic look and immediately searched the crowd for Natalie. She was nowhere to be found. "She wouldn't," Skylar said.

"She couldn't," I said.

"She did." Mia grinned.

Skylar and I had another one of those conversations with our eyes.

OMG how dare she?

I know! How could she keep this a secret?

So mad at her.

SO mad. But yay!

Yay! We'll kill her tomorrow. We'll be happy right now.

SO happy.

Mia placed us where she wanted us, and a murmur ran through the crowd. Skylar and I, as vain as this sounds, quickly appraised each other's outfits. When we'd dressed tonight, we'd thought it was just a Christmas party, but now it was our baby sister's wedding.

Skylar looked amazing, of course—a black strapless cocktail dress, chunky gold necklace, and red patent pumps. I was wearing emerald green, pearls, and strappy black heels. We gave each other the nod of approval.

"OK," Mia said loudly, addressing the room again. "Can we have Mr. and Mrs. Nixon up front as well?"

My bewildered parents appeared, and Mia placed them right in the front of the crowd. "Perfect."

They looked at Skylar and me with quizzical faces, and both of us shrugged.

"Now if I could ask everyone to clear a little path here, stand back just a bit, we can do this." She turned over her shoulder. "Nick?"

The lights dimmed so that the room glowed with the golden warmth of candles, and the dark-haired man Erin had pointed out as their friend Coco's husband stepped out from the crowd and stood in front of the fireplace, a leather portfolio in his hand. So was he ordained or something? I noticed Sebastian step out as well, standing opposite Skylar and me, hands folded in front of him. I glanced at Skylar, who was giving him a look that said *if you knew about this and didn't tell me, you are dead.*

But before she could accost him, the music started again—Frank Sinatra's "Young at Heart," which was our parents' wedding song. My mother was already dabbing at her eyes by the time Natalie and Miles appeared, hand in hand, walking through the path the guests had created. My throat closed, and Skylar and I clutched each other. How did we miss this?

Natalie wore a short, A-line maternity cocktail dress in ivory with a halter neck tied in a bow above her left shoulder. Her hair was up, her skin was radiant, and she had a smile on her face that rivaled all the strings of lights in the room.

Miles looked handsome in his dark suit, but more than that, he looked madly in love with our sister. Suddenly I realized that his family wasn't here, and I felt sad for him—I knew they weren't very close, and maybe it didn't bother him that his parents wouldn't see him get married. Although, maybe he'd invited them and they hadn't elected to come.

Miles and Natalie reached the front, and she looked over at Skylar and me, a guilty but gleeful grin on her face. My eyes teared up, and I smiled back. Nick began the ceremony, and I looked for Levi in the crowd—he was so tall, I found him pretty easily, standing a little to one side and pointing things out to Scotty. *Poor kid thought he was coming to a party and has to endure a wedding,* I thought. *I'll make sure to get him something sweet to eat as soon as it's over.*

I still couldn't believe he was here, and I blinked a few times to make sure he didn't disappear from the flickering shadows. But there he was—tall and strong and beautiful, holding his son's hand and locking eyes with me, telling me without words that from now on we would share one life together, celebrating beautiful times like this and supporting each other when things got tough. Because it wasn't about being perfect, it wasn't about having the perfect love story, and it didn't matter that it might take us a little longer to get where we wanted to go. We'd get there.

With our eyes still on each other's, he brought one hand to his ear and rubbed it—their little sign for I love you. My breath caught, my eyes filled, and my entire body hummed with assurance that I'd found—we'd found—where we belonged.

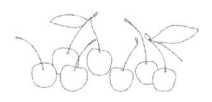

I introduced Levi and Scotty to my parents, who both insisted they come for dinner tomorrow night.

"Thank you," Levi said. "Scotty is going to spend the night at his grandparents' house, but when I drive you back after brunch, I might be able to stay for dinner."

I smiled. "Of course. However it works."

Scotty and my dad talked baseball stats for a while, and Levi laughed that finally, *finally*, Scotty had found a kindred spirit, someone who appreciated the history of the game as much as he did.

When Scotty got tired, I walked them to the door, where Levi gave me a kiss good night and pulled me close. "If Scotty is OK at my parents' house tomorrow night, I'll come down and spend it with you."

My heart beat hard against his. "I'd love that. It's been so long."

He groaned. "Believe me. I know."

I bent down to ruffle Scotty's hair and say good night, and he made eye contact for a second and said, "You and me, we're in a club now."

I smiled but looked up at Levi, a little confused.

Levi seemed baffled for a moment too, but then it must have clicked. "It's from Up, a movie he likes." His voice cracked a little. "The character that says it is named Ellie, and I think he associates her with you because I was talking about you last time we watched it."

"Oh my goodness, yes! I love that movie!" Touched, I leaned down to Scotty again. "You're exactly right, we are. We are in a club now." I held out my fist, and he bumped it with a grin.

When I looked at Levi again, he went to say something but ended up just shaking his head, and I realized he'd gotten too choked up to speak. I took his face in my hands—I'd never get enough of that beard against my palms—and kissed him once more. "I love you. I'll see you in the morning."

He nodded and whispered, "I love you too. You have no idea."

CHAPTER 32
Levi

ON CHRISTMAS MORNING, I invited Jillian to come over for coffee, and together we watched Scotty open his gifts from Santa. He usually did it at my parents' house, so it was a first for Scotty and me to be in our house, a family on our own. With Jillian there too, it felt so perfect, I knew in my bones this was how Christmas morning would be for the rest of my life.

She brought a few gifts for me—a great bottle of scotch, a new dark blue shirt, and a pair of cufflinks with the Slytherin crest on them. "To remind you," she said, her eyes dancing with mischief.

I kissed her cheek and bit her earlobe before whispering in her ear. "As if I could forget."

For her, I'd purchased a gift certificate to the spa she liked, which she could open in front of Scotty, and lingerie in her favorite shade of red from La Perla, which she could not. So while Scotty played with his new Legos, I pulled her into the bedroom, sat her on the bed, and took great delight in watching her jaw drop and her cheeks go pink when she unwrapped it.

"It's gorgeous," she murmured, holding up the bra. "Exquisite."

"I can't wait to see you in it." *But I better stop thinking about that, or I'll get—fuck, too late.*

"Want me to put it on right now?" she asked coyly. "I could wear it under my clothes today."

I jumped up and adjusted myself. "Are you trying to kill me? We have to go to brunch at my parents' house! I wouldn't even be able to sit next to you at the table if I knew you were wearing that."

She laughed. "OK, OK. I'll save it for later."

"Except now I'm hard. Fuck." I turned away from her and walked over to the window, singing the Michigan State fight song in my head, which was always my go-to trick for getting rid of an untimely erection.

"What are you doing?"

"Shh. Don't talk."

"Why?"

"Because I'm trying to make my hard-on go away, and hearing your voice gives it ideas."

"I could make it go away," she said sweetly.

"Gah! Stop!" I put my hands over my ears. "You're giving it hope!"

She laughed throatily. "Come on over here and let me get my mouth on you. You'll come so fast, we won't be missed, and I'll swallow every last drop so you won't even have to change your shirt."

"Jillian." A warning.

"What's the matter?" She put one finger in her mouth and pulled it out slowly. "You don't want it?"

And that, kids, is how the tradition of The Christmas Morning Blowjob began.

Later that morning we drove up to Charlevoix, blinking at all the bright white snow that had fallen overnight. At my parents' house, I introduced Jillian to everyone, watching with pride as she charmed them all with her kindness, her intelligence, her smile. She listened with rapt attention to embarrassing stories my mother and sister told about me, laughed and cooed over pictures of me as a kid and then Scotty as a baby, fielded a thousand questions about her family, her education, her job, and her interests with an easy grace, and complimented the meal. Monica and my mother elbowed each other incessantly, nodding at each other with *I knew it* in their eyes all day long, as if they had planned the whole thing.

Scotty seemed to be having a good day, so I asked my mother if it would be all right if I stayed in Traverse City for the night when I drove Jillian back.

"Of course," she whispered, patting me on the back. "Scotty and I are going to have a great time. We have it all planned out."

"Are you sure?"

"Yes. You need to spend time with her. A woman like that is one in a million, Levi." She turned me around and pushed me out of the kitchen. "Go. Make me another grandbaby."

"Jesus, Mom." I shook my head, glad Jillian wasn't around to hear her. I didn't want her to feel any pressure from my family—she got enough of it from her own.

We said goodbye and drove back to my house, and Jillian chattered the entire way home about how wonderful my family was.

"They loved you," I told her.

"You think so?" She twisted her hands together in her lap.

"I know so. My mother told me repeatedly how lovely and smart you are. Much too good for me." I took her hand and kissed the back of it.

"She did not say that." Jillian laughed and kept her hand on my leg. "But I'm happy she invited me today. I loved seeing where you grew up and hearing about your teenage antics."

I groaned. "You can forget those now."

"And the pictures of you with Scotty as a baby are so precious." She sighed. "I love that you're a dad. It's so damn sexy."

"It is?"

"Yes. Why do you think I couldn't control myself around you this morning?"

"Uh, I think that was *me* who lacked control this morning. But I plan on making it up to you tonight—repeatedly."

"Nothing to make up for." She squeezed my thigh. "I quite enjoyed myself."

We drove to her parents' house, where it was my turn to hear stories about smart, bossy big sister Jillian, and page through albums of her as an adorable baby, a gap-toothed kid, and a pretty teenager with killer legs and a huge smile. The Nixons were warm and welcoming, asking lots of questions about my son, my business, and my family, and I could see where Jillian got her blue eyes, her brains, her curiosity, and her sense of humor.

Natalie and Miles took some shit for keeping their wedding a secret, but the teasing was good-natured and they just shrugged and explained they'd made the decision to get married before the baby was born and Christmas Eve seemed as good a night as any, since all the family would be gathered in one place.

Around ten o'clock, we pulled up at my house, where Jillian's car was parked on the street.

"Meet me at my place?" she asked, unbuckling her seatbelt.

"Would you like to come in? Stay at my house tonight?"

She looked over at me. "I'd love that."

"Why do you look so surprised?"

"I don't know." She thought for a second. "I guess I think of this as your house with Scotty. It seems strange to stay the night."

I took her hand again. "I love you, Jillian. And I want a life with you. I don't mean that we have to rush anything, but I don't like being apart from you so often. I don't want you to be my Girl Friday anymore—I want something more."

"Me too," she whispered, her eyes shining in the dark.

I leaned toward her, kissed her lips. "So let's go in and see how it feels."

It felt fucking amazing, of course.

To be naked in my bed with her, where I'd thought of her, talked to her, dreamed about her so many nights. Where I'd chastised myself for being so stubborn and scared. Where I'd tortured myself, believing I could never have her.

To wrap myself around her and feel her wrapped around me, limbs twined around bodies like vines.

To feel free to love her and accept her love, without guilt, without reservation, without end.

To make promises.

"Spend forever with me," I whispered, buried deep inside her. "I'll make you happy."

"Yes." She held my head in her hands, her eyes shiny in the dark. "Yes."

Looking down at her, our bodies joined, I felt a euphoria beyond measure, something so much more than merely physical—something boundless and timeless and fathomless, something that made the room spin and my eyes water and my heart pound. Something that made all the pieces of me, all the pieces of my life, come together in perfect, blissful harmony.

For the first time in my life, I felt complete.

Epilogue

JILLIAN

"He's so beautiful, you guys. Congratulations." I leaned over to kiss Natalie on the cheek, and then hugged Miles, who stood by her side, dazed and beaming. At eight last night, right in the middle of my engagement dinner, Natalie had gone into labor. Twelve hours later, she'd delivered a healthy baby boy without any complications, despite being two weeks early.

"Thanks. You ever going to give him back, Mom?" Natalie called to our mother, who sat in the window seat cradling the baby, our dad right next to her.

"Never." She didn't even look up from the baby's sweet little face. "Oh God, he just sighed and opened his eyes. He's brilliant."

Natalie and I exchanged a look, and then she grabbed my hand. "Jillian, I'm so sorry about the party. I feel like we stole your thunder."

"Don't be silly! You made it more memorable. Levi and I are thrilled."

She looked like she didn't believe me. "Are you sure?"

I squeezed her hand. "Positive. He's downstairs right now getting some coffee."

"Tell him to come up!" she said.

"Are you sure? We have Scotty with us, and Levi wasn't sure if you'd want a bunch of people in here."

She flapped her hands. "It's all family. Plus I need to hear about how it went. Let me see your ring again."

I laughed. "You've seen it," I said, but I held my hand out for her anyway.

She sighed and fanned her face, tears welling. "Sorry. I'm emotional right now. But it's so beautiful. I'm so happy for you guys."

"Thanks. I'm happy too." After I texted Levi the room number, I looked at the ring again too, dazzled by its sparkle and luster, but even more by what it represented—a future with Levi. He'd surprised me with the proposal last weekend, which he and I had spent curled up in a romantic cabin in the woods with every intention of skiing, but never quite making it outside our cozy little place (that was the point of the pinky swear anyway, right?).

On our first night there, in front of a roaring fire, between sips of whiskey, and after round one of hair-pulling, toe-tingling, cabin-shaking sex, Levi had knelt before me with the ring and asked me to be his wife.

He said he didn't expect me to be Scotty's mother, but would be honored and grateful to have my help in raising him alongside any children we had. I'd nodded and cried, my heart too full to speak as he slipped the ring on my finger.

Later, when we were lying in bed, gaining our strength back after round two, he showed me a letter that Scotty had written for me. It was printed in pencil on lined paper, and there were a few holes in it where he'd erased mistakes too vehemently. *Dear Jillian*, it read. *I hope you say yes. You make Daddy smile. I like you.* It was signed, *Scotty Brooks*.

I put a hand over my heart, choked up again. "Oh my God, he's so sweet. So he knows about this?"

Levi nodded. "He does. And he understands that means we will all live together and maybe at some point buy a bigger house."

"So we'll live in your house first?"

"I hope you will. And I hope you'll move in right away… the past few months with you have been the happiest of my life, Jill. The days when I don't see you are always…lesser, somehow." He brushed my hair off my face. "That day you crashed into me at your sister's wedding was the luckiest day of my life."

I'd blubbered some more and agreed to move in as soon as I could, and when we got back, I'd called my realtor about putting my condo up for sale.

"Can we come in?" Skylar appeared in the hospital room doorway, Sebastian, Levi, and Scotty behind her.

"Sure," said Natalie, motioning everyone in. "It's a big room."

Miles went over to shake hands with the guys, including Scotty. "Thanks for coming," he said.

Sebastian thumped him on the back. "So happy for you guys. Congratulations."

"How's everyone feeling?" Levi asked, looking from Natalie to the baby. Scotty hung onto Levi's hand, but he looked over toward the baby curiously.

"Amazing," said Miles with a grin. "I've never felt better."

Natalie rolled her eyes. "We're all good. I'm exhausted but running on adrenaline right now." She turned to Skylar. "You checked in at the coffee shop, right? Everything was OK?"

Skylar laughed. "Yes, crazy. Everything is fine at work. Jeez, you just gave birth. Relax a little." She went over to Sebastian and took his hand. Together, they walked softly over to my parents and peeked at the baby.

"So what's his name?" Levi asked.

"Gotham," announced Miles.

Natalie glared at him. "We're still deciding that."

"Right, so for now, we might as well call him Gotham," Miles said, as if it made perfect sense.

"Let me have him now." Our dad reached over and took the baby from our mother. "I need a turn." Once the baby was in his arms, he looked up. "Hey, Scotty, come on over here and see my new grandson. Isn't he small?"

Scotty looked up at Levi, who encouraged him with a nod. "It's OK. Go see him. That's how small you were once."

Scotty twirled one hand in his hair as he walked over to the window, and my dad angled his body so Scotty could see the baby. My heart beat hard with love and gratitude for my dad, who'd been so good with Scotty over the last couple months.

My mother pouted. "Somebody better give us a second grandbaby, and *soon*," she said, giving Skylar and me a look, "or there's going to be trouble. One baby simply isn't enough to go around."

"Don't look at me." I laughed, holding up both hands. "I just got engaged a week ago."

Skylar cleared her throat. "Actually…"

All heads turned in her direction.

"Actually, it'll be me having the second grandchild." She grinned deviously. "And the third."

Jaws dropped. Eyes bugged. Silent seconds ticked by.

"Twins?" I finally managed.

Skylar looked at Sebastian, who appeared to be hoping the ground might open up and swallow him. "Yep," she said, giggling a little. "It was confirmed by ultrasound this week."

"Twins?" Our mother continued to gape at her, one hand moving to her heart.

"Twins," she confirmed again, rising up on her toes.

"Guess the pressure's off, huh?" Levi whispered in my ear.

I smiled up at him and whispered back. "Thank God. Now we can take our time."

"I can't believe it," Natalie said, shaking her head, a huge grin on her face. "Twins!"

"Congratulations, you guys," Miles said, sinking onto the bed next to Natalie. "And Sebastian, it's the best feeling in the world, being a dad. I never thought I'd say that, but it is."

"I'll second that," said Levi.

"And I'll third," added my dad.

"Twins," my mother said again, her eyes misting. "I can't believe it."

"Well, you know Sebastian," Skylar said, giving her husband an elbow in the side. "Two is always better than one."

Smiling, I leaned back against Levi's chest, feeling his arms come around me. I was surrounded by love, laughter, and three generations of family.

It was exactly where I wanted to be, now and forever.

The End

Thanks for reading Levi and Jillian's story! If you enjoyed this, be sure to pick up the other books in the Happy Crazy Love series, SOME SORT OF HAPPY (Sebastian and Skylar) and SOME SORT OF CRAZY (Miles and Natalie).

If you're ready for the next series, check out Man Candy—it's a sexy second chance romance that will make you laugh and swoon! Keep reading for a sneak peek!

Bonus Epilogue

LEVI

For once, I was awake before Scotty. It wasn't even six, but I heard him start rummaging around in his room, probably rearranging his dinosaurs again. At about six-thirty, he'd wander downstairs and start looking for his favorite cereal bowl—Jillian had gotten him this clock that had different colors behind the hands, and he knew he had to wait for the small hand to be in the green before he could come to our bedroom or go downstairs. It wasn't that he couldn't read a clock before, but somehow the color-coded system appealed to him. When it was red, he knew he should be in bed. Green was for morning routines. Yellow was for daytime activities like school or therapy or church or errands, and blue—his favorite—meant it was free time, which he usually spent on the iPad. Every day had a similar pattern and rhythm, which reassured him.

Except, of course, today wasn't like any other day.

It was my wedding day.

Today, instead of dressing in jeans and t-shirts and sneakers, Scotty and I would put on suits and ties and what he called our "man shoes," and we'd go over to Jillian's parents' place, where a hundred people would watch us say our vows in an outdoor ceremony next to the cherry orchard where she grew up.

I scratched my beard, trying to picture it. Other than the time and place, I really didn't know many of the other details. I'd pretty much given Jillian and her sisters free reign to plan things. It wasn't that it didn't mean as much to me—it meant everything that Jillian wanted to be my wife and the only mom Scotty would ever know—it was simply that what color the tablecloths were, what flowers she carried, and what the chairs looked like mattered much less to me than the promise we'd make each other. It had taken me so long to get to the point in my life where I felt like I could *make* a promise to someone other than Scotty, and now…I couldn't imagine life without her.

Sometimes I still had to pinch myself to believe that she was mine. *Ours.* Scotty adored her, and she was amazing with him. "We're in a club now," Scotty always said to her, and about her. She said it to him a lot too. It was from *Up*, one of his favorite movies, and at first it was mostly about the fact that they both loved me, but it had come to mean even more than that—it meant they loved each other, too. Their own little code.

Thinking about how lucky we were had kept me awake half the night. Well, that and the fact that it was the first night Jillian and I had spent apart since she'd moved in three months ago. It had been such a whirlwind—and yet, it also felt as if we'd always been together.

"He missed you at bedtime," I'd told her on the phone last night when she called to check in. After the rehearsal dinner, she'd gone back to her parents' house to stay the night, and Scotty and I had returned to our place.

"Oh no," she said, her tone sorrowful. "I knew it would

throw things off for him if I wasn't there. I should have stayed. Should I come home?"

"No, no, he's fine. I explained it to him again. He's excited for tomorrow."

"Are you sure? I hate to think of him upset."

My heart swelled with love for her. "I'm sure. You get some rest, because I am keeping you up all night tomorrow."

She laughed. "I can't wait. I love you."

"I love you too," I said, my voice catching. "More than you know."

After breakfast, I put Scotty in the shower and then let him have some iPad time while I cleaned up. Later, we stood side by side in the bathroom mirror and combed our hair, Scotty mimicking my every move. I trimmed my beard and let him rub some oil in it, then gave him some for his own face, just like we always did. After that, we buttoned up our white dress shirts and tucked them in. I let Scotty pick out a pair of cuff links for me, and he chose the ones he and Jillian had bought me for Father's Day last month—my initials on one, Scotty's on the other. When our neckties were knotted, our "man shoes" were tied, and our jackets were buttoned, we stood next to each other in front of the full-length mirror on the back of the bedroom door. Frowning at my reflection, I hoped I wasn't forgetting anything. Had I put on deodorant? Socks without holes? The right wristwatch? I double-checked that I was wearing the black Shinola Jillian had given me for my birthday.

"Well? What do you think?" I asked my son, fiddling with my tie. "Do I look good enough for her?"

"No," he answered, making me burst out laughing. When

he laughed too, I scooped him up in a hug and he threw his arms around my neck.

"Fair enough, buddy." I set him down and straightened my coat, then his. "I agree. Nobody's good enough for her, but since she said yes when I asked, let's go to that wedding before she changes her mind."

JILLIAN

My heart was pounding as Skylar fastened my dress up the back. I closed my eyes, almost scared to look.

"Oh, Jilly." Natalie sighed from where she stood in the doorway of my old room, rocking little Gotham in her arms. "It's perfect."

"I knew it would be." Skylar's tone was smug. She'd been the one to insist all along it was the perfect dress. When I'd seen it hanging, I hadn't been at all sure it was the one—my long, gangly body would look even more string-beanish in a mermaid style, wouldn't it? And all that fussy lace and the long train just didn't seem like me. I had a more reserved sense of style than Skylar, and I'd pictured something sleek and modern. But when I tried it on, Natalie and my mother had teared up, and Skylar had jumped up and down, squealing with victory. And she was right—the lace made it romantic, the mermaid silhouette gave me the illusion of curves where none existed, and the slightly ecru color gave it a modern edge.

I opened my eyes and smiled. "Thank you."

"How do you feel?" Natalie asked, coming into the room. She looked beautiful in her wine-colored bridesmaid dress, her brown hair loose around her shoulder, the front twisted back and pinned with a flower. Her son, just over three months, cooed appreciatively and reached for her face, his eyes full of love. *So sweet*, I thought, one hand unconsciously touching my stomach.

I dropped it before either one of them noticed.

Not yet. You have to tell Levi first.

I'd known for three days now, but I hadn't told him yet because I thought it would make a fun wedding night surprise—although I was a little nervous he would think it was too soon. We'd only been together for a year, and I'd just moved in with him and Scotty a few months ago. I hadn't planned on getting pregnant so quickly, but life had been surprising me left and right since we'd run into each other at Skylar and Sebastian's wedding last September.

"I feel good. But…" I shook my head, still in awe that this was actually happening. I'd watched both my younger sisters walk down the aisle already, and it had often seemed like my day would never come. "It's still a little unbelievable."

"That's because you barely gave us any time to plan," Skylar complained, moving around me, checking the pins in my hair, fussing with the strands around my face, nodding with satisfaction when she was done. Radiant, as usual, her blond hair was thick and flowing, a flower above one ear. She was a few months pregnant with twins, her belly just starting to pop. She griped about it constantly, but I couldn't wait to start showing.

"We didn't want to wait," I said without apology. "And I'm happy with the way everything turned out—even the weather is perfect."

"Are you nuts? Don't mention the weather!" Skylar's blue eyes went wide. "You'll jinx yourself."

But I didn't feel like anything could jinx this day.

It was time.

My stomach was fluttering like mad as I watched my grandparents, Levi's parents, and my mother leave the house to go be seated. Skylar, Natalie, and I held each other in a long, silent, three-way hug before they picked up their bouquets and slipped outside, both of them misty-eyed but smiling. That left my dad and me.

"Ready, Jilly Bean?"

The childhood nickname made me laugh a little. "Definitely."

He offered me his right arm, and I took it, my throat constricting unexpectedly. I made a joke to ward off the tears. "Bet you thought this day would never come, huh?"

"Oh, I knew it would come." He squeezed my arm. "But I also knew you wouldn't settle for anything less than a man like Levi, and that takes time to find."

"He is a good man, isn't he?"

"The very best. Exactly the kind I'd choose for my Jillian. Exactly the kind I'd choose for a son—and I got a bonus grandson out of it, too. I'm a lucky man."

I couldn't even speak, my throat was so tight. But I kissed him quickly on the cheek and smiled.

The wedding coordinator poked her head in. "OK, you two. Come on out."

Heart thumping with nervous excitement, I let my dad guide me out the front door and around the house toward the orchard, where rows of chairs were set up in a semi-circle at the foot of the cherry trees. Off to the left was the tent where our reception would be, and behind that the catering trucks. We followed a little brick path along my mother's herb and flower gardens, and I inhaled the fragrant scent of basil and lilacs. The sun warmed my arms as we cleared the shadow of the house and approached the white runner serving as an aisle. I took a deep breath as the guests stood and looked back at us.

Then it caught in my chest—there he was.

Tall and gorgeous and broad-shouldered and straight-backed, his dark hair smooth, his beard neatly trimmed. Our eyes locked as I started toward him.

There was music being played by a string quartet, but I didn't hear it.

The sun was so hot, people fanned themselves with their programs, but I didn't feel it.

More than one hundred people watched as I walked toward the love of my life, but I didn't see them.

I saw nothing but him, felt nothing but love, heard nothing but the beat of my heart.

When I got close enough, I saw the way his eyes shone as he looked at me, felt the strength in his hand when he squeezed mine, heard his soft, deep voice say in my ear, "My God, you're beautiful."

The temperature was probably close to eighty, but I had chills.

Next to Levi stood Scotty, adorable in his dark suit, looking both uncomfortable and proud to be standing up for his dad. His hair was tousled, as if he'd been twirling a hand in it already. I smiled at him before watching my father shake Levi's hand and then—to my surprise—his son's. My eyes filled as my heart pounded with love and gratitude for my dad. What a sweet, thoughtful way to acknowledge that it wasn't just two lives being joined today; it was a new family being created. I saw Levi's jaw twitch as he nodded his thanks at my father, and I knew how much he appreciated the gesture as well. He smoothed his son's hair and cleared his throat before taking my arm as we turned toward the officiant.

I'm sure the ceremony was touching, but honestly I can't remember one word of it.

But my heart jumped when I heard him pronouncing the magic words: "Ladies and gentleman, I give you Mr. and Mrs. Levi Brooks!"

The guests stood and cheered as Levi and I faced them before kissing once more. Music played—I heard it this time—as we headed back down the aisle with a grinning Scotty between us, each holding one of his hands. I glanced back at my sisters and saw them dabbing at their eyes as they followed behind.

When we reached the brick path, Natalie threw her arms around Levi and Scotty while Skylar clung to me and sobbed. "I'm sorry," she wept. "I'm so happy for you, but I'm just so stupid emotional!"

I laughed and held her tight. "It's the pregnancy hormones."

"And it's double," she said, sniffling. "Darn Sebastian for getting me pregnant with twins!"

"Hey, I heard that." Sebastian appeared and patted his wife on the back. "I'm not sorry, either." With a rare unabashed smile on his face, he kissed my cheek. "Congratulations, Jillian. I'm happy for you."

I grinned back. "Thank you. I'm happy for you guys too."

Skylar traded crying on my shoulder for sniffling on Levi's, and Natalie reached for me. "Oh my God, that was so perfect," she gushed.

"Was it?" I laughed as she hugged me so tight I could hardly breathe. "I honestly can't remember a thing. Did I say the right words?"

"You totally did," she assured me.

Miles joined the group, Gotham asleep in his father's arms. "He couldn't handle his joy." Miles said. "It wore him right out."

"That's OK." I brushed the back of my fingers over

Gothan's plump pink cheek. He looked so sweet and peaceful, with his chubby little legs and soft baby skin. "So cute."

Levi wrapped an arm around my waist from behind and whispered in my ear, his beard tickling my skin. "OK, we're married. Can we be alone now? Is there a closet somewhere that smells like Pine Sol?"

Smiling, I looked back at him. "Behave, you."

He groaned. "How much longer?"

"Until dark."

"I'm not going to make it," he said with certainty.

I laughed. "Try."

LEVI

I made it three more hours, and let me tell you, it was not easy.

There were pictures. And cake cutting. And pictures. And dinner. And pictures. And dancing—*dancing*, for fuck's sake. If ever two people liked dancing less than Jillian and I do, I've yet to meet them. But her sisters said we *had* to dance alone, at least to the first part of the song, so we managed to hold onto each other and sway woodenly for a minute before Jillian made eye contact with Natalie and gave her the look that must have said, *We are dying so get your asses out here right now.* Once we weren't alone on the dance floor, we relaxed a little bit and I enjoyed holding her close to me. It was the first time all day I felt like I had her to myself, even if it was in a crowd, and I inhaled the sweet scent of her neck. My dick took this as an invitation to perk up, and I was glad her body was in front of mine. "Mmm. Is it dark yet?"

"Not yet."

"I think it is."

She laughed. "We can't be the first to leave our own wedding."

"Why not?"

"It's not good manners."

"You know I have no mothertrucking manners. And you don't either."

Her brows arched. "Oh no?"

"No. If you had manners, you wouldn't still be torturing me with that dress, and those eyes, and that perfume, and those lips."

"What would I do instead?"

"You would come home with me and let me fuck you with my tongue, to start."

Her face flushed, her lips falling open. "Oh my."

"I hope someone is taking a picture right now. Your expression is priceless."

"I bet." She glanced around. "Where's Scotty?"

"He's sitting with my parents. But I think he's about done with the crowd, so they'll probably leave pretty soon. And then we have the house all to ourself." I put my lips at her ear. "And you can be as loud as you want while I make you come, over and over again."

She whimpered softly. "Maybe we can leave early."

Ah, victory. "Good idea, Mrs. Brooks. I'm ready whenever you are."

I hadn't thought she could look more beautiful than she did in her wedding dress, but when she came out of the bathroom and into the bedroom wearing some little lacy slip that was more bare than there, my jaw dropped. I was sitting on our bed, coat, shoes, and cufflinks off, but everything else still on.

"You still have clothes on," she chided, coming toward me in her bare feet. I didn't even know where to look, and I sure as hell couldn't speak, maybe not even breathe. The only thing functioning properly was my cock, which was jumping up like it needed a better view, racing for a front row seat.

And that view. Jesus Christ.

Her long slender legs went on forever. Her skin was luminous in the low lamplight. Ruby nipples peeked out from white lace. Her hair, which had been pulled back all day, swung loose around her gorgeous face. I wanted to run my fingers through those waves, slide my hands beneath that lace, run my tongue from her toes to her thighs, and then beyond. While I sat there stupefied by her beauty and by the fact that this woman was actually my *wife*, wearing the ring I put on her finger, she slipped my loosened tie from my collar and set it aside. "Why do you still have clothes on?"

"I called my mom to check in one last time while you were changing…and now I'm just paralyzed by the sight of you." Rising to my feet, I took her face in my hands. "Jillian. You're so beautiful."

Her eyes lit up. "Thank you."

"You're more than that. And before I get all caught up in your body, I want to tell you something while I still have the capacity for sentences—although this little thing you're wearing is reducing my vocabulary to very few words. Possibly just caveman sounds."

"Better tell me quick, then." She started working her way down the buttons of my shirt, pulling it free from my pants. "I have some words in my head too."

"I want you to know," I began, although now she was unbuckling my belt, and I was distracted by her pretty, graceful fingers so close to my dick. *Concentrate, asshole. This is important. You only get one wedding night.*

"Yes?" she purred, undoing my pants and sliding her hand inside.

Oh fuck. "How much I love you, and—"

"Mmhmmm," she murmured as her fingers wrapped around my shaft.

"How, uh, grateful I am that we—that you—"

"Yesss," she whispered, rising on her toes to brush her lips over mine. "That I what?"

My hands moved to her ass before I could stop them. "Grateful that—" Her fingertips swirled over the tip of my cock, her mouth moved to my neck. "That you're the one —fuck!"

Jillian started to laugh. "That I'm the one with a hand in your pants?"

"Yeah. Let's go with that." Giving up on making nice with words, I claimed her mouth with mine and ran my hands all over her body, thrilled to find she wore nothing beneath that little slip. *My wife, my wife, my wife.* I couldn't stop thinking it —she was mine in a way that she'd never been anyone else's, and I was hers the same way. She'd married me—*me*—a hairy, overgrown single dad with a son who needed special care, who would always need that care, a boy who was amazing and loving but also challenging and frustrating at times. Jillian had accepted us both, grown to love us both, and that meant everything to me. I could never tell her how much.

I picked her up and swung her onto the bed, whipped off the rest of my clothes without style or grace, and stretched out over her. Settling my hips between her thighs, I braced my arms above her shoulders and she wrapped her legs around me.

"Don't stop," she whispered, sliding her fingers into my hair. "I know you like to be all about the finesse first—and I love your finesse, I really do—but right now, I really want to know what it feels like to have my husband inside me. Don't make me wait."

Normally I argued with her when she wanted to skip the part when I got her off first with my hands or my tongue (I was forever scared of finishing so fast she wouldn't come), but tonight I couldn't resist doing what she asked, letting my body take over. I slid inside her, slow and deep, craving that sound she made when I reached her limit—and then pushed beyond.

I hadn't thought it would feel different, but it did.

More emotional, more powerful, more symbolic of what we were now—joined forever.

Jillian and I were often vocal during sex and loved shocking one another with our dirty mouths, but tonight was beyond words. Eyes locked, I moved inside her, and only our breathing filled the silence, until her breaths became those beautiful sighs and moans and gasps that made my blood surge through my veins, and my breaths became the usual barbaric grunting and cursing and choked-off sounds that was my language when I was inside her, struggling to maintain control.

I held on until I felt her climax happen, until I saw her eyes close in ecstasy, heard her long, blissful cry of release. Her fingernails dug into my ass, and I thrust hard and quick until I couldn't move anymore, my entire body clenching up as I poured myself inside her.

Nothing had ever felt better. She was mine, and I was hers, and we were a family. A whole family. I'd never been happier or more hopeful about the future. So when I opened my eyes and saw tears slipping from the corners of hers, I was taken aback. Jillian wasn't really a cryer—had I done something wrong already? But her hands were still on me, holding me deep inside her. Her legs were still wrapped around my body.

"What is it?" I asked. "Are you OK?"

She nodded, a smiled pulling at her pretty lips. "Yes. I'm just happy."

I exhaled and kissed her forehead. "Oh. Good. You confused me with the tears. I'm a simple man, Jillian. Smile, happy. Tears, sad."

She laughed and ran her hands up my back. "Sometimes tears are happy. That's what these are."

I brushed the tears from her cheeks with my thumbs. My hands looked big and masculine next to her soft skin and delicate features. "We have a lot to be happy about."

"We do." Her smile changed then—into something more sly, and mischief suddenly twinkled in her eyes. "You don't even know how much."

The back of my neck prickled. "What do you mean?"

She hesitated for just a second, but being coy wasn't Jillian's style, another reason I fucking loved her beyond reason. "I'm pregnant," she whispered, unmistakable joy in her face.

My heart, which had barely slowed after sex, boomed hard again in my chest. "What?"

"I'm pregnant." She bit her lip. "Just barely…but pregnant."

Overwhelming joy swept through me. Dizzying, thrilling joy. Tears jumped into my eyes before I could even blink. "Oh my God."

"Are you happy?" she asked hopefully. "I know it's a little sooner than we planned, but—"

I crushed her lips with mine, holding her head in my hands and pushing back against the sob that threatened to burst from my chest. When I looked down at her again, she was smiling, and I took a few deep breaths to compose myself. "Yes. Yes, I'm happy."

As I talked, I brushed the hair back from her face. "I love being a father, Jillian. For all its hardships and sacrifices and challenges, there are so many moments of pure joy. Of feeling a love so powerful, I think my heart can't handle it. Of pride and protectiveness so fierce, I think my chest will explode.

But I've been alone all this time, and…now, to think I'll share that journey with you, it's—" Again, I fought back against tears. "It's everything. I loved my life, loved being Scotty's father. And I thought that being a good father to him meant dedicating myself to only him. I thought wanting happiness for myself was too selfish. But I was wrong." Her eyes filled once more, and I kissed her lips. "I am happier with you than I've ever been, and I want nothing more than to spend the rest of my life taking care of our family." Suddenly I realized I must be crushing her belly, and I rolled off her, staying on my side and pulling her close.

"Me too," she said, turning her face to look up at me. "Being with you and Scotty the last few months has made my life so complete. I used to hope that my career would be enough to fulfill me, because I was scared I'd never meet anyone who'd love me the way I wanted to be loved. Or accept the love I wanted to give. And look—I got you and Scotty to love all at once."

"He does love you." I swallowed hard. "Even if he doesn't say it, he does."

"I know." Lifting her chin, she pressed her lips to mine. "Words aren't always the most important thing. Sometimes… you just know."

I placed my hand on her stomach, then moved down the bed to kiss the warm, taut skin of her belly. How fucking incredible that a life grew here already—one created by Jillian and me. By my *wife* and me. A little brother or sister for Scotty. This…this was everything. Jillian's hands slid into my hair, caressing softly.

I was damn glad she didn't require words at times like this, because I had none worthy of the love and gratitude and hope that I felt. Instead, I rested my forehead lightly on her stomach, closed my eyes, and repeated hers. "Sometimes… you just know."

Also by Melanie Harlow

The Frenched Series

Frenched

Yanked

Forked

Floored

The Happy Crazy Love Series

Some Sort of Happy

Some Sort of Crazy

Some Sort of Love

The After We Fall Series

Man Candy

After We Fall

If You Were Mine

From This Moment

The One and Only Series

Only You

Only Him

Only Love

The Cloverleigh Farms Series

Irresistible

Undeniable

Insatiable

Unbreakable

Unforgettable

The Bellamy Creek Series

Drive Me Wild

Make Me Yours

Call Me Crazy

Tie Me Down

Cloverleigh Farms Next Generation Series

Ignite

Taste

Tease

Tempt

Co-Written Books

Hold You Close (Co-written with Corinne Michaels)

Imperfect Match (Co-written with Corinne Michaels)

Strong Enough (M/M romance co-written with David Romanov)

The Speak Easy Duet

The Tango Lesson (A Standalone Novella)

Want a reading order? Click here!

Don't miss a thing!

Melanie Harlow

USA Today Bestselling Author

For exclusive behind the scenes information, sales and freebies, cover reveals, recommendations, and sneak peeks to what's coming, subscribe to my mailing list using the QR code below!

About the Author

Melanie Harlow likes her heels high, her martini dry, and her history with the naughty bits left in. She writes sweet and sexy contemporary romance from her home outside of Detroit, where she lives with her husband and two daughters. When she's not writing, she's probably got a cocktail in hand. And sometimes when she is.

Find her at www.melanieharlow.com.

- facebook.com/AuthorMelanieHarlow
- instagram.com/melanie_harlow
- tiktok.com/@authormelanieharlow

Printed in Great Britain
by Amazon